PRAISE FOR SARAH FINE

"As a modern-day 'Orpheus and Eurydice,' *Sanctum* will be a hit with urban fantasy readers, who will love its top-notch world-building, page-turning action, and slow-developing romance."

—*School Library Journal*

"In this well-developed concept of the afterlife, details are well-executed and the setting is described flawlessly. Without a doubt, readers will look forward to the next installment of the Guards of the Shadowlands series."

—*Library Media Connection* on *Sanctum*

"This is one of my favorite books of this year! Smart and sexy."

—*Reading Teen* blog on *Sanctum*

"Theology be damned, though: Lela and Malachi are both likable protagonists, and readers will be happy . . . this trilogy opener has a lot going for it."

—*Kirkus Reviews* on *Sanctum*

"Fans of Rae Carson's books and Victoria Aveyard's *Red Queen* will find much to love in Fine's engrossing novel."

—*VOYA* on *The Impostor Queen*

"Sarah Fine presents a fresh and fascinating magical world with its own rules and rituals, riveting action and relationships (and a sequel-worthy ending), featuring a protagonist who grows in wisdom, compassion, and self-awareness."

—*School Library Journal* on *The Impostor Queen*

BENEATH THE SHINE

Adult Fiction

The Reliquary Series

Reliquary

Splinter

Mosaic

Mayhem and Magic (Graphic Novel)

Servants of Fate Series

Marked

Claimed

Fated

BENEATH THE SHINE

SARAH FINE

SKYSCAPE

Text copyright © 2017 by Sarah Fine

Published by Skyscape, New York

www.apub.com

Amazon, the Amazon logo, and Skyscape are trademarks of Amazon.com, Inc., or its affiliates.

ISBN-13: 9781477823279
ISBN-10: 1477823271

Cover design by M. S. Corley

Printed in the United States of America

To my mother, Julie, and my sisters, Cathryn and Robin, the ones who understand my love for Percy best, I simply must say: I had a devil of a time finding a suitable basket.

Chapter One

Marguerite

Have you stopped to consider what you've become? You might have started with good intentions and some actual ideals, but now? You're just a pretty mouthpiece.

The moment the words appear on the screen of my comband, heat blooms across my chest and I feel my pulse rising. I raise my head and stare out the windshield, swallowing the urge to fire back immediately. This troll is trying to bait me. Nothing would make him happier than a public tantrum.

"Marguerite, your biostats have exceeded certain parameters. Are you in distress?" asks the car, Jenny. Back in Houston they didn't have names—or talk. "Shall I lower the environmental temperature to increase your comfort?"

"No, I'm fine." The internal rotors whir as we rise into the sky. I yawn, and my ears pop. "Just . . . tired from everything yesterday," I add, talking more to myself than to Jenny. And it's true. Not only did I speak at the president's inauguration—I got to go to the ball. That's where I made the vid that's now being trolled, while I was still wearing a designer dress downloaded directly from Hyra Urgon's winter 2069 collection.

The troll—Fragflwr is the loser's handle—is right about one thing. I looked *good*.

I glance out the rear window and see three black Secret Service cars glide into formation behind us. Apparently we've been assigned a special altitude that's reserved for the presidential fleet. A smile finds its way onto my face. Pretty or not, I'm a lot more than a mouthpiece, and I shouldn't let that idiot's comment get to me.

"There are beverages and light snacks in the cooling reservoir between my rear seats," the car informs me. "Renata analyzed your consumption and has stocked me according to your preferences."

"That was . . . nice of her." *It*, really. Not *her*, but that's a battle not worth fighting today, especially not with another it who also thinks it's a her. I didn't want a canny in the house, but Mom said it would be nice to have the help, what with all her new responsibilities, and besides, Renata came along with the apartment and was linked to its central system. When I took in the circles under Mom's eyes and the slump of her shoulders, no way was I going to complain.

Besides, Renata brought me coffee and a croissant this morning as soon as the actigraph in my comband signaled to the house system that I was awake. That part wasn't so bad. But then she asked me if I was nervous about my first day of school, as if she were my mom or a friend or an actual person or something. All I gave her was a quick shake of my head, using a mouth full of croissant as an excuse not to talk. I don't share my feelings with robots or other types of AI. I get that cannies are useful, but they're *not* people, no matter what AI rights organizations say. They're not our families. They're not our friends. And they shouldn't take jobs from actual human beings.

I've seen what happens to the humans in that scenario.

"Incoming communication," Jenny announces. "Elwood Seidel, chief of staff to the president of the United States."

"You don't have to read off his full title—" I begin, but then a three-dimensional projection of El's face fills the space above Jenny's control panel, as if he'd risen up out of her wiring. "Oh. Hey."

"So, don't be angry, but I tapped into Jenny's biostat monitors, and, well, you seem stressed."

"Yow. That's not intrusive at *all*."

He rewards my sarcasm with a wry grin that dimples the cheeks of his narrow, pale face. It makes him seem younger than his gray-streaked hair suggests. "I guess I felt guilty for stealing your mom from you on your first day of school."

"She's your primary aide, El. It's an awesome job, and we're both grateful you gave it to her. She needs—"

El clears his throat loudly, and his eyes flicker with anxiety. "Um, yes—so, *we* thought we'd surprise you."

He shifts to the side, and I realize Mom is right there with him. Her thick, curly black hair is pulled back, and she's wearing some makeup to cover the ever-present dark circles and to even out her skin. "Hi, babe," she says. She sounds slightly more upbeat than she usually does, but there's no smile. There's never a smile. I've been waiting a year to see if it would come back. "You got off on time?"

"Yep."

"And you're feeling okay about school?"

"More like grimly resigned."

El chuckles. He inclines his head so his cheek is just a little closer to Mom's. Like they're a couple or something. I don't know if she realizes how he looks at her, and I don't think *he* realizes I've noticed. "Can't blame you," he says. "But I know you understand how important the optics are here. You're the voice of our youth, Marguerite! We can't have you hiding away at home with a private tutor, not after we pushed so hard on the education plank. You have to be seen in a classroom. That's how we spur enthusiasm for the changes we're going to bring to the system."

"You can spare me the lecture, El. Going to school was my idea, remember?" I'd actually told him I wanted to go to public school, but then I found out that the *entire* educational system in the District is private. Figures. "So you think about the optics. I'm going to focus on learning—and speaking out when it's called for."

"I would expect nothing less," he says solemnly. "And you've got security there just in case things get rough."

"Can I . . . not? If you're so concerned with optics, how's it going to look if I walk into my new school with armed canny bodyguards? You know the technocrats are looking for a way to paint us as hypocrites."

El holds up his hands. "Just wanted you to feel safe as you walk into the lion's den, but if you're sure you can handle it—"

"El, I spoke to half a million people yesterday from the steps of the Capitol. I think I can hold my own with a few snooty technocrat rich kids."

El murmurs something soft and reassuring into my mother's ear. Her brow furrows but she nods. He smiles at her fondly. "I'll change their orders, then," he tells me. "They'll stay outside, and the school's cannies will look out for you. We had the school's bots scanned for malware over the weekend, so we know they're clean."

"Yay," I say faintly. "Go help Uncle Wynn make life better for the American people, guys. I'm sure I can manage a few hours of high school on my own."

"You can manage anything, Mar," El says. "Without you, we might not have won the election. We might not even be here."

"That's crazy, and you know it." But I'm smiling now, in spite of myself.

"It's true, and *you* know it. So, have a good day—can't wait to hear how it goes," El says cheerfully. The screen goes black before Mom can even say good-bye.

I sit back and sigh. I know I can handle this. It might be like walking into a buzz saw, but I know what I stand for. I'll always have that.

I glance down at the comband wrapped over the sleeve of my tunic, which was downloaded and genned just this morning. You're just a pretty mouthpiece.

I scoff and lean over so the screen registers my retinas. "And I'm guessing you're just an unfulfilled, privileged technocrat with way too much time on your hands and no concern for the 99 percent."

The words appear on the screen. "Send," I mutter. I really shouldn't indulge this troll. At this point, each new vid I post gets over a million views *a day* along with thousands of comments, and not all of them are friendly. I've become a pro at letting them slide off me. But Fragflwr has gotten under my skin, and not for the first time. I wish I knew why so I could start to ignore him—her?—like I do all the others.

The reply comes only a second later.

Well, you're right about one of those things. Maybe two. Okay, three! Brava. Sadly, it doesn't change my opinion of you. Was that your goal?

I read the comment twice and roll my eyes. I freaking hate technocrats. "That's the same smug, condescending crap that made the election such a landslide. You can't even pretend you care about normal people or even have normal feelings."

Thanks to your self-righteous babble, I'm laughing right now. Is that normal?

"Oh my god, you are so annoying and stupid. No, don't send! Log out." *Ugh.* I turn to look out the window. I hate giving a troll the last word, but I can't afford to lose it on my channel. Even if I have no official position in the administration, my words still reflect on Uncle Wynn—I mean, President Sallese. Optics, right? "How much longer?"

"Are you speaking to me, Marguerite?"

"Um, yeah? Who else would I be speaking to?"

"If you use my name at the end of any question, I will be able to respond to your requests without verifying."

"How much longer, *Jenny*?"

"We will arrive at Clinton Comprehensive Education Academy at 8:03 a.m."

"Class doesn't start until half past!"

"If you prefer, you may sit inside me until you feel comfortable disembarking. I can inform your security detail."

"No, that's all right. Jenny." I press my knees together and draw my arms around my middle, trying to be as small as possible. It's weird when cars talk about themselves like that. *Sit inside me.* Like I'm in their guts, like they've swallowed me whole. Where I come from, back in Houston, cars just go where you tell them without trying to make conversation, and they roll down the streets instead of soaring hundreds of feet above them. Of course, they also crash all the time because of operating systems and infrastructure that haven't been updated in two decades, and they're regular targets for armed gangs and hackers.

It's going to take some time to get used to this new environment. DC is a world apart from the rest of the country, save for a few other technocrat enclaves. This place is all shine, all sparkle, floating on a constructed cloud of seamless technology and unimaginable wealth. But if I have anything to do with it, someday soon that kind of prosperity is going to be within reach for the ones who live beneath the shine, the ones who have been held down by a greedy, corrupt system for way too long. It's why we came to Washington. It's why I fought so hard to help get Uncle Wynn elected. I chuckle to myself—we're not actually related, but it's pretty cool that the new president of the United States asked me to call him that.

I keep that in mind as Jenny drops smoothly from the sky and lands with a soft thump in front of my new school. I peer at its smooth, curved facade—it looks like an ocean wave viewed from above—the glass reflecting the weak January sunlight. Students are rolling in on wheelboards, and a few are landing in the queue behind the Secret Service vehicles that now offer us cover on three sides.

The stares have started. No one can see me yet—the windows are tinted—but I wouldn't be surprised if they knew it was me. Uncle Wynn doesn't have any kids, so who else would show up at high school with a Secret Service detail?

The girl who helped convince the American people that it was time to knock these kids' technocrat parents out of power, and for some of them, out of a job.

"Please tell me when you are ready to disembark, Marguerite," says Jenny. "Your security team is assembling."

Sure enough, four cannies have gotten out of the Secret Service vehicles. They wear suits complete with black collar bands, all formal, but I would never mistake them for human. Their movements are too clean and purposeful, no fidgeting, no faltering, no plucking at their clothes or scratching a random itch. And their eyes scan the horizon smoothly instead of skimming the surroundings in short, nimble bursts like humans' do.

Brian Zao, our failed president of the last eight years, whittled the number of government employees down by 70 percent, replacing people with these walking, talking, thinking automatons. The way I heard it, it was about reducing government debt and waste, something my parents' generation cared a lot about. The savings were supposed to go to people like my friend Orianna's parents, a nurse and a lab technician whose jobs had been replaced by machines. Orianna's family is still waiting, along with millions of other unemployed Americans, to see increases to the meager subsidies the government pays to people like them. But Zao's plan didn't work, because it was never about *them* in the first place—it was about his friends the tech moguls. He did a hard push to strip regulations that controlled and limited the use of cannies and other AI and then gave sweet deals to the tech companies that create them, so the number of people knocked out of jobs increased faster than the budget to retrain them or even keep them from starving.

I would think there would be families like that in DC, since Zao gutted the federal employee ranks, but I haven't seen poverty like we had back home since I left the campaign trail. Maybe those folks were forced to move somewhere cheaper than this luxurious technocrat enclave. But the Secret Service in particular is chock full of cannies, as I've come to realize in the last few months. They're perfect for bodyguard work. They're bulletproof. They don't sleep. They operate to perfection according to their protocols. Emotion never clouds *their* judgment.

And now they've arrayed themselves on either side of Jenny's door, which slides up and reveals me like a yolk in an egg. I'm sure my new pals here at the Clinton Academy would love to stab me and see if I burst. With that happy thought in mind, I plaster on the smile that has carried me through at least a hundred rallies, a thousand speeches, and a historic election night. In the last year, I've learned to smile while lights are glaring and people are screaming. I can even smile when they're throwing things, if I have to. My smile breaks only when I think it will help me get my message across, when minds can be changed.

These people don't get to see me break. I climb out of the car and smooth my hands over my new clothes. As my body heat rises, they give off the floral odor infused into the genned fabric. It's nice, but it's not really me. I hold my head high as I nod politely at the Secret Service machinemen. "Thank you. I'll be fine from here."

One of them, with a blond scrub of hair and blue eyes, steps forward. "We received the updated protocols from the chief of staff. We will remain outside the building, but we will be monitoring via the academy's central surveillance system."

I glance up at him. He'll see it all in his head, like cannies do, silent and still until it's time to move. "Okay. I'll see you guys this afternoon."

I take a calming breath. I miss my dad, who always used to walk me to school. I miss my mom, the way she was before he died. I miss home. Even though we were poor, and despite the hopelessness when one more parent lost a job, the city crumbling around us, our simmering rage at knowing we had been forgotten, I had real friends in Houston, and I could use one now. But I can't lose my temper. I can't say the wrong things. This is bigger than me—it's about my generation and fighting for each person to have a place at the table. *Stay focused, Mar. Be your best self.*

The Secret Service canny inclines his head, precise and smooth, then he steps aside, revealing a clear path to the security check at the front entrance of my new school.

That path turns out to be more of a gauntlet.

Chapter Two

Marguerite

As I walk, students gather on either side of the path, standing in crunchy brown grass. Every single one of them seems to have a Cerepin, the premier tech of the 1 percent, made right here in DC by Fortin Technology. These $10 million devices hit the market a few years ago—a breakthrough in intracranial computers. Small black nodules gleam on everyone's right temple, and each of them wears special implanted lenses that allow streaming visual data and vid capture. Sensors thread into the user's ear to manage audio. Chips implanted in their fingertips allow them to project or record themselves. A microscopically thin filament actually slides into the brain stem to enable health screening and the monitoring of vitals. All of it is tailored to the user's biological profile and powered by the body's own bioelectricity, so there's no need to worry about parts degrading or a drained battery. Users are automatically sent emergency help when their biostats warrant it. They can be located when lost. They are never alone, never in the dark, constantly updated.

The whole world is at their fingertips.

The first Cerepins came out when I was ten. I remember my dad was so enthused—he did all sorts of research to try to figure out if he could get one.

If he'd been able to afford one, it might have saved his job—and his life.

I walk with purpose toward the entrance. I'm going to get a Cerepin soon—Uncle Wynn promised. That is, if he can get Fortin Tech to cooperate. Their CEO, Gia Fortin, donated a billion dollars to the campaign of Uncle Wynn's opponent and spent countless millions on a smear campaign against Uncle Wynn himself. It was in full swing when I joined the campaign during the primary, and only got worse in the general election.

Gia Fortin is evil. I wish I could have seen her face when we won, when she realized all her money had been flushed down the toilet.

To my left, a girl snickers. "God, it looks like she styled her own hair."

"In the dark," says another.

"Ugh, what's that smell?" asks a third.

"Rancid wannabe."

I don't look. I just keep walking.

"Oh! Did you see that one video of her where she fell up the steps? Hang on—"

I can't help it. I glance over and see a tall blonde in a shiny, high-collared coat draw her finger along the round surface of the nodule embedded in her head, then tap it. Next to her, a curvy girl with silver eyelashes and silver-streaked dark hair goes still for a moment, then doubles over, laughing. "That's hilarious. Let me send it to Lara and Hannah." She, too, draws her finger over her Cerepin nodule, then taps it.

Finally I reach the door. I hold up my arms so that the school's security cannies, which are older and look less humanlike, scan me for contraband. Having none, I'm allowed into the academy's soaring atrium. There are kids sitting at tables on either side of a broad, curved staircase that leads up to the second floor. Some of them are chatting, but others seem lost in their own heads, staring at the tabletops or floor.

These kids have the most outrageous shoes, and their clothes are obviously custom-genned. I can tell by the fit and style—there's no way these were mass downloads bought at wholesale fabric generation facilities like the kind we had back home. I see a guy with slicked-back hair and thigh-high boots, his nails filed to points, and a girl with a shaved head and an outfit that looks like it's made of bloody bandages. So weird, but I guess money can buy you just about anything. Most kids are a little more toned down, though a lot of them sport little sparkly diamond-dust tattoos on their cheeks and necks. In Houston we had temp knockoffs, and they made our skin itch like crazy. My blood starts to boil as I think of how much money went into my classmates' school outfits and how it could have been put to better use.

Be your best self, Mar.

Using my comband, I pull up the map of the school and my schedule. My homeroom's on the second floor, so I make for the steps—and almost immediately stumble. The girl who made me trip flips her shiny sheet of brown hair over her shoulder as she bounces past. Her arms are at her sides, but the middle finger of her right hand is extended, pointed at the ground yet clearly meant for me. Oh, this is crap. I'm *not* going to be bullied.

"Excuse me," I say.

She stops. Looks over her shoulder. "Are you talking to me?"

I walk forward with my hand outstretched, offering to shake hers. "Yeah. I'm Marguerite Singer. I'm new here. And you are?"

She snorts as she looks down at my hand. "Oh, sorry. I have a feeling I know where those hands have been, and I'm determined to stay disease-free."

My hand drops to my side. "Is this really how you treat new students? It's not very nice."

She gives me a bemused look. "Of course it's not how we treat new students. It's how we treat destructive haters. Like *you*."

"That last bit was kind of obvious, Bianca," drawls a boy who is leaning against the wall, narrow hips cocked. Whoa. Even in this sparkly, stylish crowd, he stands out. His lips shine with gloss, and his pale skin is perfect—not a zit in sight. I think he might be wearing blush? His blond hair swoops up from his forehead like a cresting wave and glitters under the light like it's flecked with metal. His clothes are a riot of color and prints that somehow go together perfectly—and he's wearing a jacket with *tails*, like he's from the 1700s or something. He looks totally out of place and time yet completely at ease. He also looks vaguely familiar, but maybe that's because he reminds me of an anime character, all exaggerated lines and sharp eyes—which are focused on me.

"Obvious to all of us, maybe," Bianca says, turning to the boy. "But we all know she's a bit slow without her scripted talking points, Percy. I wanted to help her along."

Oh, here we go. There has been a rumor for months that Uncle Wynn's campaign wrote out scripts for my vids and all I did was read them off a screen. "Just a pretty mouthpiece," I mutter.

Percy tilts his head to the side as he watches me, as if I'm an animal in a zoo. I shoot him a glare. Interesting or not, he is definitely not on my side.

Bianca's eyes are unfocused now, and her fingertip is sliding over her Cerepin nodule. "Oh, here it is. Have you seen this one?" She taps the nodule. "It's a compilation of all the times she got nailed by protesters. Paint, fruit, oh, there's pee!" Her laugh is like breaking glass. "I'm even in one of them—it's from the rally over in Arlington last summer."

Percy continues watching me.

"Must be nice, having instant access to the entire Mainstream in your head," I say to Bianca, since she's the most obnoxious. "There are so many important, useful things you could do with that privilege instead of trying to tear other people down."

Bianca rolls her eyes. The swirling diamond-dust tattoo that resides along her collarbone winks at me in the light of the atrium. "Maybe I think it's important and useful to put conceited, greedy social climbers like you on notice—I'm capping every move you make, so there's going to be a record. You're not the only one who can stream a vid."

And unlike me, she can do it with a blink of her eye—the lenses connected to her Cerepin will do the rest. She can even boost the vid capture to the Mainstream so her followers can watch us live—my dad went on and on about the possible uses, including letting other humans remotely witness lectures, groundbreaking surgeries, weddings, personal disputes, or accidents. He said it even has a feature that instantly coms for police assistance when it detects violence or danger approaching.

But Bianca is using it to try to intimidate and hurt me, because of course.

"Go ahead and cap, Bianca," I say. It's a great reminder to me that I have to be *on* at all times. "And please stream all of it. Your followers might need to think about how many American people have either lost or can't get jobs they need because they don't have Cerepins and can't compete with the cannies, and yet this amazing technology has a price that no average American can afford. I'm happy to raise their awareness. They might want to think about the income inequality that—"

"I'm sorry, what?" She's fiddling with her Cerepin again. "I was too busy watching a video of you showing off your wretched dance moves." She gives me a lacerating fake smile. "Is that what attracted sleazy Sallese?"

My cheeks burn—now she's talking about a vid I posted before everything happened. Me in my old life, innocent and clueless and happy. For some reason, I glance over at Percy, the fancy boy who's still leaning against the wall. He's still watching me, still wearing a smirk, like he's just waiting for me to lose my temper or fall apart.

He doesn't know me at all. "You're trying very hard to be mean in an effort to upset me," I say. It's working, but I'm stronger than that.

The movement is bigger than her. "But no matter how hard you try, you won't change the fact that Wynn Sallese won the election, and he's our president now. It won't change my belief in his agenda or my understanding of just how badly everyday Americans need an advocate after what eight years of greed and corruption have done to this country."

"Of course you won't stop believing in him—you have to do whatever he wants to hang on to your free ride," Bianca says. She taps out a little rhythm on her nodule. Several other kids get up and amble over. She must have just messaged them or something.

Bianca puts her hands on her hips. Now she's blocking my way to the steps. "I'd like to introduce all of you to Marguerite Singer," she announces. "As she has told us in vid after vid, she comes from a humble family and a humble place." The pitch of her voice swings from high to low, all drama and mockery. Her full lips pout, and she bats her gold-flecked eyelashes. "Because of this, she feels entitled to have everything for free, and she thinks other losers like her should have it just as easy as she does. She got lucky when she attracted the eye of the man who would be president. He scooped her out of the crap pile where she was living, and as long as she's his dirty little girl, he'll be her sugar daddy." She skims the tip of her tongue along her lips, all suggestion.

"Got lucky?" I ask in a trembling voice. "You think I'm here because I was *lucky*?" Rage spirals up my backbone, turning it molten. "And how dare you—"

"Dirty little girl." A stocky boy with sandy blond hair and a red jeweled collar band has come to stand next to Bianca. He lets out a giggle. "I love it. Can we call her that, B?"

"I think we'll have to, Winston." Bianca doesn't take her eyes off me. "I've already forgotten her actual name."

"I don't care whether you remember my name. Because I represent the millions of Americans out of work and trying to support their families. The government subsidies are enough to get by, but by that I mean barely survive. So what do your fellow Americans do, Bianca?

They numb the pain however they can. If that doesn't work, they end it." I swallow hard, because the lump in my throat threatens to steal my voice. "They don't know how to keep their children safe. They don't see themselves as having a future." My fists are clenched, but I'm speaking quietly enough that several of the kids around me tap at their ears, probably upping the volume on their auditory chips. "You don't have to remember my name so long as you remember that."

"So you think Fortin Tech should just give the Cerepins away to these people?" asks Bianca, suddenly more vicious than before. "You think the billions they poured into research is worth nothing? That sleazy Sallese should be able to barge into their facilities, take the 'Pins, and hand them out on the street? You think businesses that develop or use cannies should be punished for wanting to be successful and efficient? You think we should live in the past, because things were so much better then? You act as if all these people are left on the street to starve, when in actuality they're sitting on their couches all day, eating chips and getting fat off *our* parents' tax dollars!"

"You're so out of touch, it's scary," I tell her.

"And you're so brainless and classless that you'll wrap your arms— and legs, probably—around anyone who promises you a better deal."

"Ah, Bianca, when the appallingly sordid becomes your go-to attack, you're doing it wrong," says Percy, finally shoving himself off the wall. The tails of his coat flap against the backs of his thighs as he saunters forward. "You'll have to be a bit savvier if you want to knock our Marguerite off message."

"Is that a challenge?" Bianca asks.

"It's just . . . you're using more of a club," says Percy. His eyes glitter as he looks me up and down. "This job calls for a scalpel."

"Cut it out," says a voice I haven't yet heard.

Percy turns to someone behind me and arches one eyebrow. "Literally?"

"You know what I mean, Percy. Quit egging Bianca on."

Standing just behind me is a girl with brown skin, white hair, and white eyebrows. She's dressed in all white, too, a crisp tunic and pants. Subtle but elegant. Obviously super expensive. Her dark eyes look past me and focus on Bianca. "We're not bullies. Stop acting like one."

"Actually, Anna, Bianca *is* a bit of a . . . ," Percy begins, but the white-haired girl holds up her hand, and his mouth twists into an amused smile. With a flourish of his hand—one that draws my eye to the lacy cuffs and ruby cuff links at his wrists—he cedes the floor to the girl in white.

Anna moves to stand next to me. "This isn't the way to prove a point," she says to Bianca before turning her head and speaking to the other students who have gathered around. "We're all upset about this, but it's no excuse to act like jackals."

"Come on, Anna," Bianca says, her lip curling. "You know I'm just saying the things everyone else is thinking."

"Thankfully, no you're not," says Anna. "How about you step aside and let Marguerite walk to her homeroom in peace, instead of making us look like the soulless monsters more than half the country already thinks we are?"

Kids are backing off now, tossing hateful looks at me over their shoulders. Bianca rolls her eyes when she sees her audience abandoning her and blows a kiss at my new white-haired friend. "You'll bulk up your shoulder muscles, toting this extra baggage."

Anna doesn't say anything, but her jaw works beneath her skin, and her eyes are wide and steady on the mean girl. A classic *shut up shut up shut up* look. Hmm.

Bianca puts up her hands in surrender. "See you tonight?" she asks.

"Maybe," Anna replies. "Mom may want me home."

Bianca sighs. "I know. Dad said it might not be safe on the streets now that Sallese is bringing all sorts of low-class trash into the District. The beatings, people being attacked just because they have Cerepins. Dad says it's only a matter of time before we're rounded up and—"

Anna groans. "Stop. Just stop."

"Fine. Whatever." Bianca looks toward Percy, as if she's wondering if he's leaving with her, but he's not looking in her direction.

He's looking in mine—I can see it out of the corner of my eye. I'm not going to return his gaze. Out of all the people in this scene, he's the one I can't figure out. With one last eye roll, Bianca pivots and heads up the steps, dragging the stocky blond guy—Winston, I think she called him—along with her.

Anna looks over at me. "Our parents work together. I've known her all my life."

"Okaaaaay." Once I've given Bianca a respectable head start, I trudge up the stairs with Anna next to me. Percy falls in behind us. I resist the urge to glance over my shoulder at him—it seems better to ignore him.

"She's usually nice," Anna insists.

Percy laughs quietly.

Anna drops her head back, looking tired. "Well. Nic*er*."

"Yeah," I say. "She seems like a sweetheart."

"Everybody's just intimidated by you."

"Right. They seemed absolutely terrified." If Anna hadn't shown up, I might have needed the Secret Service after all.

Anna starts to respond, then seems to think better of it.

"I'm sure I can find my homeroom on my own, even without GPS in my head," I tell her, holding up my comband. "You don't have to be the welcoming committee."

"It's okay. My mom told me to look out for you. But I'd have done it anyway. Someone has to."

"Why?"

"Marguerite, I *care* about my classmates, even when they're acting like idiots. Don't even think about it, Lara." She lightly shoves away another girl who was about to collide with me. "We don't need vigilantes coming in and firebombing our school because they think you're being bullied. One tearful video from you and—" She makes a little explosion sound.

"I wouldn't—"

She holds up a hand. "I saw what happened in Silicon Valley."

Not my best moment. Some protestors threw a bucket of pee on me as we headed into a rally. Wynn's security quickly got me inside, where I sat in the women's bathroom and fed a vid to the Mainstream, gagging on the stench, my hair dripping. It had just become a habit at that point to tell everyone what was happening to me at the moment it happened. Plus, I was scared and frazzled and needed the comfort of the strangers who'd become family. But this time, my vid got more than just views and comments—Uncle Wynn's supporters went on a rampage that lasted for days. When they were finished, some of the Valley technocrat enclave's nicest neighborhoods were nothing but smoking ruins. "I didn't want that to happen, and neither did the president. He called for calm."

"Mm-hmm. And that fixed everything right up."

My fingers grip the banister, anger turning my knuckles bloodless. "So basically, you're being fake-nice right now to save your own ass?"

"No, I'm being real-honest right now because I want you to understand where I'm coming from."

My eyes flick to her Cerepin. I wonder what it's doing for her right now, and for all these other kids who have them, too. I bet they can see the tiny beads of sweat on my upper lip. I bet they can hear the frantic swish-thump of my heart. And I bet they're still hoping I lose it and embarrass the president. After a deep breath, I smile at Anna. "I'd like to understand, Anna. We're all a part of this country. Everyone has a perspective. President Sallese believes that, and so do I."

Behind me, Percy snickers. "I don't know about you, Anna, but I totally get the appeal."

His condescending drawl is getting under my skin, making me itch with irritation. "You're *very* good," he says when I finally turn to look at him. "Much better than I thought you'd be in person, on the fly. I think I'm jealous."

Anna rolls her eyes. "No you're not, Percy. You have almost as many Mainstream followers as she does."

"Oh, stop flattering me. It's not even close." But he looks like he's eating it up.

I look him over with new suspicion, my brain churning as it tries to identify him. This is where a Cerepin would come in handy—instant facial recognition that automatically opens a person's Mainstream mention results and social feed. "Did you campaign for the technocrats or something?"

Anna chuckles, but Percy looks horrified. "Lord, no. I'd rather have my teeth pulled. *Politics.*" He shudders, but then his blue eyes flash as he looks me over. "I must say, though—I'm not a huge fan of Hyra's, and I thought her winter collection was positively provincial, but your ensemble for the inauguration was divine. I did think it skewed young for you, but I suppose they wanted to project innocence."

I'm opening my mouth to ask what the heck *he's* trying to project with his ridiculous outfit when Anna's head jerks up. She stops right there on the steps. "Accept." After a few seconds, she says, "Excuse me," and jogs up the stairs.

Percy looks down at his fingernails, filed square and polished dark purple with a deep rich sheen, like a night sky. "Probably an incoming com on her Cerepin from Mommy dearest. Poor Anna's family is under siege, new threats daily. It's had a rather devastating effect on her social life, I'm afraid."

"What? Why are they being threatened?"

He stares at me incredulously, then breaks into a wide smile, as if he'd just gotten the punch line to a joke. He inclines his head toward Anna, who is at the top of the staircase, frowning as she stares into space. "You really don't know who she is, do you?"

"I don't have a Cerepin to give me all the answers."

"Then let me help you out." He joins me on my step and nudges my shoulder with his in a conspiratorial way. "You have just made the acquaintance of Anna *Fortin*." There's that smirk again. He looks like he thinks this whole situation is hilarious. "You may have heard of her mother?"

Crap. Gia Fortin strikes again. "She said her mom told her to be nice to me," I mumble.

"Ah. Well. I'm sure a political animal as cunning as yourself can puzzle this one out. This"—he tugs at his cuff—"is why I stick to fashion." Each of his cuff links is a flower, as it turns out. The rubies are the petals. "*Slightly* less likely to result in bloodshed. Shall we?" He offers his arm.

I gape at him.

He lays his palm over his chest. "You have slain me with a glance." But his expression is one of barely restrained laughter. "Welcome to DC, Marguerite. The city is at your feet." He glances down at my new boots, and I am suddenly very aware that I've already managed to scuff them. He is smiling as he meets my eyes again and leans forward to whisper, "Do watch your step."

Chapter Three

Marguerite

I sit in the cubicle and put on the goggles, already feeling queasy. With unsteady hands, I slip in the two earpods, and the noise from the learning room—thirty voices all having one-sided conversations—cuts off abruptly.

It's been a year since I was in school. When El came to Houston and invited me and Mom to join the campaign and travel around the country with them, he made sure to tell her that they would provide a tutor for me. He also made sure to specify that the tutor would be human, not virtual.

There were reasons.

I wipe my clammy palms on my pant legs. I was fine during the homeroom discussion—there, we sat in a circle and Mr. Cordoza said everyone had to turn their Cerepins to "blank." He walked us through a discussion of AI accountability in light of a few recent incidents in which cannies committed crimes after being infected with malware. Most of the kids in the room ignored me, looking away whenever I spoke, but Anna and one other girl, Kyla, kept talking right to me, so it ended up being a conversation between the three of us and the teacher. Fine by me.

Mr. Cordoza went out of his way to be nice to me, without being a stooge about it. I think he and Anna are on the same page—they both handle me a little like one would a loaded weapon.

When he dismissed us to our individual learning sessions, my gut started to churn. I mean, I knew it was coming—Clinton is actually notable for the amount of time spent in what is called "organic learning," which basically means that you get to interact with an actual human teacher like we did in that discussion with Mr. Cordoza. Research has proven that humans pick up social skills in complex interactions with other humans, who are not nearly as accommodating as cannies, so places like this one, swimming in the tax dollars of the 1-percenters, provide teachers who have a heartbeat.

My school in Houston did, too, once upon a time.

"Marguerite Singer, welcome to my classroom," says a male voice as my goggles light up, revealing an empty room containing just a stool and a screen. When I look down, I see my own hands on the surface of an old-fashioned school desk.

When I look up, Aristotle is sitting on the stool in front of me. He has thinning white hair and a goatee. Teacherlike. Nothing about his appearance is designed to distract from the learning process.

It is all I can do not to rip the goggles off my face.

Aristotle rises from his stool, steepling his fingers. "Your previous tutor's lesson plans have been uploaded, so we'll simply continue our discussion where you left off. Later, we'll do some games and exercises to assess your problem-solving style and strengths, as well as your learning needs and preferences."

He keeps talking. I'm just . . . lost in this. All I can think about is Dad and how excited he was when he first heard of Aristotle. "Margie," he said to me, "this is going to revolutionize my classroom." He had the biggest smile on his face, and he was gesturing with his big hands, his hair shaggy around his face, his beard long and bushy. His students joked that he was a bear trying to disguise himself as a man. They loved him. His energy and passion were infectious.

Aristotle is still talking. "You've clearly covered a great deal of the French Revolution, so we'll focus on the Reign of Terror for today, beginning with its political and social catalysts."

"The people were sick of being mistreated," I say flatly. "They wanted equality and fairness in their society. And that is something I can totally get behind."

"Actually, one of the causes of the Reign of Terror was widespread frustration that the early promises of the revolution—measures to end poverty and increase that equality you mentioned—had not been fulfilled. The external threats to the country had largely been resolved, and so the revolutionaries focused on the internal threats to their hoped-for changes."

"Right," I say. "The nobility. The people lucky enough to be born to the right families, so they got to live a life of wealth and privilege while their neighbors starved." Bianca's face flashes in my mind, along with her diamond-dusted collarbone. Between that and the way she was attacking me, I'm guessing her parents are technocrats of the highest order. Probably racking up billions while not giving a crap about the jobs they're costing working Americans.

"—used violence as a deterrent for counterrevolutionaries," drones Aristotle. He's gesturing at the screen behind him, where images from the revolution are being displayed. One shows a guy with a frilly thing around his neck and a long crimson tailcoat, and I instantly think of Percy. I'm betting he would have loved revolutionary French fashion—until they chopped off his head for being a pretentious idiot.

"Marguerite?"

"Huh?"

Aristotle smiles. "Your biostats indicate your attention has drifted."

I can't bring myself to care. I used to love classes, but this guy's not a teacher. He's not even a person.

He leans forward. "Would you like to take a break?"

"Yeah." I strip off my goggles and rip out my earpods, then glance around. I'm in a big room lined on three sides with cubicles, each filled with one of my classmates staring at the blank white walls. Unlike me, they're using their Cerepins for their learning sessions. With their lenses and auditory chips, their tech seamlessly meshes with their bodies. They can access the whole virtual world, the entire Mainstream, any channel, any experience, any information, with a literal blink of their eyes or a simple flick of the gaze, tilt of the head, murmured command—even, I've heard it rumored, a simple thought for the newest versions. The richer you are, the more like a machine you can become.

Bianca is sitting a few seats down. As If she senses me, she leans back from her desk and looks my way, then smirks and blinks, just once.

She's recording me, I'm sure.

My goggles are flashing on my desk, a warning that Mr. Cordoza will be alerted if I don't get back to it.

I make it through my lesson, with my AI teacher using the French Revolution as a classic example of how initially noble ideals can be corrupted step by step and how power speeds up that process. By the time it's over, I am so badly in need of a voice from home, some sense of the familiar, that I can barely hold back the tears. I bow my head and whisper, "Com Orianna."

My comband screen goes fuzzy for a moment and then hums as it tries to reach my best friend back home. I haven't talked to her since just after the election, when I told her I wasn't coming back to Houston. I sag in my seat as her face appears, too pale, sleepy eyes, hair mussed and spread across her pillow. "Hey," I say. "You're still in bed? I thought I might catch you between learning sessions."

"It's an hour earlier than where you are," she mumbles.

"But it's almost noon here."

She starts to sit up, then winces. Her fingers slide up the back of her neck and poke at her neurostim device. She shivers from head to toe and blinks fast. "There we go. Now I'm up." Clear-eyed now, she peers at her comband. "You okay? Saw your vid last night. Looks like you had fun at the ball."

"Yeah, but my carriage turned into a pumpkin at midnight. I'm me again."

"You look thrashed. I saw that King Troll got up in your comments this morning. Saw you start to get into it with him."

I roll my eyes. "Not for long. I shouldn't ever reply, though. It doesn't help."

"Frag-flow-er," she says, exaggerating each syllable. "What kind of stupid name is that?"

"I'm sure it was chosen by committee. He's probably just a flack on Gia Fortin's payroll." I bite my lip and glance around as I realize someone might hear me. Everybody seems immersed in the lessons.

". . . just ignore," Orianna is saying. "Sore loser."

I lean my head on the side of the cubicle. "I'm trying."

"Hey. You look like you need one of these." She lifts her hair from her neck to show off the little black pod attached to her skin just below her hairline. "Screw Cerepins—I'll take one of these babies any day."

"You got a new one. Was it pricey?" I squint to try to see her new neurostim device, but the image is pixelating randomly, either because the network in Houston is so crappy or because her comband is too old to manage the data, or both.

"You kidding? Each new version is cheaper! Which is good because they wear out fast. But boy, do they help. Everyone in the fam has one now."

"I'll tell Uncle Wynn you said that," I tell her. "That'll make his day."

"Good. Tell Mr. President that Orianna Ross approves." She draws out that last word, syrupy smooth. "So, you gonna stick it to those technocrites?" Her lips stay pouty even after her voice falls silent and her eyes half close. For a moment I wonder if her screen has frozen, but then her eyes shut all the way.

"You sure you're awake?"

"Almost." She reaches up and taps her device again, then lets that shudder run through her. "There we go." She gives me a goofy grin. "I miss you, you know that?"

My throat goes tight. "I miss you, too."

"You might miss me, but I *know* you don't miss being here. When is our new commander in chief gonna fix us up?"

"Is it bad?"

She shrugs. "Another shooting."

"Someone we know?"

"I think it was Trey's older brother."

"The one who moved to Chicago?"

"Came back in the fall after he got laid off. Don't know why he thought it'd be any better there. Only place it's better is where you are. And maybe California. Boston."

"We'll make it better everywhere," I say to her, but it doesn't look like she hears me.

She rubs her eyes. "That's three shot since the new year." She touches her neurostim. "Only reason I'm not crying all the time."

Her eyes meet mine for the first time, and even through the pixelation I can see they're bloodshot and shiny, her pupils small, like her comband is on the brightest setting. "Listen. Don't you forget about us. Don't get so used to all that fancy tech that you become one of them."

"I won't! You know I won't."

She scowls and taps at her screen, which freezes.

"Orianna? Can you hear me?"

The screen stays fixed on her frowning face. I end the com and try to reconnect, but all I get is a This user is busy message. I'm alone again.

Actually, not really. When I turn around, I realize that Anna is waiting behind me with Kyla, the only other student who didn't ostracize me in homeroom. She has plain shoulder-length black hair and no visible diamond dust, making Kyla instantly more approachable than most of my classmates.

"We just finished and wondered if you wanted to sit with us at lunch," Anna says.

I glance around, as if another, better deal is going to come my way, and notice Bianca staring at me again. "Sounds good."

We join the flow of glittering, perfumed bodies moving toward the cafeteria. Kyla and Anna walk with me between them, and only one person kicks my heel as I pass, so it's a definite improvement on the morning. For now, I've decided to put aside the fact that Anna is Gia Fortin's daughter. I'm on guard, sure, knowing she could use anything I say as some sort of ammo, but as long as I don't actually trust her, we should be fine.

Once in the cafeteria, I grab an eerily perfect-looking salad and a protein bar and head for a seat at the table Kyla has staked out. "My parents are scientists at the Department of Artificial Intelligence Regulation," she tells me with a smile.

"Oh," I say as I sit, my stomach sinking. "Are they still . . ."

"Employed?" Kyla asks. "Sure—they're not political appointees."

"How are they with the change of administration?" I ask as Anna joins us.

Kyla gives me a nervous smile before dipping into her yogurt. "They just want to do their job, you know?"

It hits me in too many ways. "Yeah. I know all about parents who just want to do their jobs. I get it."

Anna opens a bottle of sparkling water. "How was Aristotle this morning?"

I frown. "Like, what kind of mood was he in? I don't—"

"No, I mean were you okay being in there?"

"You know what happened to my dad," I say quietly.

She nods. "I think a lot of people here don't—they didn't pay a lot of attention to the campaign."

"I wanted to say something before," Kyla says quietly. "I'm really sorry for your loss."

"Whose loss?" Percy leans on the table, holding a tray containing steamed fish and a protein bar like mine.

"My dad," I say.

"Ah," Percy says and lifts his coattails as he plops into the seat next to Kyla's. "You're a vision in cobalt," he says to her.

Kyla's cheeks glow pink as she runs her fingers down the arm of her blue sweater, which fits her like a second skin. "I watched your vid on winter blues."

"And here I get to reap the benefits. Payment in full."

Kyla turns to me. "Have you seen Percy's fashion vids? They're almost as popular as yours!"

"Wow," I say in a voice that shows I'm not at all wowed. "Cool."

Percy just looks amused. "I'd be happy to give you a makeover, Marguerite. Sallese's consultants have not done you justice."

"That's a nice way of telling me I look like crap."

He leans back and slaps his hand onto his chest, showing off those dark purple–painted fingernails. "You do me a disservice, darling."

"Don't call me 'darling.'"

"I apologize, my dear."

"Oh my god." I turn to Anna, who has her sandwich halfway to her mouth.

"He's an acquired taste," she offers.

"I'm not really into fashion."

She nods without looking at me. "Obviously you have other priorities."

Just then, Bianca and company stride in. "Here we go again," I mutter.

"She's harmless," Kyla says. "Just hasn't gotten over the regime change."

I chuckle. "You think I'm afraid of her? Have you ever been to Houston?" A streak of bitterness cuts right through me. "You guys really have no idea what it's like out there."

"Oh, do tell," drawls Percy.

I grit my teeth. "Everything's a joke to you, because you don't see the murders or the home invasions. It happens all the time now—people who have been kicked off the subsidy rolls get desperate sometimes. Before the sponsored neurostim programs started—"

Percy's eyes flash. "Neurostims. The magical cure-all . . . that our current president made his fortune selling."

"I didn't say they were a cure-all," I snap. "But I've seen them help people through the rough patches! And, by the way, it's the one piece of intracranial tech that people like me actually can afford."

"Because Sallese is so very generous," Percy says. There's something glinting in those blue eyes of his. Literally glinting. Like silver chips. He *would* be that vain. "I am certain that the fact that those charming little devices wear out after a few months and must be replaced by now-desperate individuals would have nothing to do with why he runs a charity program to give away the devices to first-time users." His lip curls. "The first hit is always free."

"That's totally unfair," I say, "and totally rich coming from someone who . . ." I peer at his temple, and that is the first time I realize he doesn't have a Cerepin.

"Yes?" Percy leans forward.

My nostrils flare. "Someone who doesn't have the slightest clue how most people live. There's hunger, and there's violence—"

"Violence is everywhere, *darling*." His voice is the slice of a knife. "I don't care if you are from Houston or Hawaii—don't kid yourself into thinking you understand it better than I do."

Anna and Kyla look stricken, and even the kids at the nearby tables have fallen silent. Percy has shed his amused detachment like a coat. Now he's a live wire, incandescent and dangerous.

I clear my throat. Then I look at each of my new classmates at the table and down to the untouched food on my plate. "I forgot to wash my hands." I get up and walk away, feeling Percy's gaze on my back like a laser beam.

Behind me, I hear someone jump up from the table, and then Anna tugs at my arm.

"What the heck just happened?" I ask.

"You hit his one sore spot," she says.

"Which is?" I'm the one who gets to be mad. What in the hell does Percy, king of the fashion vids, know about violence, about death?

"His parents."

"Okaaaay."

"They were murdered."

My breath leaves me in a rush.

"It was this random thing, apparently," she tells me. "It happened about two years ago. Percy didn't come to Clinton until about a year after they died. We haven't known him for that long, except through his vids."

I've never seen them, but that explains why he looks familiar—he's actually famous, just not for something that I think is important. But he probably thinks the same of me.

"It was a big deal when it happened. His parents were both scientists. His dad was kind of a controversial figure." Her cheek dimples as she gives me a wry smile. "My mom hated the guy."

That actually makes me prone to like him, but I certainly don't say it. Anna Fortin is being nice, and today, that's a blessing. As we cross the atrium I see a quiet corner and sink down. Anna sits down beside me.

"Anyway, they were at an addiction treatment clinic for some kind of business meeting, and one of the patients just . . . attacked."

I cringe. "That sounds awful. Percy wasn't there, was he?"

She shakes her head. "But don't ask him about it directly unless you want to hear his theories about who's responsible."

"Not the violent patient, then?"

She shrugs. "That's what it was, but he doesn't accept it. He thinks his parents were targeted. And silenced."

"Why?"

A group of girls walk by and wave at Anna while glaring at me. She waves back. "Like I said, his dad was a controversial guy. I just wanted to give you a heads-up. He's not usually keen to argue, but you kind of raised the temperature in the school today. Maybe that's what's getting to him." She stands to go.

It's a kind way of blaming me for upsetting the guy, who seemed perfectly willing to goad me into upsetting him.

Suddenly, I'm feeling very tired. I don't want to be *on* anymore. But the daughter of the enemy—an enemy who could be very useful, if she were to cooperate with the president's agenda—is standing right next to me. "Anna?"

"Yeah?"

"Thank you for being nice to me. I know we've been on opposite sides."

She offers me a ghost of a smile. "I campaigned hard against Sallese. I was president of the DC Young Technocrats. Kyla was a big part of it as well." Maybe she translates the curiosity on my face, because she adds, "Percy wasn't—he hates politics. But Winston was our social organizer—his mom is the outgoing secretary of AIR."

No wonder he wanted to call me names. His mom just lost her job to the new administration. Uncle Wynn appointed a fiery guy named Ron Gould, who is way more committed to AI regulation, and the Senate is spoiling for a fight. The technocrats in Congress are terrified of him.

"—and Bianca was our vid editor," Anna is saying. She bites her lip. "Her dad is CEO of Parnassus."

I can feel the blood draining from my face. "Oh," I whisper.

Parnassus Inc. Creator of the Aristotle program.

"I know you've probably hated Aristotle since it was released."

"You're wrong," I say hoarsely. "When we first got word of it, my dad couldn't wait to work with it."

Her brows draw together. "But he was a teacher."

"We had no idea what would happen. He thought it would be a supplement, like it is here." I blink fast to hold in the tears. "He thought it would help his students learn. We needed every advantage we could get."

"After Congress made tailored individual learning a federal mandate, the Zao administration made sure the program was cheap. That was supposed to make it easier for poor districts to get it."

"Right," I say, anger hardening my voice. "So what did cash-strapped cities like Houston do? They laid off all their teachers and made Aristotle the *only* teacher. My dad lost his job to AI on January 4, 2068. He killed himself on January 5."

I clench my fists to ward off the sharp smell, the sight of him slumped against the door, my ragged scream. My nostrils flare and I swallow hard, fighting the sudden urge to puke.

"That was the day you fed that first vid," Anna says. "The one that went megaviral."

The one where I howled my grief and rage into the electronic wind. The five minutes that changed my life. "Yeah."

"And that's how the Sallese campaign found you."

I nod. "It hit a nerve, that's for sure, and El—he was managing the campaign—felt like I was a symbol for what Wynn Sallese could offer the American people. What happened to my dad wasn't fair, but it's happened to so many others. Not here, maybe, but . . ."

"You really believe in him, don't you?" she says softly.

"He's never given me reason not to."

"I guess we'll see how his first hundred days go. He's made a lot of big promises."

Our eyes meet. Those promises include twisting the arms of tech moguls like her mom to try to get some price controls and inventory increases, limitations on canny manufacturing, new laws restricting use of cannies in certain positions, restrictions on Cerepin use as a job requirement—an agenda technocrats like Anna must hate. "He sure has."

There's an electronic hum that reverberates through the atrium. Aristotle is waiting.

Chapter Four

Marguerite

I've just gotten into Jenny for my second week of school when she alerts me that I have a com.

From the president of the United States.

My voice is shaky as I say, "Yes, I'm available!"

President Wynn Sallese's face appears above the control panel. "Good morning," he says with a smile. His blue eyes twinkle with pride and fondness. He has thick, graying auburn hair and a smile that suggests everything's going to be just fine. It instantly dissolves some of the dread that has been sitting so heavy in my stomach at the thought of going back to school this morning. "Before they left for their tour of the Department of AIR this morning, El and Colette let me know that your first week of school was a little rocky."

"And you're comming me with a pep talk? Don't you have . . . I don't know, briefings? Or meetings with important people?"

"You *are* important, Marguerite. I didn't bring you here to Washington to be miserable, but I also know you can take on anything you set your mind to. I wanted you to know that I'm proud of you."

My eyes sting with happy tears. "That means a lot, Mr. President."

"Uncle Wynn," he says with a reproachful shake of his head. "You're the daughter I never had, and although I know I could never come close to standing in your father's shoes, I like to think he'd be happy, knowing you had me looking out for you."

"He would," I whisper. "I wish you two could have met."

"Me too," he says sadly, and then clears his throat and throws his shoulders back. As he does, I can see he's sitting in the Oval Office. This is crazy. I'm talking to the president. *The* president. "Now—you haven't made a vid since the inauguration."

Anna's words about me being a threat to my classmates if I post my hurt and rage on the Mainstream have kept me from uploading. Not that it hasn't been tempting—since last Monday, most of my classmates have just offered me more of the same bullying, shunning, whispering grossness. I'm not going to break or whine, and I'm not going to let anyone silence me forever, but I also don't feel able to hold it together in the way I'd need to if I were to post to my thirty million followers. "Well . . . I've been focused on my schoolwork. And last night, El came over for dinner. We were up late, talking." My mom crawled off to bed early, claiming a headache, and we stayed up, talking politics—and what might help Mom finally climb out of the pit of her grief. El said he was looking into possibilities, but wouldn't tell me what he meant. "He told me he was headed to the Department of AIR this morning to have a tour with the future secretary."

"Yes. We're going to be making big changes over there, assuming the Senate confirms Ron. I know he was a controversial pick. But when he is in that seat, it's going to be a lot harder for people like Gia Fortin and Simon Aebersold to get anything from this government unless they start thinking of the American people instead of their own bank accounts."

A chill runs down my spine. Simon Aebersold is CEO of Parnassus Inc. Bianca's father. "That's good," I say. "They've created such amazing things—I hope they'll work with your department."

"They're going to have to, Marguerite. The days of cushy exclusive contracts, development grants, and shameful under-regulation are over."

His bushy silver-flecked brows are low. "I have a sacred trust to fulfill. This is part of why I wanted you to stay on the team. You deserve to have a front-row seat to the changes that are going to start this very week. Whenever I think of compromising, I'm just going to remember Dan Singer and his love for teaching. I'm going to remind those tech moguls that AI is meant to serve us, not to steal our reason for being."

"I'm honored to be a part of it," I say, wiping a stray tear from my cheek.

"Oh, look what I did," Uncle Wynn says, clucking his tongue. "You can't head into school with tears in your eyes! I meant to cheer—" His brow furrows, and he looks down at his desk as a quiet voice emanates from its screen. "Marguerite, I'm sorry. I have to go. You have a good day, and we'll talk soon."

His holographic image disappears, and I sit back, reminding myself that the president is responsible for a million things. He could be talking to world leaders or have the Speaker of the House on the phone, but he took the time to com me and try to cheer me up. My chest swells. No more feeling sorry for myself at the thought of dealing with people like Bianca and Percy and Winston. Maybe I can make friends with Anna and Kyla, and since they're so politically involved—and yet also seem like decent human beings—I can help them understand what Uncle Wynn's agenda is going to achieve. Both of their parents are critical to the mission, and both of my new, friendly-ish classmates seem like they could have some influence if they wanted to.

With that goal at the top of my mind, I smile as we descend to street level, and for a moment I watch my classmates flowing like ants toward the school. From up here they seem pretty harmless. The Secret Service is a little pulled back today at my request, and the cannies don't even get out of the car as I slide out of the backseat, telling myself today is a new day.

As Jenny's door slides shut, I hear someone gasp. I look around to see my classmates suddenly frozen on the sidewalk, some of them midstride, some of them with their hands plastered over their mouths. Students stand on wheelboards that have stopped moving, perhaps sensing the distraction of their riders. I walk to the entrance and peer into the school. I see the same thing in the atrium, scores of kids just staring into midair or at the ground.

"What—"

A flurry of movement startles me, and I turn to see Percy burst through one of the front doors and run toward a landing black car. His gait is smooth and swift, and he dives into the backseat with his tailcoat flapping. The door closes, and the car rises into the sky an instant later. I am the only one who seems aware that he's gone. Stillness and silence reign until they're shattered by a scream.

"No!" Kyla staggers out of the school, Anna and Bianca flanking her. Anna has tears running down her face, and Bianca's gaze lasers over to mine. For the first time, there's not hatred there. I see only fear.

Shuffling sounds behind me are my only warning before I'm grabbed and carried backward. "For your safety, Ms. Singer," says one of the canny Secret Service agents. He and two other agents surround me, pushing me toward the open door of one of their black vehicles. As soon as I'm in, we're off.

"What just happened?" I ask all of them.

"There has been an incident."

"Yeah, I gathered!" We're not flying, I realize—we're rolling on the car's spherical magnetic wheels, over the smooth streets of the city. "What's going on? Why aren't we airborne?"

"The skyway has just been closed down."

I close my eyes and pray for patience. "Okay, but why?" I bet this was the reason Uncle Wynn got off the phone so fast and why everyone was frozen like that—they were all getting news via their Cerepins, while I was in the dark. "What's the incident?"

"An explosive device appears to have detonated at the Department of Artificial Intelligence Regulation."

"What?" Panic rises in me so fast that I can't keep my voice level. "My mom was there today!"

"We are taking you to a secure facility at the request of the president."

Oh my god. Oh my god. I can't lose both of them. This can't be happening.

"—will wait for further instructions once you are secured," the agent is saying, but I can barely hear him. The buzzing in my ears is too loud.

Wait. That's my comband buzzing. Hoping to see my mom's face, I look down and find myself looking at Anna. Her brown skin is ashen. She's streaming with the fingertip-cam connected to her Cerepin, holding her arm out in front of her. "Where did you go?" she asks.

"They're taking me to—"

An agent covers my band. "You are not to disclose your location."

"I won't," I snap. "Now, if you don't mind." I poke the back of his hand and draw back quickly at the feel of his synthetic skin. He removes his hand, his face blank.

"Sorry about that," I say to Anna. "This is crazy."

"Tell me about it," she says. "They herded us inside, and now we're on lockdown here in the cafeteria. I've been trying to reach people, and the comlines are jammed because everyone else is trying to do the same thing. I was just hoping . . . have you heard anything?" In the background, I can hear all sorts of things—someone is crying, and it might be Kyla. There are distant sirens and the hum of anxious conversation.

"You know more than I do," I say, tapping my temple at the spot where a Cerepin nodule would be.

"Kyla needs to reach her parents." Anna's voice is hushed, and she moves the cam closer to her face. "The streams from people in the area of the Department of AIR are horrifying. There's nothing left."

Oh my god. "I'll com you if I find out anything I can share."

She sighs. "Okay. I'm just . . ." She turns, and in the gap over her shoulder I see Bianca with her arms around Kyla, practically holding her up. "Worried."

"Me too," I say quietly. "My mom was supposed to be there this morning."

"Oh, Marguerite, I didn't know." She sounds genuinely concerned. "Have you heard from her?"

I shake my head. The distress on her face is amplifying mine. It must be real. It must be bad. "I have to go," I manage to choke out. "I'll com you later, okay?"

"Please. Stay safe."

"You too." I end the com and gulp in a deep breath. It comes out as a low sob.

I might be an orphan. Like Percy, I guess—I'm remembering what Anna told me about his parents. This is a club I so do not want to join. As we race down the streets of DC, I can't get my mind off my mom. "Colette Singer," I say to the agent on my left. "Is she accounted for?"

"I am not authorized to send inquiries via the president's channel," he replies.

I clench my fists and face forward. This is why I hate cannies. If this were a human being, he would have some understanding of what it might be like to wonder where a loved one is. But this robot next to me? He probably doesn't even have a basic empathy chip installed.

Anna would understand. She wanted to get answers for Kyla. It occurs to me as I mentally review my convo with Anna just now that I was talking to her as if she were a friend. Am I actually starting to like the daughter of a woman I absolutely hate? We streak through red traffic signals and past a ton of stopped cars. Patrol cannies stand in the intersections; they have thick arms and wide-set legs to help them maintain crowd and traffic control. Everywhere I look, robots have replaced people.

My fingers grip the seat as we swerve to the side and descend a ramp leading to a municipal parking structure—and then speed straight toward a concrete wall. I scream, then gasp as a door slides to the side. The car glides through it and stops. My stomach bobbles—we're descending. Another door opens, revealing a tunnel. We go down a sharp dip, and then darkness surrounds us. When the lights come up, the car has stopped in a small parking area next to a row of maybe ten other vehicles—and from the seal on the side of the one next to us, I know it's the presidential motorcade. My heart beat kicks against my chest as one of the guards gets out and opens my door. I avoid his dead eyes as I slip past him. The other guard leads me through a doorway with a brush of her palm against a sensor.

"Oh, thank god!" My mother's arms are around me before I can look around, so all I see is thick black hair and a flicker of light through her curls.

She grasps my shoulders and holds me away from her, and I touch her face. "I'm so glad you're okay," I say. I can't stop shaking.

"Me too," she says in a thin voice. "We had just left when the explosion happened. Ron was a few minutes behind us." She swallows and winces like her throat hurts. "He was hit by debris and is at the hospital, but he's going to be all right."

We're in what seems like an office space, cubicles in the center, a hallway that reveals several other rooms with closed doors, and a conference room on the other side of the hallway entrance. Its glass walls reveal the president meeting with a bunch of people, including El, who excuses himself when he sees me. He looks exhausted, his hair standing on end. "You okay?" he asks when he reaches us.

"Yeah. Mom said you guys had a close call."

"We had decided to get some coffee at a nearby café," he says. "We'd just gotten there when the explosion went off." He sighs and rubs his hands over his face. "All the windows shattered."

"We didn't know what was happening," said my mom, her eyes glazing with tears. "But we knew it was bad. The fire—"

El puts his arm around her. "It's okay, Colette. You're safe," he says gently before looking at me. "It was pretty scary. You two can go home tomorrow, but I think it's better if you stay here for the night. We're trying to assess what happened and ensure that there are no other targets. The president is coordinating with his security council now, and the VP is participating in the virtual." El lets out a little laugh. "She's not happy about it, either."

"Oh, I bet she's not." Audrey Savedra was just a rebel technocrat from California—a moderate in a place where tech is worshipped like a god—when Uncle Wynn forged an alliance with her that won him the state. Now I'm hoping she gets pushed to the sidelines. She's always been snide about my vids. If she had her way, I'd probably be on the first flight back to Houston.

Good thing El is closer to the president than she is. "We have to get her back here, or she'll eat us all for breakfast," he says in a tone that indicates he's not the slightest bit afraid of her.

"I wouldn't mind if she had to stay in New York for a while," I mutter. "So—when will we know about casualties? I have some classmates whose parents work in that building."

"It's chaos down there right now, and the DC police are in charge, but we've also got FBI agents in there because it's a federal building. It's probably going to be at least twenty-four hours before any victims are named." He lets out an unsteady breath. "But the building was packed today. People wanting to meet us, wanting to bend our ear, make sure we weren't going to toss them out on the street."

"They might all be dead," my mom says, shaking her head as the tears flow again. "Excuse me. I need a moment." She turns and walks abruptly toward a restroom.

"Do you have any idea who's responsible for this?" I ask.

"I'm sorry I can't share, Marguerite, given that you don't have a security clearance. But I can say we've got a few ideas."

"Technocrats?" I ask. It would make so much sense in some ways.

"I bet there's one name you just want to shout right now."

"Who—Gia?" I think of how upset Anna looked. "This is terrorism, right? It doesn't seem like her style, I guess?"

He arches one eyebrow. "Who are you, and what have you done with Marguerite? Don't you want to cut out her heart and wear it as a trophy?"

"I thought you'd be happy if I toned down my Gia hate."

"On the Mainstream, sure. We've planted our flag on the moral high ground, and there's no way I'm letting them take the hill. But right here and now it's just me, kid. You can be honest. Admit it—you kind of think she's capable of something like this."

"Her daughter goes to my school."

"And does she take after Mommy?"

"She actually seems kind of nice."

"You're smarter than that, Mar."

I look toward the conference room and stare at the back of the president's head. "I didn't say I trusted her."

"Good." He's quiet for a moment. "Actually, this could be good. *Really* good."

I lean my head back. "You are so predictable."

"Bear with me on this—"

"I'm way ahead of you."

"You're predictable, too." El touches my comband. "This might be a good time to tell your fans you're alive and well, and how relieved you are that the president is handling this crisis."

"Then I'll go do my thing." I smile and pivot, eager to dive into the place where I'm most comfortable. Sometimes I feel like a sea turtle forced to march across long stretches of beach, awkward and slow—but then, once I plunge into the Mainstream, I turn into something graceful. And now that I know Mom's okay, it'll be nice to spend time with my fans. I need the support.

Instead of using my comband, I sit down in a cubicle and wave to alert the ID scanner. I lean in as the blue line of light skims my face and retinas, and then my home display appears. "New vid," I murmur, and then I smile as the screen flashes to let me know it's capturing.

"Hey, everyone, you've probably heard about the bombing by now." Some of them probably knew before I did. "It was at the Department of AIR, and I don't have any info about casualties or anything, just that it's bad. But in case you were worried, I wanted to let you know that I'm okay. I had just gotten to school when the bomb went off, and that's at least a few miles away. I'm alive—but it seems really likely that others have lost their lives." I let that sink in, and I allow myself to feel the tragedy of it. What if Kyla lost her parents? How many others did we lose? "Like you all, I'm bracing for news. The one thing I do know is this: our president is on it."

I watch my own gaze become intense, a reflection of my resolve and confidence. "But as we wait to hear more, I want you all to think about something. You sent Wynn Sallese to Washington to do a job for you. You sent him here to make your lives better. This is *your* time. *Our* time. Whoever is responsible for this bombing . . . they're trying to mess that up for-for-for *all* of us, as if we haven't gone through enough already!" I pause, knowing the best stuff needs to ripen in the silence. Then I drive it home. "But it doesn't matter. Whoever did this is no match for the president, not with all of us standing behind him, am I right?" I can almost hear the cheering. I smile. "Wynn Sallese is here for you guys. He always has been. And he won't let you down when it counts—I can tell you that from personal experience. Let him know you're with him, okay? Let him know."

I flick my finger, and the vid stops capturing.

"Would you like to edit your vid?" my channel asks. "Select 'Stutter-Smooth.'"

I shake my head. I always upload the raw stuff, mistakes and all. It works better that way—people know I'm seventeen and real, not some invention of the campaign. No matter what anyone says, no one has ever written a script for me. "Feed it, baby."

I release the vid into the stream and watch for a few minutes as the views skyrocket and comments start to roll in.

I see the new-comment icon blink as FragFlwr drops by.

Using this tragedy to score political points? How typical.

My mouth drops open. "You are such a jerk," I mutter.

"Publish comment?" the channel inquires.

"No!" I sit there and stew as I reread the comment. "You're making a lot of assumptions about me that simply aren't true," I finally say. "Publish."

I assume you will use every opportunity to convince people that Sallese is working on their behalf. I assume YOU actually believe he is. I'm thinking that's better than assuming you're evil, but feel free to let me know if that's what you prefer.

"Of course I believe in my president and his message," I say through gritted teeth. "I know and trust him. And I've experienced the technocrat agenda firsthand, too. I *don't* trust them." I publish this comment with an impatient flourish of my hand.

So if the technocrats are wrong, he must be right? Isn't that a logical fallacy?

"You tell me," I snap. "Can't you access that kind of information instantly on your Cerepin?" I publish it before I can think better of it.

44

Now you're the one who assumes.

"You're a technocrat without a Cerepin? And they still let you into the clubhouse?"

So many assumptions, lovely hypocrite. So very many.

Oh my god, this idiot is driving me nuts. "You've admitted to being a technocrat."

Not really, though I suppose it's a fair conclusion. Also, I've remembered what your fallacy is called! A false dichotomy. Particularly apt, considering how Sallese made his money. But I apologize for carrying us off track. I'm sure you'd like to return to spouting propaganda now. *chin hands* Let's hear it, mouthpiece.

"Arguing with you is sucking away my energy on what has already been a really sad day, and I'd like to save it for people who actually deserve it." My heart is beating so fast that I can barely catch my breath. My face is hot with rage and regret at even starting this comment war. Tears are fighting to break free, but even though this troll can't see me, I'm not going to shed them. "Be safe, FragFlwr, and take care. Publish. Log out." This troll will get nothing else from me.

Chapter Five

Percy

The user has logged off.

Well, I've had my fun. Worked off a bit of the savagery I try to keep in check most of the time. Now I have to sit here and think about what's happened.

I kick off my shoes—they're not as comfortable as I'd like, but they look damn good—and start to pace.

"Your heart rate is rising, Percy," says Sophia, the voice of the house. "Are you in distress?"

Lovely. My aunt has increased Sophia's empathy and intervention settings again. But it's good I'm finding this out now instead of tonight. "I know what my heart rate is, Sophia."

I always know.

"I am here for you if you would like to talk."

I lean over my desk and press my knuckles to the polished surface. "I'm not distressed, darling."

"Distressed" is a silly and entirely inadequate word for what I am.

"Bianca on vid," says another voice, this time emanating from beneath my knuckles. I look down to see Bianca's pretty face in the center of the display. I waggle my eyebrows, answering the com, allowing the projection of her to inhabit the space over the desk.

"I hardly ever hear from you these days," I say to her as I lean back.

"That's because I broke up with you."

"Ah. Of course. I remember now."

She flips her hair. Really, her hair is the thing I enjoy most about her. I liked sliding my fingers through it. I liked clenching my fist and pulling it when I kissed her. She seemed to like it, too. Now, though . . . "I'm only comming to see if you made it home okay." She eyes me. "Nice hair."

I smooth my hand over the new blond streak—the only gold that's left, because my hair is now ebony. "You noticed."

"Percy, honestly, who cares that you got your hair done? The freaking world is exploding."

"And yet here we stand."

"You can cut the act. I know you better than that."

"If that were true, you would know not to say that to me."

"Chances are Kyla's dad was killed in the attack. The building is completely obliterated—my intel says there are no survivors so far. Not even any injured except for a few people just outside of the three-block radius that was flattened. He was probably incinerated instantly."

I clench my jaw. "Her mother?"

"Wasn't at the department today. I just found out."

"And Kyla?"

"Mr. Cordoza came and took her out of the cafeteria, and the look on his face was just . . . ugh. She thought both of her parents had been killed. She started screaming for her mommy and daddy."

Grief twists hard inside my gut, but Bianca's watching me now. I don't know why she thinks I'll give her more than I did when we were together. "Poor Kyla."

"Seriously?"

"Did you com just to try to get a reaction out of me?"

She presses her lips together. But after a moment of blessed silence, she says, "So, is she what you expected?"

"Who?" I know exactly who.

"The president's attack puppy. I still think she slept with him."

"Are we onto this again? How grandly retrogressive of you."

"Are you actually defending her?"

"No, I'm insulting *you*."

"Whatever. She's nothing special. Did you watch the vid I sent you last week?"

"I have more exciting things to do with my time." And I prefer the raw, unedited versions.

"She's exactly like she is face-to-face. Self-righteous and stupid and boring."

"I can't disagree with the self-righteous part." It's amusing in both milieus.

"Oh, come on! She's where she is because she had a sob story and got lucky!"

I laugh. I can't help it. "Yes, lucky. That is *exactly* how I would describe her."

Bianca's eyes narrow. "Wait. Do you *like* her?"

"Madly in love. I think it's forever this time."

"Can you ever be real, Percy?"

"Not when such unpleasantness can be avoided."

"She's the puppet of sleazy Sallese! At our school! I thought you would at least want to help me make her miserable, just for the freaking sport of it. I thought you were on my side, but you've been totally avoiding me for the last week."

"And I've disappointed you yet again. One would think you'd be braced for it by now."

"Well . . . you could make it up to me. I've got a little vid project that I'm working on for our new friend, and I need a fashion consultation."

I look her over. She is immaculate, as always. "This is what you're focused on in the wake of a heinous terrorist attack?"

"You know those populist thugs are behind this somehow."

"Do I?" The thought had occurred to me, but would they really bomb a government building they now control? To what end?

"Oh, you're the only one who gets to spin conspiracy theories?" She sighs. "Percy. Believe it or not, I'm not interested in fighting with you, especially not today. I just need to do something. This is crazy."

"So your brilliant plan is to provoke a Mainstream darling, a dazzlingly effective spokeswoman for a landslide president?"

"He's not that popular."

"Not in our circle, dear. I may not dabble in politics, but did he not win the election with over sixty percent of the vote and carry forty-seven states? What do you hope to accomplish?"

"She's going to push Sallese to punish Parnassus—"

"Don't tell me your father's on board with your revenge fantasy."

"He said to be nice to her!"

"How silly of him. Or . . . oh, perhaps he feels some responsibility over Marguerite's father's untimely demise? Does he feel he had a hand in what happened afterward?"

"Because some wack job killed himself?"

"My darling, sometimes you do a brilliant impression of a psychopath. Might there be a glitch in your empathy chip?"

"Ugh! I don't know why I commed."

"Allow me to help. You wanted to use Kyla's unspeakable loss as a way to get under my skin, and you were hoping to co-opt me in a plan to torment someone it would benefit you to be very, very nice to."

"I hate you."

"One of the key ingredients in our breakup, as I recall." I soften my tone as her face turns red. "Bianca, I know you're scared about what's going to happen to Parnassus. What's going to happen to your father and your family now that the winds of change are blowing."

"You don't understand. You're untouchable."

"If that were true, perhaps I wouldn't be an orphan."

Bianca grimaces and looks away. "She needs to get the hell out of our school, Percy. She doesn't belong there."

"A fact of which she seems keenly aware. But she doesn't seem petty to me. She doesn't seem cruel." Quite the contrary. She seems . . . *earnest.* But true believers are often the most dangerous. "Now, if you'll excuse me, darling, I need to go interact with people who actually like me."

I end the com while Bianca is in midreply. As her face disappears, my display returns to my channel. My subscribers have come aboard to watch the vid on hair color that I posted when I got home—and the comments have started to roll in.

Muchacha17: Love the new color! You were sooo cute as a blondie, tho ☹

CREMdela: You couldn't be ugly if you tried.

SlzySally451: Divine, baby. Wish I had your skin.

ClintRock: Seems like it's the season to make some changes, but you can only do it if you're willing to go out on a limb.

I read the comment twice. Then I reply. "Good thing I'm very *secure* with myself. Publish."

ClintRock: If that's true, now is definitely the time.

Here we go. "Sophia, privacy," I say, the order that essentially makes her blind and deaf until I reinstate her. My heart rate is climbing as I open a portal to my secure channel and activate my "ghost," autonomous AI that conveniently erases any trace of my activities in real time by slicing up my data and scattering it to the electronic wind. The tech is a gift from the man with whom I'm about to commune in the virtual world.

"It's been a while," I say. And it has, too long. Of all my online relationships, this is the only one that commands my attention.

"After what happened today," comes his electronically distorted voice, "we need to meet."

"Does this mean—"

"I repeat, we need to meet. I'm still assessing the new administration's security, and until I know, I'm not saying anything on the wires. Usual place, usual time. You bring the chips; I bring the dip."

"And what party games shall we play?"

There's no reply. He's already gone.

"Percy," says Sophia. "Dinner will be served in ten minutes."

"Privacy off. Is the ambassador home yet?"

"She arrived twenty-two minutes ago."

"Marvelous." I need to see how Aunt Rosalie is faring. I put on my satin slippers and slide out of my room. The corridor chandelier senses my approach and greets me with an intensifying glow, and I blink, letting my implants adjust the aperture of my pupils. I love being able to see in the dark, but it's the devil on my peepers in the light.

I can already hear my aunt in her office. She is anything but subtle. Sophia is issuing white noise, but my audio implant cuts through the static like a razor through silk. My aunt is speaking French, of course, as befits her position, but this is not a problem for me.

The implant in my middle ear is also equipped with full translation. *I've put everyone on alert,* she is saying. *We're ready, if it comes to that.* Uh-oh.

No, the administration has not reached out, though I sent a message that the French are ready to support them. I don't think they were ready for this . . . Yes, I'll do that. The vice president might be the best contact. We've identified Audrey Savedra as the most moderate senior administration official so far. I'll reach out tomorrow.

Suddenly I'm wishing I had upgraded audio tech, so I could hear what her conversational partner is saying. My chips haven't been updated for over two years. What I have is what I have, until I figure out how to get more.

I'm trying to find out more about the damage assessment, Aunt Rosalie continues. *No one's saying anything. I'd wait to pull personnel until we know Sallese is blocking access.*

Mm-hmm. Sounds like the French president is more than a little skittish about her new American counterpart. Then again, she was always savvy. I skip back several steps and start forward again as I hear Auntie offer a curt *au revoir* and sign off. She bursts out of her office a second later to find me strolling down the hall toward dinner.

"Ah, Percy," she says, smiling, though she looks unusually frazzled. Short silver wisps, like antennae, wave around her hairline, begging for a touch-up. "How is my darling boy?" She's speaking English now—she doesn't know about all my augmentations.

The only people who did are dead. Well, except for one, and I'm meeting him tonight at eleven.

"Thank you for letting me have the car this afternoon," I say, so loudly that it makes my aunt jump and then mutter "Volume level four" to her Cerepin. "I escaped the academy right before the blast walls lowered."

She shakes her head at my turn of phrase. "*Oui, oui.* A very sad day indeed."

I wait for her to tell me more, but she never does. This is why I'm forced to eavesdrop. I'd be honest about it, but I don't think she'd take well to my *extra* extracurricular activities. She likes to believe I could be a normal boy if only I'd admit I am devastated and move on. Poor

Auntie has no idea how not-normal I really am. Moving on isn't really an option.

"Some of your classmates may have lost parents in this catastrophe," she continues, giving me a cautious, probing look.

She wants me to spill my insides out for her to examine, rearrange, and stitch back together, so very *cathartique*. "They probably did. It's so tragic," I say, eyes wide, pupils authentically dilated with concern.

If I admit I already know there are bodies, like Kyla's father, she'll ask for details, and just like Auntie, there are secrets I must keep. I glance at the walls, silently daring Sophia to ask if I'm distressed. I exhale and loosen my muscles. It would be a shame to punch a hole through the wall's intricate trompe l'oeil.

"Such a waste," Auntie says, then clutches my arm. "Are you sure you're all right?"

"Fine, as always." There is no other answer that does not involve broken glass and splintered furniture and all the rage that's in me. I offer her my airiest smile. We can't slide over this edge. We can't ever. Instead, I bring my hand up to frame my face. "I had my hair done this afternoon."

"And you look so handsome." She regards my new jacket, a simple cut adorned only by a thin silver piping that matches the miniskirt I'm wearing over my black pants. "Too handsome to stay home."

"I think tonight it might be too dangerous to go out."

She grins, looking relieved. "*Oui*. Staying in is a good plan."

I stretch. "An early evening for me. Must have my beauty sleep. But first, our meal." I wink at her. "I'm famished."

"We can eat in the dining room," she says. "We have gentlemen in the sitting room."

Extra guards, she means. Because we are waiting for the whole city to explode. When Sallese won, my aunt said this country's downfall would happen by a thousand cuts. Now she seems to be reconsidering.

I offer her my arm, glancing at the antique clock on the hallway mantel. Four hours. Plenty of time. "Dining room it is, Madam Ambassador." I use my best terrible French accent.

She winces.

We head for the dining room, where Louis, the chef, will serve us fresh baguettes and cassoulet, his bare synthetic hands deftly managing the searing pot. I will babble about stockings and mineral powder, and she will ply me with stories of Paris in her youth, and after she has had two glasses of wine, she will sigh and tell me I look so much like my mother that it hurts her heart.

At that point I will excuse myself, because she lost a sister, yes.

But I lost my mother.

I register the stress response, and it takes me several seconds to slow my breathing. I focus on lowering my heartbeat from 172 beats per minute all the way to an even 100. I need to control my legacy.

My parents wanted me to live, and they equipped me to survive.

I smile and think of the sun, bright and blank and certain. Aunt Rosalie returns my smile.

We survive in very different ways. And both of us hold our secrets close. The only difference is that I need people to believe I don't have any at all.

Chapter Six

Percy

At ten to eleven, I shimmy out the window undetected. I redirected the beams of Sophia's sensors, and my Mainstream feed is set to a channel that mimics bio-sounds, including breathing and heartbeats. It even farts from time to time. It's not perfect, but it's easy enough to elude the embassy AI. It hasn't been upgraded since I moved in two years ago, and I've spent all that time studying the system in order to win myself a little freedom to indulge my . . . hobby? No, my quest.

The canny guards and building-mounted surveillance scanners are a bit trickier, but I am still prepared. Truly, all one has to do is stay one step ahead, and all one needs for that is the Mainstream and an untraceable funding source. Check and check. The prisms on the top of my head and on my shoulders, thighs, and back project a visual and audio mirror of whatever I'm walking past. I am invisible to cannies until I reach the edge of embassy property, when I have to remove these rather gaudy patches.

Humans aren't so easily fooled, see.

Well, good riddance, because the silver patches don't match my current outfit at all. Horror show, to tell the truth. I don't look like myself, but I suppose that's the point. *Myself* is noticeable. I usually draw the eye, and this outfit is made for melting into the night: plain black slacks, a gray T-shirt, a black jacket. No makeup. A black cap on my head, smashing down my hair. I've removed the polish from my fingernails. I feel like an exposed nerve, shivery and thrumming with a current on the air.

And now to make me . . . *really* not myself. I reach up and slide my fingers under my cheekbones and along my brow, pressing firmly to trigger what lies beneath. I wince as I feel my face changing, stretching, just enough to evade facial recognition. I'm taking a risk tonight—after the bombing, security will be tighter. Police patrols will be more frequent.

I head east along Reservoir. There are more people out walking and on wheelboards. Word on the Mainstream is public transportation and the skyway will be suspended until tomorrow morning, and private vehicles are doubtless being monitored as they travel along the grid. Hence the need to be on foot. If I had a Cerepin, I could be tracked that way as well.

That's a feature Fortin Tech has always spun in a positive way—instant emergency assistance! You'll never be lost!—but lord, it has its pitfalls.

If anyone wants to monitor *me*, they have to lay eyes—real or synthetic—on my person. I jog along the embassy fence, knowing I'm cutting this close. Ricard, my aunt's favorite aide and "secret" lover, always leaves a few minutes before eleven. I press myself against the ivy as I see his car roll along the private road. No flying tonight, lucky for me.

As they sense his approach, the gates to the embassy grounds slide open. I have to time this perfectly, or I'm caught. I lope along in the darkness and reach the gate just as Ricard's vehicle glides toward it. I drop to the ground and crawl through on all fours just as the car silently rolls by. With my patches on, the gate doesn't "see" me, nor does it detect my body heat, because of the vehicle. I fold myself against the wall as Ricard departs.

After I pull the silver patches from my clothes and place them back in their case, I head up the block, now fully visible but less suspicious looking. Better to be caught *without* patches than with, for reasons both fashion related and not. I don't walk quickly or with too much purpose. I pretend that there are weights strapped to my wrists and ankles. It feels ungraceful and unnatural, but this is part of the game. I've practiced in front of a gait analyzer, and I know that if I walk this way, no one can match it to my usual stride. Every step takes intention, but that is something I possess in spades. Dad always used to say I had it in me to be a chameleon. He would know, because what I have in me? He put it there.

I blink to widen the aperture of my pupils and let in more light. I tell myself that's why my eyes sting. It's the only reason.

The streets are humming tonight. With no air travel allowed, each car skims the street, maintaining that perfect two feet of distance between it and every other moving object on the road. Each electronic brain flickers and calculates, controlling braking and acceleration. Each living organism inside churns with far less linear thoughts.

I am fond of linearity.

As I walk, I press the tiny bump beneath my left ear—one of my augmentations, an audio chip. *Recording,* says a voice only I can hear. The street noise is minimal, but my implant will capture the whisper of magnetic wheels, the occasional passing conversation, the hum of the city. Perfect.

When I reach the intersection of Reservoir and Thirty-Seventh, I stretch and yawn, and then turn left and stride up Thirty-Seventh, along a lovely residential Georgetown street lined with old trees and reeking of money.

"Lovely night," says a man who's pulled even with me. His strides are short and uneven, as is his breathing. He's clad in a thick jacket with the oversized, ratty faux-fur hood pulled so tightly around his face that all anyone can see is his eyes.

A travesty, and how very subtle.

I want to tell him to get some self-control before his indelicate huffing and puffing gets us noticed, but that will just jangle his poor, frayed nerves even more. "I wonder why more people don't stroll the boulevards like they used to," I say.

"Probably because they know their every word is being monitored." His gaze darts back and forth, and he pulls his hood even lower. "Did you bring me a snack?"

"You're so clever." I tap the chip beneath my ear twice. *Playback,* I hear, and smile. I tap it one more time. *Projecting,* it says. Now we have a bit of privacy. "I've got us covered, as always, Chen."

"Good thing, because my auditory interface is gl-gli-glitching."

"Are you sure it's not your vocal—"

"It was a joke, kid."

I glance over at him. I know what lies beneath that hood—he let me see it the first time he introduced himself to me in person after a few months of intriguing cat and mouse on the Mainstream.

How did he hook me? He said he knew my father, Valentine Blake. He said my father had told him about me, that he knew things about me that my father wanted me to know, and he'd tell me when the time was right.

That was a year ago. He'd fed me enough, bit by bit, for me to know Chen was the closest link I had to my parents—and to the real me. I have to wonder if the fiery little surprise at the Department of AIR this morning might have goosed Chen into giving up more information.

Tonight he is twitching more than usual. His thumb and forefinger tap together constantly, as if he's aching to work a pair of tweezers. "New add-on?" I ask, perfectly casual.

He gives me an irritable glance. "Made a go at thought-controlled volume toggle and Mainstream navigation," he says as his shoulder starts to jerk up and down. "Ukaiah said I was dumb to try."

"Ukaiah is wise." His partner is definitely the more prudent, based on my dealings with her. "Is this even legal?"

"If I want to install a computer in my head, how am I different from any Cerepin user?"

"The FDA approved Cerepins for installation by certified med-tech professionals only. This . . . well, is not that."

"It's all part of the racket, kid. Zao was in the tank for Fortin, and you know it. She wanted a monopoly, and he gave it to her genned with a bow. Oh, Perce, I thought of a name for these babies." He gestures at his fur-covered noggin. "Incomps."

"As in incompetent?"

He stops so suddenly that his hood falls off his head, temporarily revealing the misshapen helmetlike technical interface that covers his skull, sprigs of black hair sticking out here and there like weeds in an abandoned park. "Internal computers!" He looks genuinely hurt as he yanks the hood back over his head, twitching the whole time. "Ukaiah didn't like the name, either."

"Once again, Ukaiah outshines you."

"And you of all people shouldn't be judging me. I mean, look at *you*." He jabs a finger at my newly configured face. "That stuff you have on board is not exactly government sanctioned."

Touché. My heart rate spikes to 167. "I have twenty minutes before I have to be back at the embassy. What did you want to tell me?"

"Your parents' case is gonna be officially closed. The detective uploaded the order this morning."

One eighty-five. *Breathe.* "He was supposed to be tracking down the doctor. Weisskopf."

"Apparently the good doctor has disappeared."

I rub my hands over my altered face. "So first the murderer disappears from his cell—"

"Technically, the accused. He was awaiting trial. And he wasn't charged with murder."

"Yes, yes. Because a crazed addict who *randomly* decides to stab two people to death as he waits for his morning hit in the recovery clinic is guilty only of manslaughter." My insides twist again. "And now the man who supplied him with the weapon is also in the wind."

"Dr. Weisskopf always claimed Kasabian stole the scalpel from his exam room."

"And you and I both know that's too convenient to be true. How did he manage to get through the retina scan on Weisskopf's office door? My parents were onto something, Chen. I know it." Now I'm sweating, and my rate of respiration is up to twenty-five breaths per minute.

Chen notices me starting to lose my composure and clutches at my sleeve. I'm not in the mood to be comforted, but when I jerk away, a canny patroller swivels its head in our direction. I shut down my thoughts and slow my stride. We can't afford to be noticed.

Chen doesn't try to grab my arm again. "You're right that the whole case is shady, Percy, but now it's bigger than your parents. They were the vanguard, though."

"You mean the cannon fodder."

"They were killed because they were dangerous."

"But to whom?" I say, strained and quiet. We're past the canny and headed west on T, essentially walking in a loop back to the embassy. "I thought their research was on neurostim devices. They were trying to *help* people."

Chen's darting eyes go still as he looks into mine. "You're right on both counts. Let's say your father was asking some very probing questions around the use of neurostims. And the Cerepins, well . . . He had an agenda, and he and your mother were collecting data someone didn't want them to have. So who might they have harmed with all that 'help'? That's always the question to ask. Always, always, always."

"Weisskopf ran the clinic. He had a stake in it."

"Right. He was using neurostims to treat addiction, demonstrating they were more than simple mood enhancers. That was something companies like NeuroGo and Fortin Tech were *very* keen to prove."

Ah, NeuroGo, the trillion-dollar start-up founded by none other than Marguerite's hero, President Wynn Sallese. He sold his shares three years ago, though, as he prepared to run for office. Since then he's hailed himself as a man of the people—and for some reason, those people ate it up.

"The police report said that Weisskopf had invited my parents there to show them the clinic and discuss collaboration. He *asked* them to be there that morning," I say.

"And then one of his patients nabs a scalpel from his office and . . ." Chen bows his head and shakily *crosses* himself, of all things. *Mon Dieu!* A rebel hacker who prays the rosary. A day full of surprises. He continues. "Perce, why didn't the police ask why he had a scalpel in his supplies? It was an addiction clinic, not a hospital!"

I look away, watching a bus silently glide by full of glassy-eyed drones tapping at their Cerepins. "And now Weisskopf is gone, along with anything he might have known about who guided Kasabian's hand—or his own."

"Now ask yourself, kid. Really ask yourself. It's been two years since your parents were killed. Eight months since Derek Kasabian vanished from that cell. Now the one person left who could have explained what really happened that day has flown the coop—case closed. Just as the Sallese administration takes over." Chen places his hand on his jerking shoulder to try to keep it still. He does not succeed. "Coincidence?"

"You think the president's involved? Why?"

He puts up his hands. "I didn't say that. I'm just saying that if you dismiss a possible connection simply because it's not obvious, then you're one of the sheep." His eyes narrow. "And if you're truly Valentine and Flore Blake's son, a sheep is the last thing I'd expect you to be."

We've reached the corner where we must part ways. I have to get back before Sophia notices the slight drop in temperature in my room, the tiniest decrease in carbon dioxide levels, and realizes there is no actual breathing body in my bed.

"You'll contact me again when you have more information?" I ask.

Chen looks up and down the street. "Yeah. But—we have something else to talk about."

"And that is?"

"You turn eighteen in a few weeks. And your dad wanted me to give you something."

I catch my breath. I've been waiting a year for this. But I know I can't force it out of him—I've made the mistake of losing my patience a time or two with his meager trail of breadcrumbs, and his response is always to threaten to disappear. And I've reviewed his ghost AI program—Chen could really do it. "I'm ready."

But he only shakes his Incomped head. "Not here and not now." He lets out a loud sigh. "I'm not even sure I should be doing this at all."

No. No way is he backing down. "Chen, if it's rightfully mine and it came from my father, you can't keep it from me."

"That's what Ukaiah said, too."

"Majority rules."

"Maybe you're right. Things are getting serious now. Sallese and his buddies are no joke. Their response to this bombing . . ." He whistles, and spittle flies from his mouth.

"I would have thought you had voted for Sallese, Chen. Technology for the masses and all of that?" This is the first I've heard from Chen since the election.

"Ever ask yourself how deep the ties go between Fortin and Sallese? You think they're really at each other's throats?" He snorts. "That's what they want you to believe."

It certainly seemed that way after watching Marguerite Singer's vids. And the way she reacted when I told her who Anna really was—that seemed genuine . . . genuine disgust, that is. An emotion I happen to know a little something about. "Well then, the Oscar goes to Sallese. He has convinced the 'real Americans' that he has their best interests in mind . . . and made a lot of enemies in this town in the process."

"Has he?"

I roll my eyes.

"Gotta figure out what their game is, kid. Sallese and Fortin are at war, but what's going on underneath?"

I scan the night with my augmented vision and listen to the hum of the canny patroller one block behind us. I adjust my heart rate so it doesn't catch his attention. I tap beneath my ear to increase the volume on my auditory shield. "Frankly, Chen, I don't care about their game. All I want is to find my parents' murderer. I want justice for them."

"Answers will come to you from the strangest of places. But first you might want to dig down and explore what's right under your nose." He smirks. "I'll be in touch."

And that's it. Another unsatisfying conversation that brings me no closer to understanding. I don't know who or what is more elusive— Chen and Ukaiah or the answers I'm looking for. "Chen, thank you for helping me."

"Is that what I'm doing?" He stretches, even though his fingers are still twitching and his shoulder is still jerking. "I thought I was just out for an evening stroll." He turns and walks away, his steps just a shade too quick.

As soon as they fade, I'm aware of the canny watching me from across the street. I zoom in close. His eyes are scanning my face. No. I can't run now—if I avoid him, he might decide to follow me. I can only hope I am hidden as well as I need to be. Just to be on the safe side, I tap my Adam's apple and feel my vocal cords swell. Then I cross quickly, controlling my strides, my breathing. "Thank you for your service," I say in my new deep and raspy—and completely untraceable—voice. "You guys don't get nearly enough credit."

This canny looks less human than many of them; his face is flat, no nose, no eyebrows. He has broad shoulders and fingers that fold back to expose a neural disruptor or a gun, depending on what level of force he is authorized to use. Right now his arms are at his sides. "You are welcome, citizen."

I smile, but not too broadly, just a friendly, bland curve of the lips. He's still watching me, probably still probing the Mainstream, looking for my face, but I'm not doing anything suspicious and he's already scanned my body for weapons, no doubt, and therefore has no reason to detain me. I'm no threat.

Not at all. I let him stare at my back until I turn the corner, and then I jog to the embassy. I arrive and press my silver reflective decals back into position just in time for the delivery canny bringing in fresh croissants and *pains au chocolat* from Auntie's favorite bakery for the morning. As the gates swing open, I slide in, knowing all that will show up on the cameras is a slight warp in the air.

I make it back into my room and dive into bed, letting out my breath slowly.

"You are awake now," says Sophia.

Sophia, queen of the obvious. I quickly reach over and wave off the bio-sounds channel within the desk screen. "Bad dream."

"You have many bad dreams," she says. "You often cry out in your sleep. If you were to enable the actigraphy sensor in your comband, I would be able to—"

"No *thank* you, Sophia."

"Your volume indicates you believe I might have trouble hearing you. I assure you my settings are quite sensitive."

"Aren't you saucy tonight?"

"Your tone indicates that you are frustrated."

I sit up abruptly. "Sophia. Please stop talking to me." Good lord. I'm going to have to speak to my aunt. I had no idea she planned to sic the house on me.

It makes me wonder if she knew about my parents' case being closed before I did.

"Engage privacy settings," I say. "Wouldn't want you spying on me in my birthday suit."

"Privacy settings engaged." That's when I remember that I still have my patches on. I am still invisible. I slide my fingers along my cheekbones and brow, pressing until I feel the release of pressure that tells me my face is returning to its normal configuration. I push back the memory that keeps trying to surface. My father's eyes, his hands on my face, his frown of concentration.

I get up from my bed, go to my closet, and dig under the mound of discarded jackets, trousers, wigs, skirts, shirts, some imprinted with loving little digicards from the designers, mostly from Europe or Asia, thanking me for downloading their creations and letting me know what huge fans they are. All of them hope I'll wear their designs in a vid. They'd probably scream if they knew I use their precious garments to hide my most treasured possession.

I reach the bottom of the pile and feel its smooth edges, its warmth. I pull the box into my lap and press my thumb to the circle in its center. The lock releases as the box senses my DNA and fingerprint. I open it and stare down at the contents. It's a time capsule in many ways.

My fingers tremble slightly as I reach down and trace the fragile edge of the paper on top, then the petals of the flower embossed onto its surface with a handheld metal press. My mother's handwriting is smooth and graceful on the page.

Off to do some good in the world. We'll see you for dinner!

In a completely digital world, she and my father loved to leave notes for each other and for me, written with soy ink on a special paper they sourced from overseas. No one really used paper anymore, of course. It was so anachronistic they might as well have been writing with feathers dipped in inkwells. I used to find it both cute and tiresome, in the way so many parents are, but now I wonder if it was just one more way to avoid being tracked, recorded, monitored.

If so, it didn't help them much.

I pick up the sheaf of paper and carefully remove the sheet at the very bottom. The fountain pen inside the box rattles. A gift from my grandfather to my father, it bears my father's initials, VPB. Though it's completely dark, I can read it easily. Thanks to him.

I press my thumb to the flower at the top of the paper, retrofitted by my dad to contain a chip coded to my DNA alone. My father's words appear. It's been ages since I read this.

It is my intention never to leave you, Percy, but I've learned that one man's strength means little in this world. And with that lesson hard earned, I feel the need to tell you things I so hoped to explain to you in person when you were older.

Do not be afraid of what you are, and trust your body. But please treat all of it, both what you come by naturally and what I've given you, with respect and care—I haven't yet tested it as thoroughly as I wanted to.

I've never gone further than this before. It's too painful. Too eerie. But like Chen said, I'm almost eighteen. Bombs are exploding. People are dying. I want answers and justice. And he told me to dig deep. He told me to explore what's been under my nose this whole time.

"Here we go," I murmur. I press the raised flower again, and my father's words are erased—and replaced with code. My eyes lock onto it and scan, and then I clutch at a nearby chair and hang on tight as I sway with dizziness. A menu is floating in front of my face, telling me to select an option.

<u>Sense Management:</u>
Ophthalmoception
Audioception
Olfactoception
Tactioception
Proprioception
Thermoception
Nociception
Equilibrioception
Mechanoreception

"Oh my . . ." This is all inside my head. Literally inside my head. Carefully, I spend a few minutes navigating through the menus, which is as easy as the brush of a thought. I turn my sense of equilibrium up a notch—it's always good to have a keen sense of balance—and dial my sense of smell down. This will make my school days easier, given that most of my classmates wield perfume and cologne like cudgels. I leave nociception, my detection of pain, alone. I think it's necessary. Besides, even if I dialed it to nothing, I don't think it could save me from the ache of missing my parents. My parents, who did this to me, even though I'm still figuring out exactly what *this* entails.

So far, these notes, these menus inside my head, are all I have from my childhood. They stand in place of my memories, because I have nothing from before the accident. Just me looking up at them, me unable to move, me hearing their voices but never my own. Me listening to all their cautions—for secrecy, for protection—their promises that I would understand all of it when I got older, and their strict instructions for how to be and to live.

And then me having to do all that without them.

I go back to the main menu, planning to exit, when a menu item catches my eye:

<u>Health and Safety:</u>
Bioscan
Site management
System update (option disabled)
Self-destruct (option disabled)

I read the options again, and then again. An odd sense of frustration washes over me.

(option disabled)

It's just the kind of thing a good parent would do, like DNA-locking the starter on the car and capping all the screens to enable monitoring of Mainstream activity.

My face crumples as I bow my head. The menu disappears, burning white then black behind my closed eyelids. My fist clenches around the pen, which my mother used to write me that sweet little note only a few hours before she was killed.

For two years, I've been trying to find out why she was. I waited for Derek Kasabian's trial. My aunt wanted to ship me off to France, but I threatened to file for emancipation and never speak to her again if she tried, and I think the poor dear actually believed I would. And then Kasabian vanished into the ether, and no one would tell me why or how or where. So I waited for the detectives to question Dr. Weisskopf and follow that thread, hoping for answers. I have been told that was the only thing I could do. That was my only option.

I stopped believing that months ago, even before this new development. When Chen and Ukaiah first contacted me, it felt a little more my style. Finally I had the power to find answers on my own. But then? More waiting! And now? I can't for a moment believe this string of catastrophes—the murders, the disappearances—is coincidental.

I close my box and slide it beneath a pile of silk stockings. I glance toward my desk screen. I need answers, but I know the Mainstream won't offer them. Except . . . I walk over to my screen. "Anna Fortin," I say.

I stare down at her face, impeccable white brows stark against her brown skin. We've been almost-friends ever since I started at Clinton, moving through circles that touched but didn't quite overlap. She's a fiercely loyal cub to mommy tiger. But I need to know if Fortin and Sallese are working together, as Chen seemed to suggest. If they are and I don't know how or why they would—I need to find out whether either of them is linked to my parents' deaths.

It sounds crazy even to me when I string it together like that. But nothing is making sense anymore. And now that the sole remaining link to what happened—Dr. Weisskopf—has vanished, I really see only one option.

"Marguerite Singer."

Her channel comes up immediately. I trigger her latest vid and watch her hover, life size and vibrant, before me. For the second time today, I listen to America's young hero reassure all of us that President Sallese will find out who attacked the Department of AIR and will bring the terrorists to justice. It's very moving. Her eyes, warm and brown, seem to be looking right at me. Oh, she's good.

I am itching to start another comment war with her. She takes the bait so readily. One thing holds me back, though: Could *she* help me find out what I need to know? Is she a puppet, or is she really part of the inner circle?

I smile. It looks like I have some work to do. I need to get closer to Anna. And it is time I make Marguerite Singer my very good friend.

Chapter Seven

Marguerite

My eyes pop open when I hear footsteps thumping down the hall past my door, and for a moment I'm not sure where I am. I take in the soft glow coming from the gray-blue walls, simulating dawn in the window-less room. The sheets are white and soft beneath my fingers, too soft for me to be in my bed in the apartment in Houston.

Oh. I'm in a secret bunker with the president of the United States, and DC is in flames.

The night comes back all at once. I was up past one interacting with my followers, talking about what I knew of the bombing, trying to stay somewhere in that perfect zone between authentic supporter of the president and actual spokesperson. I've learned the power of words in the last year. Right now, it would be disastrous to be any-thing but sad and angry on behalf of people like Kyla and her family, even though what I want to do is point the finger at the technocrats responsible. There were no terrorist attacks on the Department of AIR when they were in power, but the moment the American people take that power away? The whole thing literally explodes. But I have to constantly remind myself of how this plays for Uncle Wynn as he starts his presidency and tries to improve the economy. He wouldn't want to look weak, like he can't keep people safe.

Because a crisis wouldn't be complete without trolls, several waded in just after midnight to attack, accusing me of being the "sexy jailbait puppet" of "Sleazy Sallese's" corrupt regime, describing what they thought had happened between me and the president on the campaign trail.

In graphic, extensive detail.

I looked over every handle—oddly, FragFlwr skipped the party. I guess our last argument satisfied his need to torment me. Maybe he asked his friends to stand in. And . . . I can't help the next thought that enters my head: What if some of these new trolls are my classmates?

Bile rises in my throat as I remember the look on Bianca's face when she made the same kinds of accusations.

My comband vibrates as I stretch, sensing I'm awake. I get up quickly and toss on the freshly genned clothes one of the attendants offered me last night. Plain black pants, black shirt, per my request. Then I flick to my channel and scroll through comments, just to see if I missed anything important. I skim until I see one tagged with a very familiar face.

ScarletP: People over politics. Bravo. Really.

I reread it. Is Percy being sincere or sarcastic?

The door slides open as I approach, and I look down the hall. El is in the mazelike work area, standing in one of the cubicles, probably watching the Mainstream chatter about the bombings. My mother stands next to him, her hands folded around her narrow frame, her hair pulled back from her face. As I approach, El takes a step away from Mom and gives me a quick nod. He hasn't shaved; his beard is brown shot through with silver hairs. "They've got breakfast in the conference room," he says to me. "More importantly, coffee."

"I need it," I say, rubbing my eyes. "Any news? The good kind, preferably?"

Mom puts her hand on my back, and I lean into her. "They've determined it was definitely an explosive device that caused the damage," she says.

"Have they pulled any survivors from the rubble?"

She sighs and shakes her head. "Only bodies."

"Sixty-eight and counting," El says. "It's an outrage! We need to find out who did this and make an example of them."

"Any leads?"

"Marguerite," Mom starts to say, but El holds up his hand.

"It's okay, Colette." He has a shrewd look on his face that I know so well. "Why don't you tell her who *you* think is responsible, Mar?"

"Well, a lot of my followers wonder if the bomber is sympathetic to the technocrats," I say. "I do, too. I mean, here we are, poised to actually give that department some teeth. We'd stop handing out free-pass contracts to places like Fortin Tech and Parnassus unless they made changes to protect ordinary Americans—quotas maybe, actually address some of the monopolies . . ."

El smiles. "I like the way you say 'we.'"

"So it makes sense that some deranged technocrat sympathizers might want to punish us or stop us from making those changes, I guess," I finish, standing up a little straighter.

"It's way too early for us to know anything," El says, "but your reasoning is definitely sound, as far as I'm concerned."

Mom gives him an uncertain look. "Just be careful about what you say on the Mainstream, Marguerite. Right now that's just speculation. Plus, the last thing we need is backlash toward technocrats."

El nods solemnly. "We want them to stay right where they are."

Mom frowns. "We have a strategy meeting later this morning, after the president has a chance to get briefed. If there are administration actions or policies that we want to publicize, we'll let you know."

"The one thing I can tell you," El says, bouncing on his heels, "is that now Ron Gould is probably going to sail through his confirmation hearing. We'll celebrate once the poor guy is out of the hospital. Because no one's gonna want to block the president's choice while he's dealing with this."

"I have to go, or I'm going to be late," I say.

"Mar goes to school with Gia's daughter," El says to my mom. "They're gonna be good friends."

"Really?"

I shrug. "She seems nice. Serious, actually. Some of my classmates, though . . ." I roll my eyes, thinking of Blanca and Percy and Winston and all the rest.

Behind Mom, El looks triumphant. "She's probably the one who matters most. Keep us posted."

Stomach growling, I head for the conference room. If I'm going to survive this day, I need major caffeine.

Walking into school is different today. Even though it looks like at least half my classmates decided to stay home, there are twice as many security cannies at the doors, some of them Secret Service. El told me I'd be protected, and I guess this is what he meant, but once again, he can't protect me from the stares. They're different today, too. Since my first day of school they were accompanied by half-concealed snarls and nasty grins, but now they're blank. Shocked. Or coldly hateful, as if all of them are the victims and *I'm* the terrorist. I pull my jacket tighter around my body and try to make a quick march from the security check to the stairs, but then I catch sight of Percy sitting with Anna on a memorial bench near the hallway to the cafeteria. He's handing her a coffee and whispering into her ear. Both of them are wearing black like me, like half of the student body.

For a moment, I'm frozen midstep, because all I want to do is run up the stairs, but then I remember El's confident grin. He's counting on me to get closer to Anna as a back door into Fortin Tech, except . . .

Anna's with Percy, and that boy leaves me feeling flustered and irritated and intimidated like even Bianca can't. Of course, at that exact moment, he sees me standing here like an idiot, and he smiles and gets to his feet. He's wearing a tailcoat again, and for pity's sake, this ruffled lacy thing around his throat just like the guy in that pic from last Monday's history lesson. He sees me looking at it and flutters his fingertips along one of the edges.

"It's a cravat. I have a weakness for French tailoring."

Is he for real? I turn to Anna, who seems to be suppressing a smile as she moves in next to him. "How's Kyla?" I ask.

Her gaze meets mine. "I haven't talked to her. My mom's been trying to com her mom, but they've got privacy settings on."

"I totally get that," I say. "For days after my dad died, all my mom and I could do was hold each other."

Percy shifts uncomfortably from foot to foot. "I get it, too," he says quietly.

For a moment, we just look at each other. He gives me a fleeting, sad smile before looking away.

Anna puts her hand on his shoulder. "I know you do, Percy. We should get to class."

She marches ahead, leaving me to walk next to Percy. "I'm sorry," I say. "Anna told me about your parents last week. I had no idea."

He sighs. "Sometimes a gorgeous facade belies a cracked foundation, I'm afraid."

He actually sounds sad, so I don't scoff at his cockiness. We walk across the atrium in silence, and then I stop and put my hand on his arm. "I really *am* sorry," I say. "I think I might have jumped to one too many conclusions about you, and that was crappy of me."

He gazes down at the place we've connected, and then, very lightly, traces a fingertip across the back of my hand. "I think I might have done the same," he murmurs.

"There she is." Bianca is standing at the base of the steps. Her eyes are wide.

"Bianca, darling, I'm not sure Marguerite is ready for her close-up," Percy says. When Bianca doesn't move he adds, "Stop recording." He doesn't sound nearly so breezy this time.

"Oh, shut up. It has nothing to do with you, right?" she replies, keeping her gaze fixed on me. "So, Marguerite, how's the president? Did you give him a massage yesterday after that tough day he had, pretending to care about all the people who died?"

Percy moves in front of me, but I step around him. "We're all upset about what happened, Bianca," I say.

"You didn't answer the question," she says, all singsong. "Does he pay you, or is it enough that he rescued you from that slum you came from?"

"Bianca," Percy snaps.

"Oh, what's wrong, Percy? Are you still trying to get into her bulletproof pants? Don't you know where she's been?" The few students who have gathered around us snicker.

"Dirty little girl," murmurs Winston, then waggles his eyebrows at me.

"Cut it out," barks Anna, who is behind Bianca on the stairs. "You're just being mean for the sake of being mean, Bianca. You're not helping anyone." Anna comes down the stairs and steps around Bianca to stand next to her. Bianca keeps her eyes trained on me.

"What about Kyla's dad, Anna?" Bianca says. "What about Drew Phillips? His older brother was interning at the department. She got him killed, too."

"I know, Bianca," says Anna. "I read the list of names this morning. But you're not going to bring the dead back by attacking Marguerite. It's not like she wanted this to happen."

"Or maybe she did—what better way to make the prez look like a victim?"

"How does this help him?" I ask. "It only makes his job harder!" Of course, then I remember El saying his nominee for secretary will sail through confirmation, but that seems like a tiny consolation prize given the state of panic across the country right now.

Not to mention the growing panic I'm feeling right here. There's a huge crowd now, like every single one of my classmates is pressing in on me. I'm outnumbered and surrounded. And then Bianca does something that I understand only later. She slides her finger along her Cerepin nodule and then taps it, and all the students around her, including Anna, go still.

Winston is the first to start laughing. "Oh my god," he says between guffaws, tears leaking from his eyes. "Is this real?" He whistles. "If it weren't for the fat old dudes, this would definitely be on repeat. Mar-gerr-*eeeeeeet*."

Laughter echoes through the atrium.

"Share it with everyone you know," Bianca says loudly. "It's a billion times more interesting than her other videos—that's for sure." She glances over to see Mr. Cordoza coming our way, then waves cheerfully at me and bounces up the stairs. Everyone else is still laughing and tapping at the black nodules on their temples, some making surprised *O*s with their mouths.

Anna's eyes meet mine, but then she quickly looks away. "We'd better get to class."

I look around at my classmates, too close to me, too many of them. They're clearly watching some vid; I just don't know which one. I don't know why they're all laughing. I glance at Percy, whose gaze is riveted on Bianca's back. I can't read his expression. Then he curses under his breath and looks down at me. "Perhaps you'd like to talk to Mr. Cordoza about skipping our group discussion today," he suggests gently.

Oh, god. It must be bad. I know better than anyone how things go viral. "Just tell me what vid they're watching. I'd rather know," I say, then glance at his temple. And I remember he doesn't have a Cerepin.

Some tiny connection is made just then in my overloaded brain, but it's drowned out by the rest of the chaos.

"Apparently," he says, drawing me back to the present, "there is now a vid in existence that . . . appears to document . . . your"—he clears his throat—"with the president. *And* some of his personal security detail."

"What? But that—wait, how do *you* know?"

He glances up the stairs. "I may be able to help you, but Bianca is really quite skilled with vid fabbing, and I think—"

"I need to get out of here," I say as my stomach shudders and pitches. Ignoring Mr. Cordoza as he asks me if I'm all right, I head for the one place where I can have a moment of privacy. But as I burst through the door of the bathroom, a half dozen girls look up from their Cerepin trances, and when they recognize me, they dissolve into a fit of giggles. I back out as the sound echoes off the walls and run, just needing to get away from the sound of their gleeful hatred. The lights brighten as I fly past and hook a right into the first empty classroom discussion space I find. Panting, I press myself against the wall and sink to the floor.

This is stupid. It's just so high school. Not national security–level stuff. But that doesn't keep me from putting my mouth close to my comband and saying, "Com El."

He accepts the com instantly. "Amazing. I was just about to com you." His face falls as he looks at mine. "Are you all right? I had security doubled!"

"They can't stop what goes on inside people's heads."

"What happened?"

"I think one of my classmates is a pretty talented vid artist. One who thought it would be funny to . . ." I can feel my cheeks turning red.

"Do I want to search the Mainstream for this work of art?"

"I'd say no, but . . ." I swallow hard. "I don't want Mom to see it."

His eyebrows are halfway up his forehead. "How bad?"

"I haven't seen it. I don't want to. But I'm guessing it's as bad as it possibly gets. And if it spreads, it's going to be a mess."

Now El has a cold glint in his eyes. "Who did this?"

"Her name is Bianca Aebersold."

"Oh, god, that's not a surprise. The daughter of Simon Aebersold? Since her dad's the CEO of Parnassus and the father of your favorite AI, I guess that makes little Bianca Aristotle's sister?"

"Yeah, Anna Fortin told me who she was."

He nods. "Lovely family, am I right? Wouldn't you love to take them down?"

"At the moment? Hell yes. She's so freaking awful."

El just smiles. "But so is karma, Marguerite. And I have a feeling it's going to come back to bite Ms. Aebersold. Trust me on that." His face goes serious. "Hey. *Hey.* Chin up. I'm going to fix this for you. I promise."

I lean my head on my knee. "Why were you going to com me at school? It seems important."

"Hmm? Oh." He lets out a weary breath. "Yes. We're in a state of emergency, and I think you can help. I need you to let me know if any of your new friends let slip any information about the bombing, any detail, even if it doesn't seem important. It all might help. I also need to know if any of them have plans to leave town. Any shady behavior at all, you com me directly."

I just blink at him. "You think some of my *classmates* are involved?"

"Not just me. We've been over the school roster with the FBI. You're there with the children of the most powerful technocrats in Washington. I'm not making any accusations, but if someone bank-rolled a terrorist group, it would have to be an individual with a lot of cash, right?"

"Okay, but I'm not a spy, El. I'm not sure—"

"Just as a favor to me. I know you want the president to get through this unscathed. We all want him to be able to do his job getting this country back on track. Catching whoever is responsible for this slaughter would help. The FBI believes asking for tips in your vid, too, might be very effective."

He leans forward so his face is close to the screen. "You're our face. Our voice. Our connection to the young voters counting on us for change. Now we just need you to do work in person instead of with a screen between you and your audience. That's all we're asking."

"I want a raise," I grumble.

"I'll do you one better. I'll give you what you really want."

"And what's that?"

Congress should make a law against El's smile. "Just trust me."

"Okay," I say, getting to my feet. "You've never steered me wrong before."

Chapter Eight

Marguerite

When I walk out of the classroom, Anna is leaning on the wall just outside. My heart races as I wonder whether she heard any of my conversation with El. But she simply looks at me with solemn concern. "I told Mr. Cordoza you needed a mental health break. He said I could come make sure you're okay." She pushes herself off the wall. "And if it helps at all, the vid is obviously fake."

"I wish that mattered more than it does."

"I guess you would know."

I can't tell how she means that, but I let it go, too tired to fight. "Yeah. So. Is it viral yet?"

Anna taps her Cerepin. "It's gotten about three thousand views so far. Lots of shares. But plenty of megavirals die quickly, and this one . . . it's probably going to get content restricted. I've already reported it."

"Thanks, but all that means is that it's harder to search."

"I had to try. That was a pretty classless move, even for Bianca."

"What's her deal?"

Anna presses her lips together and lifts one shoulder, a half shrug. "You're kind of a lightning rod."

My eyes narrow. "Because I think the rich don't have a right to ignore their fellow citizens?"

She laughs. "Look. This sucks, and I'm sorry. It's been, like, the worst week ever."

Suddenly, the fact that there is a fake scandal vid being passed around the Mainstream seems like a stupid problem. "It really has."

She nods. "I'm just so grateful my family is all right. My mom used to have regular meetings with the secretary of AIR—Winston's mom. What if . . ." She starts to walk back to the main atrium of the school.

I follow, thinking about how she basically just admitted to the cronyism we all suspected. "She must be pretty upset now that there'll be a new secretary."

Anna shrugs. "We'll see. Mom's pretty persuasive. But right now we're just trying to keep a low profile." She glances over at me. "In other news, Percy seemed pretty determined to defend you this morning."

"I don't know why he's suddenly trying to be my friend. A few days ago he was totally happy watching Bianca pounce. What's his deal?"

"Like I told you, I don't know. I haven't known him for all that long, and he's kind of hard to read. He only came to school after . . . after the thing with his parents."

"Who does he live with, then?"

"His aunt, who happens to be the French ambassador."

"I guess that explains his love for fine French fashion."

"Kyla's a big fan of his," she says. "I think he's let her get as close as anyone."

"Are they together?"

"No. Percy and Bianca dated for a while, though."

"You're kidding."

"Nope. It was right after he started here. She went after him. They were a couple for longer than I expected, considering how unhappy she was with him most of the time."

"Why?"

"Because she wanted to be the one to figure him out, and Percy isn't about to let that happen."

"*You* seem to have figured out quite a bit about him." I glance at her, taking in the elegant curve of her cheekbones and the somber intelligence in her dark eyes.

Eyes that hold my gaze. "Maybe. But I'm not interested in boys. I'm not your competition. And I have a feeling Kyla isn't, either."

"I-I-I—" My face is blooming with heat. "Can we reach out to Kyla?" I blurt out, needing to steer this convo to a more reasonable, realistic place. "Maybe send her a message? I don't know her well, but I know how it is to lose a dad."

"We can try. Our parents were actually really good friends back in the day. Her parents were some of the earliest employees at Fortin, right when my mom was starting out. Brilliant, really. And they were a great team. I don't know how her mom's going to do without him."

"What did they do for the department?"

"Evaluating safety and setting operation parameters for the industry. They were collaborating with Fortin on the new cog-link version of the Cerepin. No more voice commands or eye movements, just brain waves to control the display and activity."

"That sounds pretty revolutionary. I hope their work wasn't lost in the bombing."

Anna snorts. "Right. Sorry, but you do realize who brought you to DC, don't you? You guys don't want Fortin to succeed. My guess is the cog link will die a swift death under a mountain of new regulations now. Why be excellent when you can sell mediocre technology for cheap?"

I give her the side-eye. "The president wants to make sure Cerepins are affordable for ordinary people—he doesn't want to cripple the business that makes them!"

"Oh, come on. He's an old tech mogul himself, and he seems more than eager to take control. We're just waiting for it to happen."

"Except that his company made beneficial technology normal people could afford!"

Anna scoffs. "Is that what you believe?"

"I guess people here in this little wealthy enclave are too good for neurostims?"

"I didn't say that."

"They make people's lives better. People who can't afford Fortin's products."

"Do they really, Marguerite? My mom says they could mess up people's brains if they're used the wrong way."

"And Cerepins don't?"

"No, actually. They . . ."

We make it to the atrium. Percy is at the base of the stairs with Bianca. Both of them are flushed, and his fists are clenched. We've caught them midargument, apparently. Suddenly, Bianca and Anna bow their heads, staring at the floor, and the telltale way their eyes are moving tells me they're getting news on their Cerepins.

"Did you hear that, Anna?" Bianca says as both of their heads come up at the same time. "You still want to defend her?" She gestures at me.

"What happened?"

"The FBI is going to start questioning 'technocrats of interest,'" Anna says, giving me a wary look. "They've generated a list, along with a registry of unique Cerepin IDs based on who's connected to the DC network, and they're matching them to individual users and their locations. Did you know about this?"

"Is that official news?"

"I suppose you could call it that," says Percy, holding up his comband. I squint and move closer. On it, a pale, dark-haired woman is standing next to the president. "That's Kyla's mother."

"Wait, what is she saying?"

"As a federal employee, she's begging the culprits to turn themselves in, and she's asking that the technocrats wanted for questioning do the same," Anna says, her voice hollow. "Excuse me." She turns abruptly and heads out the front doors, her strides stiff.

"Classy, twisting the arm of a widow," Bianca says, glaring at me.

"You're going to talk to *me* about being classy?" I snap.

She takes a big step closer to me, and Percy lunges between us. "I think it's time for a little fresh air!" he announces, then slides his arm around my shoulders and steers me toward the cafeteria. "There's a lovely courtyard right this way."

I'm so rattled by the developments that I allow Percy to shunt me away. He moves so smoothly, like he's gliding, and I feel clumsy as I stumble along next to him. He smells good. Rich. Like money and flowers. He ushers me down the hall until we reach a security canny at the door to the courtyard. It lets us pass but follows us out, positioning itself right by the entrance as we walk into a wide area with a tree at the center.

"What a day, yes?" says Percy, tapping absently at a spot just beneath his left ear.

"Why are you being nice to me?"

"Aren't you worthy of kindness?"

"Not according to your ex-girlfriend in there."

He smirks. "Bianca is a wounded soul."

"More like she had it surgically removed. And she seems more likely to do the wounding. God, she's toxic. I'd like to rip that Cerepin right out of her head—all she seems to want to do with it is hurt people."

"She hasn't been at her best today, poor dear."

"Jeez. You do flippant better than anyone I've ever met. Have you seen the vid she's spreading?"

He purses his lips. "Would it help if I told you it doesn't do your beauty justice?"

"God, no! That just grosses me out more!" Tears form in my eyes, and I turn away.

"Sorry. I'm sorry. I'm an ass."

"It's not true," I say in a choked voice. "The rumors. Uncle Wynn would never do anything like that. I would never—"

"Darling, you don't have to say another word. It's obvious how you got here and that it has nothing to do with your body and everything to do with your spirit. You have such presence."

I stare across the courtyard, watching a gust of wind blow dry leaves into a spiral. "And luck. I know that."

"Bad, you mean."

I look over my shoulder at him, and he gives me a sad smile.

"You parlayed a tragedy that would devastate most people into something powerful, something bigger than yourself. I'd say that has less to do with luck and more to do with strength. Conviction."

"What about you?" I turn all the way around again so we're standing face-to-face. For a moment, that's all we do, and yet it feels like a collision.

"Me? I'm a fool. And I'm very, very good at it." He breaks our locked gazes and chuckles.

The canny walks over to us. "Marguerite Singer, I will escort you to the front of the building. There is a car there for you."

"Why? What's going on?"

"Classes have been canceled for today."

"Huzzah," Percy says quietly. "I think I'll go have my nails done." He holds them out for me to see. "They're monstrously ragged, don't you think?"

"What is it with you? Why won't you drop the act?"

He has the bluest eyes. "If you get to know me better, you might find out." Then he whirls around and strides toward the entrance to the school, leaving me standing with the canny, which hums in quiet monotone as it waits to walk me to my car.

Chapter Nine

Percy

I walk back into the school and find students milling anxiously, waiting for their rides home. I heard the canny get its marching orders and knew what was happening when I was with Marguerite, of course, but I'm used to pretending I can't hear anything and everything.

Today, that has come in handy.

Bianca stomps down the steps and narrows her eyes when she sees me. My efforts on Marguerite's behalf appear to have caused a rift. "Another free afternoon," I say to her. "We have all the luck."

"You're a jerk," she says, glancing around. But she moves in closer, rift apparently healed. She continues talking but more quietly, her lips barely moving. "Everyone's freaking out. Dad totally called it—he said that they'd find a way to hunt us down and lock us up. We've got a chalet in Switzerland. We're out of here."

"How patriotic."

I said it to provoke her, but she looks genuinely hurt. "You have no idea what this feels like."

Oh, how many times I've wanted to say that to her. Instead, I bow. Rising back up, I say, "And how could I? Not everyone has the thrill of being a victim."

"When my family gets disappeared, I hope you remember you said that." She stalks past me and out the door as a Parnassus corporate vehicle lands in front of the school.

I poke my comband and see that my own ride is just forty-three seconds away. My nose picks up the warm scent of Marguerite behind me—there's something sweet and deep about that smell, like honey but with a tang of iron, and it makes me want to turn my olfaction settings back up to the max. I turn to see her looking frazzled, her eyes darting from face to face as she follows the canny's stiff march to the exit.

I don't blame her, poor lamb. I did see the vid—Bianca was kind enough to send it to my private channel. It was completely disgusting, Marguerite in the back of a limo, in flagrante delicto with a person who could have been the president and two others who clearly were not. The most enraging thing about it was that I could tell instantly that it *wasn't her* and it probably wasn't the president. My augmented vision picked up the enhanced definition, but normal eyes won't. If Marguerite sees the video, to her it will look like herself, doing things she can't possibly have done. Things perhaps most normal people could not do if bound by the laws of physics.

I would say I can't believe that Bianca did this, but . . .

Marguerite walks by. She gives me an uncertain, vulnerable look. It's tempting to overplay my hand here, damsel in distress and all that, but she's suspicious enough of me that I simply give her a reassuring smile to see her on her way. I need her to trust me, and she won't if I try too hard. She's too savvy for that. She's already called me out—both in person and online. She'll see right through insincerity.

I am surprised to find, though, that I'm not quite as insincere as I'd like to be when I'm around her.

I trail behind her to catch my ride. Aunt Rosalie clearly was in the loop, because I got the alert that I was being picked up less than a minute after the canny in the courtyard got its orders. She must be worried, even though I have an ace up my perfectly tailored sleeve that my classmates do not: as Aunt Rosalie's ward, I possess full diplomatic immunity.

Despite that lovely bit, she's still going to suggest packing me off to Paris. I always enjoy that conversation.

It's impossible to miss the motorcade that arrives to pick up Marguerite, presidential seal and all. As she moves toward the open door, I catch the flush on her cheeks and the defeated slump of her shoulders. There is something so genuine and open in her manner. As though she knows she caught lightning in a bottle, knows she has the world on her shoulders, and worries she might not be worthy to carry it. I like that. It means she's smart.

It's also why I don't trust her.

My own ride, Yves, lands not fifteen seconds after hers takes off. I hop aboard, wondering if Bianca is already landing at her parents' estate, where another, larger car is waiting to fly them to the airport, where they can catch a hypersonic and be in Geneva in two hours. It was a story played out by several of our classmates' more connected families over winter break, just before the inauguration. Easy to do and explain away for these types—taking a year abroad, extending the ski season and all that. I will admit that at the time it seemed like paranoid whispers or perhaps even sour grapes, this theory that Sallese would actively persecute technocrats who had worked alongside President Zao. Would Zao's cronies be on the political outs? Of course. That's how the game is played, darling. Winner takes all. But surely that doesn't mean the winners must behave like utter brutes. They did seem too sophisticated for that—and besides, they had some genuine points.

My parents, strangely enough, were not fans of Zao. *If we were meant to be this connected, we'd be dolphins,* my mother used to say. *Or maybe bees.*

My father would merely smile, then tell me I couldn't ever have a Cerepin, because it was a trap, because I wasn't a sheep, because men and women should be alone in their own heads, the monarchs of their own kingdoms. I only ever understood half of what he was telling me. Now I'll never get to ask him what he meant.

Chen's words ring in my augmented ears. Just because there isn't an obvious connection doesn't mean there isn't one. What if Fortin and Sallese are actually frenemies? What does that explain? What I do know is that suddenly the pre-inauguration paranoia doesn't seem that far off the mark. There is definitely a chill in the air.

"Welcome, Percy," says Yves. "The ambassador requested confirmation of your pickup."

"Confirm."

"Very good." Yves rolls forward, pauses, then receives the signal to fly from the central grid, rising smoothly to the cruising altitude before banking toward the embassy. I like this car; he isn't programmed to ask pointless or vapid questions, like how my day was or whether I have homework.

Yves lands outside the embassy gates, which slide open in welcome, and tools up to the carport. I walk in and greet Sophia so that she'll let Auntie know I'm home safe. "But I want quiet and privacy settings in my room, Sophia. It's vid time."

"I understand, Percy."

I get ready in the same methodical way I always do. Each article of clothing is chosen carefully for fit and style, color and pattern. Today I choose a more austere look to match the mood of the District. I skip the blush and wear only a streak of white on my eyelids. I use my manicure box to paint my nails black. I don a jacket of bottle-green velvet over an ebony shirt, and even though they don't complement the ensemble, I put on the floral cuff links, the ones that signal a meeting with Chen. Each is a ruby primrose, a "pimpernel," my mother said they were called. She and my father gave them to me for my sixteenth birthday. That was just a week before they were killed.

I create the vid. Not sure if my heart is in this one, but it's beating at over 120 throughout. I have to work the signals to Chen in while flirting with my followers. I do adore them, and I adore this. I started my channel just before my parents died, and in the aftermath, it was everything to me. My vids, those moments, were a way to wear a mask or maybe shed my skin. Either way, I could be what I wanted to be instead of the destroyed wreck of a boy I always had been.

Yes, the augmentations weren't an enhancement. I was rebuilt. In fact, my father made it his life's work to fix me.

He might have succeeded, had he lived. As it stands, all I have to understand his efforts are my scattered memories and the letter he wrote me. And Chen. None of it is enough.

My rage twists so hard inside me that I clench my fist and press it to my lips. I catch myself and pretend it's an elegant gesture rather than an expression of pain so intense I want to throw my desk across the room. My ruby cuff links glitter in the sunlight, filtering through Sophia's "half-drawn shades" setting as I talk about spring fashion, as I joke about searching for inspiration, about craving something entirely new, about wanting to be impressed—and how all the tired old florals won't cut it for me this year. I'm guessing next week there will be twenty hand-tailored and custom-genned shirts on my doorstep, courtesy of my favorite designers, all of whom keep my measurements on hand. Most people in this country might not be able to afford what they make, but there are plenty overseas who are dripping cash.

I lay down each cue, needing to make sure they match the specific signals I scrawled onto one of my precious pieces of paper and left at the dead-drop site this morning. The time of the meeting. The place. I had no idea I'd be using them this soon, but these are the times I live in, I suppose.

I launch the vid and wait.

Chen is always online, or else one of his wired-in friends is. They live in the ether. So the seventeenth comment on the vid is from one of them, confirming. Except I had proposed we meet at eleven tonight, and the comment says, I think you need a shirt for each weekday at least—yesterday! Send those designers a note and tell them that.

Five shirts minus one day. They want to meet at four. They've never moved up the meeting before, but it's all right with me. I'm relieved I don't have to wait.

My face is untraceable when I reach the corner and sit on a bench in the shade. This early, with so many people on the streets, I don't bother with the reflective patches. I have every right to sit here and sip my fresh orange juice. It was devilishly expensive, seeing as there are only four remaining orange groves in the country. But I do have my auditory shield on, projecting the ambient street noise I recorded on my walk over here.

The people who walk by are nervous. Visibly so. They frown as they stare at the ground. Their steps are a little faster than usual. Instacars, summoned through their Cerepins, swoop down to pick up people, who run to the curbs as if it's raining. My comband whispers to me that the FBI is now tracing anyone who was within a mile of the Department of AIR yesterday and tracking them down for questioning. A mile radius includes most of the Anacostia Technology Zone, home to Fortin Tech, Parnassus, and at least a dozen other companies that produce canny and AI tech. The focus of their investigation seems clear enough.

At five after four, a woman sits down at the other end of the bench. Like her partner, she wears a hood wrapped around her head. Unlike Chen, she's also wearing a surgical mask. I catch a glimpse of brown skin and glittering dark eyes as Ukaiah looks me over.

"Where'd you get the juice?" she asks.

"Plenny's. And I nearly had to hock one of my kidneys to afford it."

"That's why god gave you two, I suppose."

I offer the cup. "Want some?"

She grunts. "Chen sends his regards. We adjusted one of his sensors last night, and he can't move the left side of his face at the moment. Lots of drool. But he's pretty worked up. Wanted to make sure you're crystal on what's really going on."

"I'm all ears," I say, making sure I reflect back the street noise I recorded on my walk over.

"He says anyone who voted technocrat in the District might want to contemplate a little European vacation starting yesterday, especially if they've got Cerepins . . . but we're talking a Venn diagram that looks like a single circle."

"What do the Cerepins have to do with it?"

"What better way to wipe out your enemies than a bloodless blow to the head?"

"You think this registry of Cerepin users is the start of some kind of political revenge, not an investigation into the bombing." A chill starts in my chest and radiates out. "Do you have proof?"

"We're digging. We have some strategically placed friends. But it'll take time to get the evidence we need."

"Why did Chen want *me* to know about this? I don't even have a Cerepin." Rosalie does, but she also has diplomatic immunity. They can't touch her.

"He thought you might want to warn your friends—carefully, on the DL. Also, you're one of the only people we know who could actually help people get out of Dodge."

I squint at her. "How?"

"Because of your embassy connection. Embassy staff have immunity chips. Immunity chips mean unrestricted travel out of DC."

"No one's restricting travel."

Those darting eyes. "Matter of time."

"This is insane."

"A major terror attack offers the perfect cover for instituting martial law, Percy. It's worked before—2022 in Italy after that virus bomb in

92

Rome, 2047 after the dirty nuke in Johannesburg . . . Not original, but effective."

"Okay, but—"

"We're not paranoid. These people will stop at nothing to get what they want, and rest assured it's not sharing power. If we don't do our part, we're part of the problem—and so are *you*. So. You know innocent people whose biggest crime is their zip code or their profession, am I right? We can help you get them out. We know how to erase and disconnect people when they need that—but the security network in the city is airtight. Immunity chips would get them to the other side, and from there we can activate our web. We've been working on this for a while. This was only a matter of time."

I set my elbows on my knees and stare down the straw of my cup at the orange center. For so long I've been fighting my own private battle, looking for justice for my parents. It's a small arena, and the prize for victory is answers, not lives—it's too late for that. This whole hero thing isn't really me . . . is it? "You need a knight in shining armor? Well, Chen said he has something for me—something my father wanted me to have. I want it. Now. No more waiting, no more games. That's the price of my help."

"I'll let him know." Ukaiah stretches and gets up, but then stops in front of me. Slowly, she reaches down and takes my cup from my loose fingers. She pulls the corner of her mask aside, revealing a maze of fused plastic and glittering data chips across her cheek. She slips the straw under the mask. I wince as I listen to the stuttering slurp that vacuums up the last of my juice. She hands me back the empty cup. "I strongly suspect you have a soul, but that's one thing that can't be augmented. You have what you have. If you decide you want to join the cause, you need to get on board."

I glance at a canny patroller who has just turned the corner. "I'll think about it."

Her dark gaze is unforgiving. "Your parents wouldn't have thought twice."

I flinch. "My parents spent a lot of time and effort trying to keep me *safe*."

"Yeah, when you were a child. Is that what you are now? Or are you a man? Because what your father wanted Chen to give you? It's meant for a man. Not a scared little boy."

I am on my feet so quickly that I don't remember having the thought. Ukaiah takes a step back, though I suspect she's smirking behind her mask. "Your friends might be used to luxuries, but time isn't one of them, not anymore." She turns and walks away.

The fear in the air is electric, and I'm not sure whether it's the attack or this new roundup of "technocrats of interest." Part of me wants to go home, talk to Rosalie, fly away to Paris.

The rest of me clings to this: *Your parents wouldn't have thought twice.*

She's right.

I tap my comband. "Kyla," I murmur. Her lovely face pops up as I wait for the com to connect. But instead, a message appears: This user has engaged privacy settings.

Hmm. "Anna," I whisper to my screen. My heart accelerates to 144 beats per minute as I wait for her to pick up.

Chapter Ten

Marguerite

Alone in the apartment with my Secret Service detail outside, I start to drive myself crazy. I com Orianna, but the only thing she wants to talk about is that awful scandal vid Bianca made and posted to the Mainstream this morning. When I tell her who Bianca is, her face turns sour. "I ever see that bitch, I'm gonna pull her stupid head knob right outta her stupid skull."

I laugh. "I think I said the same thing earlier."

Orianna nods, her fingers rising to the nape of her neck, to where her neurostim device is implanted. She got her first one about six months ago, and it's helped her mood a lot. "Great minds. We're from Houston. We don't mess around."

If she were in the same room with me, I would hug her. We chat a little more about what's going on here, but I think it's so hard for her to really understand the vibe, what it's really like in DC. Then she says she has "stuff to get done," and I let her go. I try to com Kyla, but she's still not online. I try Anna, too, but get a message that she's unavailable, maybe on another com.

I watch a few vids on other channels, some of them so paranoid that it's funny. Some people even accuse the president of using the terrorist attack to bend the technocrats to his will, not realizing that it's made his job a hundred times more difficult. I think that might be what my next vid needs to be about, because it's easy to forget that we need Gia Fortin and the other tech moguls on our side now that the people have spoken. We want them to keep doing their thing; we just want more people to benefit from the results. I hate when I see that fact twisted by people who don't know the first thing about Uncle Wynn or the team he's put together.

Renata announces my mom has arrived home, then the door in the hallway beeps. "Marguerite?" It's not my mom's voice. It's El's. I come out of my room to see him holding the door open for her. She heads into the kitchen without greeting me.

"Mom?" I start to follow her, but El puts his hands up and positions himself between me and her.

"Mar," he says softly. "It wasn't a good day."

For me, either. I want to see her. I crane my neck around him. "Mom, are you okay?"

"Yeah, baby," she says, all choked up. I watch her toss her head back. Taking a pill and downing some water.

I glare at El. "You'd better tell me what's going on."

He glances at my mom. "You okay, Colette?"

She doesn't answer. Her palms are on the counter, fingers tapping the side of her empty water glass.

He clears his throat. "I'm going to fill Mar in. Take your time." He nods toward the living room, and despite my desire to walk past him and go hug my mom, I do as he indicates. I've seen her like this before, and I can't help her.

I walk straight to the chair by the window and sit. "What the heck is going on? They canceled classes and the Secret Service comes to get me, and then everyone was furious at me because they said the FBI was rounding people up . . ."

He rolls his eyes. "Gross overreaction. People are blowing this way out of proportion."

"Then what's going on with Mom?"

"She's sensitive." He casts a longing look toward the hallway. "I totally get it. I appreciate it. She's like our canary."

I stare at him. "What the heck does that mean?"

"Long before your time, I guess. Mine, too, actually. But anyway, all I meant was that she cares a lot, and if she's upset, we need to pay attention."

"El, you're scaring the crap out of me."

He closes his eyes. "One of our federal employees attempted suicide today, which of course is troubling—but she was also important to the investigation into the bombing."

"Who was it?"

"Dr. Wendy Barton."

"Oh my god! Kyla's mom? What happened? Wasn't she doing a press conference with you just a few hours ago?"

El puts his finger to his lips. "She'll hear you."

"Sorry. Jeez. Just tell me."

"Her husband was killed in the attack, which I think you know, and she had pledged that she was going to help track down the culprits. She gave us a lot of information about who came to the department and why. She wanted to convince people to cooperate with the investigation—she'd been part of the technocrat community for ages."

"But then she tried to kill herself?"

"Hung herself while in a car after overriding its safety settings," El says. "She meant to have it deliver her body to the hospital." He sinks into the couch across from me. "She was still alive when she got there—but she's in a coma."

I put my hand over my mouth. Kyla and her little brother have already lost her dad. What if I lost Mom, too? How would I react? "And?"

He shrugs. "The medical team is top-notch, but it looks bad. Her brain might be irreversibly damaged. Mar—" He looks toward the hallway again and lowers his voice even further. I have to lean forward to hear him. "This is top secret right now, okay? No one can know."

"How on earth are you going to keep it from getting out?"

"We're working on that, but if it does, it's going to cause panic. You understand this is for the public good? The last thing we need is more anxiety. The city is already in bad shape because of the attack and all the rumors about the FBI's investigation. We're taking the very best care of Dr. Barton. We're doing all we can. We just can't imagine what was going through her mind that she would do this."

We both go quiet as we glance toward the hallway. The door to Mom's bedroom clicks shut. There have been times I thought Mom might hurt herself, and each time, I've had to shove down anger that she might be willing to leave me. Kyla must be in agony right now. "Her kids—"

"We're taking care of them, obviously. Wouldn't wish this on anyone."

"And what are you guys going to do to calm everyone else down?"

"Well, the president is going to do an Oval Office address, for one. And we need you to follow it up. More than ever, we need our frontline surrogates giving this the right spin."

"I need to talk to Mom."

He sweeps his hand toward the hall. "Be my guest, but make sure you don't upset her more."

God, somehow Mom and I have switched roles, and it sucks because right now I need her so badly. "I don't know if an Oval Office address and a couple of vids are going to fix this. Some of my classmates were practically running out of school, El. I heard one say they're moving to South Korea."

His mouth twists. I can tell he's biting the inside of his cheek, thinking.

"What?" I narrow my eyes at him.

"Nothing. It's just . . . I wish you had called me like I asked you to." He sees the look on my face and makes a *calm down* gesture. "I'm not criticizing you. I just wish people weren't so prone to panic. It undermines the president right when he needs support. He should be riding a wave of high favorability right now!" He leans his head back and heaves a weary breath. "Who was it, exactly, that said they were going to leave?"

"A bunch of people."

His head pops up again. "'A bunch of people'? Are you sure? Not a certain little twit who happened to release a fabricated scandal vid not twelve hours ago?"

I look out the window. I'm too embarrassed to admit it, but I watched it after I got off the com with Orianna. And then I went into the bathroom and puked. It wasn't really me, but even knowing that, there was something about watching it that sent my body into full-on revolt.

"I have our Mainstream technical team looking for ways to make it disappear, Mar."

"Didn't we always say we were against suppression of speech?"

"For god's sake, you're a kid."

"Seventeen isn't really—"

"It *is*." His voice is sharp. "And people can say whatever they want. This kind of thing? It's evil."

I can't disagree. "Then lucky for me she'll be on the other side of the Atlantic soon."

El is quiet for a moment. "You're handling this with a lot of poise. But I guess I should have expected that."

"One of my classmates might have lost both her parents. I can't really whine about some video."

"Yeah." He stands up. "Like I said, we're trying to make that right. But we still need people like Gia Fortin to cooperate." El puts his hand on my shoulder. "This is why I'm trusting you to keep everything we've talked about here secret, Mar. It's a matter of national security."

"Then why did you tell me in the first place?" I mutter.

He squats in front of me. "Your mom needs you. And I care about both of you. I know you can handle it."

I look into his gray eyes. In them I can read how much he cares about Mom, how worried he is, and I sit up straighter, knowing he's trusted me with something this big.

He watches me with a gentle smile. "I know full well how influential young people can be. That's why I need you to talk to your friend Anna. See if she might go in and talk to the FBI herself. Set a good example. She was very politically active during the campaigns, you know. She led a student group that vandalized some public buildings and coordinated protests and attacks during our rallies. I'm sure she'd like her name cleared as a suspect in this attack."

"Wait—Anna? There's a huge difference between defacing a building and blowing it up."

He nods. "It's just a few questions, Mar. To rule her out so they can find the real person responsible. She might know something, though. And the smallest bit of info can help."

Anxiety makes me squirm. "I don't know what I'm supposed to say to her."

"You always know what to say. You open your mouth, and the right words come out. Just remember that all of this stuff that's happening? It's out of our control, but we're still gonna try to govern the way all Americans need us to."

"When is Uncle Wynn going to do the address?"

"Tonight. And he wants to meet with *you* after."

I smile in spite of myself. "Really?"

He grins. "I'll send a car for you at eight." He stands up again. "And on that note, I'm going to let you take care of your mom." He squeezes my shoulder and heads out, and a moment later I hear murmuring just before the door opens and closes.

"Mom?"

"Bedroom," she says, her voice muffled.

I pad in and see her curled up under the covers. I sit on the edge of the bed. "El told me about Dr. Barton."

"I talked to her right after her vid announcement. She's an amazing woman," Mom says quietly.

I stroke her hair, smoothing down the curls. "Sounds like you really connected with her."

"I told her about Dan."

Of course. They both lost their husbands. And they're both trying to honor their memories. "Did you talk to Kyla? Was she there?"

"El said they're taking good care of the kids. I didn't talk to her. I asked him if I could, but he said it might be more upsetting."

"For Kyla, or for you?"

Mom's brow furrows. "Sometimes El is a little protective."

I want to shake her a little. He's protective because she seems so fragile. And I want her to be strong, for me, for herself, but I know why she's not. But it also means I can't fall apart . . . because who would take care of either of us then? Fatigue rolls over me. "I'm going to go watch some vids and relax. Are you going back to the White House for the speech?"

"El said I should take the night off." She looks up at me. "I think he thought I'd worry the president, and El wanted to make sure he was confident."

"Wait—does Uncle Wynn know what happened today?"

"El said he's managing that."

Doesn't answer my question. But El has been managing Uncle Wynn for years, so I guess they've got a good thing going. "Okay. Well. You rest. I'll get dinner for myself."

As I rise, Mom's fingers close over my wrist. "Hey. I overheard El talking to you earlier. Did something happen at school?"

I smile weakly. "Nah. Just fallout from the election and stuff."

"Oh. As long as you're okay."

"Totally fine. As always."

"You're so strong, baby. I wish I was as strong as you are."

I lean forward and kiss her forehead, unable to speak the truth aloud. *Me too, Mom. Me too.*

As soon as I get to my room, Anna's face fills my desk screen.

"Hey," I say. "What's up?"

Anna's eyes look huge from this angle, full of questions. Or maybe fear. "You haven't talked to Kyla, have you?"

"No. Why?"

"I still can't reach her."

God, my heart is beating so fast. "Same here. I tried to com her. No luck."

A long pause, like she's waiting for me to spill. But I've been media trained, and I'm not that easy to crack, especially when I'm looking into a screen. This is my home turf. So she breaks first. "Does . . . um. Do any of your contacts in the administration know?"

"How to reach Kyla?"

Anna's eyes narrow, just slightly, but she might as well have screamed her suspicion.

"Anna, I make Mainstream vids. I'm not in the cabinet or anything."

Her shoulders droop. "I'm just really worried. I haven't talked to her since the attack, and now her mom did that weird press conference . . . Sorry, since her mom called for leading technocrats to turn themselves in for questioning. My mom's on that list."

"Is your mom mad at Kyla's mom for supporting the president?"

"Mom thought Sallese took advantage of her. She's in shock."

"Of course she thought that. Why not always think the worst, after all?"

"She was *worried*, Marguerite. They've been friends for twenty years. Since graduate school. Mom is grieving, too, and not just for Kyla's dad. She lost a lot of people she cared about."

"I'm sorry."

Anna dabs her cheeks with her sleeve. "I just found out that *I'm* on the list to be questioned, too," she says with a husky laugh. "Did you know?"

Here, I can't lie. "Yeah, I just found out. But it's not what you think." Her eyes flick to mine, so intense. "I mean, they want to clear you as a suspect. It won't be hard—you were at school when it happened!"

"But this is more complicated than that, Marguerite, and you know it. They know very well I didn't plant some bomb."

"You think this is some kind of payback."

She looks so weary. "Can you honestly tell me you disagree? You're smart, Marguerite. Come on."

"If you go in and talk to the investigators, they'll clear you. It doesn't have to be a big deal." And it'll show others that it isn't a big deal, which is what the administration needs—to prove to Washington and the rest of the country that it's being fair but thorough.

"Yeah, well, I might not have a choice," she mutters. "Anyway— Kyla is who I'm really worried about right now."

"I could ask around. I'm not sure they'd tell me much." My throat is so tight. I want to tell Anna the truth, but the phrase "national security" is sitting on my shoulders like a patrol canny—much heavier than it looks. "But I'll try."

"Thanks. It's just—things are crazy. People are scared."

I scoff. "Seems like everyone and their brother has a house in Europe."

Anna's cheeks get a little pink, which tells me her family does, too. Knowing how rich they are, they might even have more than one.

"Hey—are you guys thinking about taking off?" I ask.

"Should we?"

"What? No! Seriously, this I know. The president wants to work with your mom. If the Department of AIR hadn't been destroyed, they'd probably be meeting this week! I don't understand why your mom doesn't want to collaborate to get more Americans tech that they so badly need. I mean, it's a bigger market for her, right?"

Anna's mouth drops open, then snaps shut. "Just because she doesn't want to do it *his* way doesn't mean she doesn't want to do it at all. And just because he claims to be serving the American people doesn't mean he really is. Or that he can't be serving his own interests, too."

I bow my head and say through clenched teeth, "I'm sure the president would like to hear her ideas."

"What makes you think she hasn't shared them with him already?"

I look up at her. "Has she?"

"She's trying her best, Marguerite. You don't know my mom. She's a good person."

Who funded a smear campaign last fall that was about as low as what Bianca did to me today. "Okay. I believe you."

Anna lets out a short, harsh laugh. "I've gotta go. Let me know if you hear anything from Kyla?"

"I totally will. I'm worried about her, too." And that is no lie. "Hey. I want you to know that even though it feels like the world is going crazy right now, and I know it might be weird with your mom and Uncle Wynn, I'm glad I met you."

Her brow furrows. "Thanks."

"You don't have to say the same." I laugh. "Though it would be nice."

Now she smiles, and it seems genuine. "I'm glad, too, Marguerite."

"My friends call me Mar."

"Mar. Okay. Look, I'll talk to my mom, all right? But she's really suspicious of Sallese, because she thinks the administration is just trying to grab her company and they're using the bombing to their advantage."

"I've heard those rumors, too. It's pretty pathetic." I let out a bitter laugh. "Almost makes me wonder if Bianca planted it."

Anna sighs. "I told her to take that vid down, and it looks like she did. Just before I commed, actually. I checked a few places—it's totally gone."

"Huh." That had to have been El's doing, not hers. "That's a relief."

"Yeah. I wish everything could be solved that quickly."

"I'll talk to you tomorrow?"

"School's already been canceled—too many students were going to be absent, from what I heard. Want to meet for coffee if we're off the hook?"

"Absolutely. I'd love to know where to get some decent caffeine."

"I know where we can get the good stuff."

"It's a date. How about eleven?"

"Sure. I'll send a car."

I give her my address, and then she signs off and my screen goes dark. I sink into my bed, letting the tension in my muscles ease. Well, at least she offered to talk to her mom. I know El wants me to get her to cooperate with the investigation, too, but I'm not sure I moved the needle just now. Maybe tomorrow I could offer to go with her to the FBI offices. It would help if I could give her more solid reassurance that it was just a formality—it's ridiculous that she'd be a suspect, but nobody asked me.

I change clothes and settle in to wait for my ride to the White House. I'm looking forward to having a face-to-face meeting with Uncle Wynn. He'll take my questions seriously, and he'll listen. He always has.

Chapter Eleven

Percy

Aunt Rosalie is in the sitting room with an open bottle of white Bordeaux and two glasses when I join her. "Shall we?" she asks, pouring.

"Lord have mercy, Auntie. We're starting already?"

She waves her hand, and a projection appears over the table. It's the Seal of the President of the United States. "Sallese is scheduled to address this great nation, and I hoped you might watch with me."

I sit next to her and cross one leg over the other. "You sound so very enthusiastic."

She chuckles and takes a deep pull from her glass. "Sometimes I feel too old for this job, my boy."

My chest tightens. "But you do it so well."

"Percy, I am thinking of retiring."

There's that twist of pain again. "You're a lady of vigor and action, though, my dear. Retirement would absolutely bore you."

She smiles down at the bottle of wine. "My apartment in Paris is really very nice, you know. I'm sure you would love it there. There is a *magnifique* patisserie only a minute's walk from the building. Nothing touched by canny hands. All natural."

"Well. As natural as anything gets these days, I suppose."

"You could be happy there, *mon chéri*. You're not happy here."

"Are you joking?" I pick up my glass and sniff deeply. I don't drink, but I like the smell, and Auntie doesn't like to drink alone. She'll cluck her tongue at me and finish my glass when we're done here.

She pats my knee and taps her Cerepin nodule. "You could make your little movies in Paris. Even more people would watch them, because everyone has one of these, instead of the endless fighting about who can have, who cannot."

Because the government subsidizes them. The European Union abandoned any pretense at capitalism before I was born, according to my mother. "One problem: my little movies aren't in French."

"Oh, all the Cerepins have automatic translation. It unites the world. Percy, you could get one yourself if you wanted."

I set my glass down and lean back, giving her a casual smile that belies my fury. "Darling, we've talked about this. My parents were quite clear on this point."

"Yes, but why? They never told me, and neither have you. It really is odd that you've never gotten one."

We'll tell everyone the truth when the time is right, but until then no one can know, my mother's voice whispers in my ear. "Ah, just old-fashioned, I suppose." I pluck at my cravat and give it a horrified look. "Lord, my cravat has gone limp."

She gives me a playful slap. "So cheeky, boy," she says.

"Well, I don't think you should worry too much about my opting to go au naturel, Auntie. When the Sallese administration is done with Fortin, Cerepins might not even be available for purchase overseas."

She takes a generous gulp of the Bordeaux. "The French government is well aware. Our importers have been contacting the trade offices in Paris. This uncertainty is good for no one." She grunts. "And how it's being handled . . . using Cerepin registrations to track down technocrats for questioning? Such a violation of liberty! At least you and I are safe. I am relieved to have diplomatic immunity—I can tell you that."

Immunity . . . "Auntie, that immunity extends to our embassy vehicles, doesn't it? As a logical exercise, is your car, for example, the same as this house or your office?"

"But of course. We must be free to conduct official business without interference, and this includes our vehicles."

"How would they interfere?" I pretend to take a drink.

She grins, happy to have company, and does the same. "Well. Zao prided himself on his technical operators, but some of them have a weakness for *une partie de jambes en l'air*, you know how they say? And we used that to our advantage."

My auditory chip translates as she speaks, and I fan my face. "Auntie. How risqué."

Her cheeks are getting pink, and she giggles. "Oh, governments like to listen in on each other, darling, but we ensured our buildings and vehicles are cloaked in absolute secrecy."

This is promising. "Now I feel foolish asking if I can borrow something from the fleet a bit more often."

Her eyebrows rise, wrinkling her forehead. "Ah? You need a car?"

"There's a girl." I do my best to look sheepish.

Now she's positively glowing. "A girl? Percy." She chortles. "Of course you may have a car. *L'amour* is the most important thing. Tell me her name, my boy!"

I say the first name that comes to me. And then I wonder why.

Auntie looks like she's about to explode with joy. "Marguerite! She is French?"

"Um."

"Oh . . . is this not a relationship with much talking? My boy!"

"I'll have to ask her."

"I hope she is nicer than that skinny one you brought here. Her face had the look of one who has smelled something bad."

I snort. "Bianca does have that look! An excellent observation." I wonder if she's made it to Switzerland by now. I wonder if she would let me know, or if she only coms to torment me.

"Tell me about this Marguerite!"

"She . . . has lovely skin. And eyes. Her sense of fashion . . ." This is starting to get funny. "She isn't from the District."

"Who are her parents? Would I have met them? Do we move in the same circles?"

I clear my throat as the presidential seal dissolves with a flourish of trumpets, and not a moment too soon. "Perhaps later, Auntie. I think my president wants to speak with me."

She finishes the wine in her glass and pours herself more. My gaze stays riveted on the three-dimensional projection in front of me. It's as if the president is sitting between us and the antique fireplace.

"My fellow Americans, I had not anticipated addressing you so soon after taking office, but life rarely cooperates with an old man like me."

The president is at his desk, his large hands clasped, shoulders hunched. He looks too big for the seat. His face is simultaneously soft and strong, his thick head of auburn hair flecked with gray. He projects an aura of vigor while still managing to appear both gentle and fatherly. Take it from a pro: he is simply made for streaming—either you want him to take care of you or you want to please him or both. This man would not have gotten so far if he were scrawny and bald, for example. These things matter more than they should, but this is why I'm so popular.

"As you know, on Monday, our Department of Artificial Intelligence Regulation building was the target of a terrorist bombing. The loss of life has been significant and unacceptable: eighty-two people are confirmed dead. Rescue efforts are ongoing, and I assure you that this administration is providing every scrap of assistance we can offer."

"He is very good," Auntie murmurs. "You can almost believe him."

He does seem sincere. He has that earnestness that Marguerite also projects. I can see why she is under his spell.

"Throughout November and December, as we prepared to assume the responsibilities of the White House, I worked with President Zao to create a seamless transition. I believed we succeeded, but it seems we underestimated the level of contempt that exists for economic equality and prosperity for all Americans. Because that's what these attacks were—an attack on hope. Let me be clear: I will not let that stand."

Now he's leaning forward, looking right at me. Well, not me, of course, but I feel his stare like a hard scrape along the inside of my skull. He is so very good.

"But we have some obstacles to overcome." Then he moves on to what I've been waiting for. He tells us that we need all patriotic technocrats in DC to cooperate with the investigation and to submit to questioning if the FBI contacts them. Next he says that while the culprit is being identified and brought to justice, he will continue his work with the nation's tech conglomerates to push his agenda forward.

So the tech moguls are expected to cooperate with the president—and I wonder if the level of cooperation is linked to how hard the FBI leans on them.

"You might be wondering who would be willing to attack us on our own soil in so cowardly and vicious a way. Such attacks haven't been a part of our daily life since the anti-android bombings of twenty years ago, and I had hoped we would never see it again in my lifetime. But I will tell you that my administration is cooperating with federal law enforcement to mine every clue and follow every lead. We will find the individuals who perpetrated these murderous attacks, and we will offer them the full measure of American justice."

His fists are clenched. His jaw is, too.

"For those of you who are afraid right now, afraid that technology like the Cerepin will never reach you, afraid that these setbacks will deter us from our promises to restore American jobs to *human* workers,

I speak directly to you now. When you voted for me, you were casting a ballot in faith, with trust. When you voted for me, you stood up and said that you wanted a better life for you and your family, that you wanted a chance to thrive in this, our new reality, where cannies can do so many of our jobs and where the gap between rich and poor is larger than it has been at any time in our history. You wanted a voice here in the White House, and a future. I tell you now: nothing has changed. You have that voice. That hope will not be diminished. That trust will not be squandered. And this is not an empty promise. I am backing it up with the power of this office and my own personal determination."

He smiles. It is welcoming and reassuring. He has marvelous teeth. "In the private sector, I built a technological empire on one wish, one dream: that I could make the everyday lives of the American people better. That I could ease pain and stress, that I could increase concentration, energy, potential. Many of you can testify to the power of that dream."

"Ha! He speaks of his former business with the neurostim devices. How tasteless," my aunt says. "He only serves their stockholders."

"He had to sell his shares, didn't he?"

"This is what he wants the people to believe."

The president is still talking. "And that is the power of this dream and of this effort."

"He is not even speaking about the crisis now!" my aunt says. "He is still campaigning."

"Maybe he is. For public opinion."

"Tell our technocrats in Congress that you want them to take action," Sallese says. "Tell them you want emergency funds to support this effort. Tell them you want access to Cerepin technology to improve your lives, your options, and your chance of success. Tell them to work with me so that we can increase access to our best technological advance since neurostim devices."

"Bah! Neurostims were banned overseas a year ago."

I lean away so I can see her face. "Really?"

She nods. "It was not pretty."

"How Sallese handled it, you mean?"

"No, he was out of the company by then. But his board was very ugly about the whole business. Distasteful." She sniffs. And then she finishes her second glass of wine.

I pour her another. "But he seems to think very highly of them still and talks up what they do."

"When he was the CEO, they marketed them very aggressively."

"Do you think he believes the claims about their benefits?"

Long ago, my parents told me the difference between the stim devices and my own augmentations was as vast and deep as the Atlantic. Later, I wasn't sure if that was good or bad.

"I think he believes in whatever brings him profit," says Auntie. "He worships the almighty dollar."

"But now that he's president, how does that work?"

Her eyes are wide. "Dear, we're all wondering that."

"Thank you. And all bless America," says Sallese. The channel returns to the display of the presidential seal.

I stretch. "Well, he has marvelous hair. But did he actually say anything?"

Auntie has her nose in her glass as she says, "To Americans, he said everything, didn't he?"

"I wouldn't know. I've been too long here in the embassy with you," I tease. Although perhaps it's true. Neither American nor French. Neither human nor . . .

"Then talk to this Marguerite." Now her eyes are glinting with mischief. "If you have a chance to talk. If she is not from the capital, perhaps she is charmed by him."

That's not even the half of it. "I'll ask her. Can I go see her now?"

"Oooh, dear boy. Is it like that?"

"Perhaps. I'll let you know." I get up. "Until tomorrow, Aunt Rosalie. This was a true pleasure. Bonsewer."

She winces, as she always does when I (intentionally) slaughter the language of my ancestors. *"Bonsoir, mon lapin."*

I head back to my room, letting Sophia know I am not in distress and would simply like noise canceling. I go straight to my desk and call up Marguerite's channel. I wonder how she would feel if she knew I'd just hinted to my aunt that she and I are *fous d'amour*, or at least that we love to *faire l'amour*, which might be worse.

Especially if she knew who I really am, to her.

No new vid yet in response to the president's address. The president's favorite surrogate is slow on the upswing tonight. I swipe away from her channel. I'm sure it will be there by morning.

Right now, though, I have questions.

Wynn Sallese is the former CEO of NeuroGo. Everyone knows that. But the bigger story was when he relinquished control of the company to run for president. The man who gave up his fortune to fight for the people. He self-funded his campaign and didn't ask for a coin from the commoner—he asked only that they turn out to vote. There were charges of corruption, but none managed to stick. And no one has raised concerns about the safety of neurostim devices, not in this country, at least. This even though hundreds of thousands of people have them, just not in the District. By some accounts, that is because they can conflict with the signals from the Cerepins, and many consider the Cerepins to be superior tech. By other accounts, neurostim devices are used more for mood stabilization, a little pick-me-up, and many say the District inhabitants don't have as much need. They're doing just fine.

But Auntie said that his neurostim devices were banned in Europe a year ago. This was news to me.

The day they were slaughtered, my parents were at a clinic that used neurostim devices to treat addictions to various substances. Derek Kasabian, the man who killed my parents, stabbed them over and over again with a scalpel, tried to blame the neurostim device Dr. John Weisskopf had installed at the base of the man's skull the previous week, saying it drove him to a burst of impulsive violence. No one listened, because Derek was caught on surveillance stealing the scalpel over an hour before he attacked, pointing to some degree of premeditation.

No one listened, because he disappeared before he went to trial for the killings.

No one listened, because his doctor, John Weisskopf, insisted he had shown violent behavior in the past.

No one listened, because random violence happens, and people are quick to blame an addict.

But if you knew who my parents were, then it might behoove you to listen. My parents specialized in neural augmentation and were trying to collect information about these devices. My father commented to me the week before he was killed that he thought the neurostim devices might disrupt the connections between the prefrontal cortex, the thinking or logic part of the brain, and the limbic system, our most basic fight-or-flight survival center. Of course, at the time *I* was barely listening. Probably too busy painting my fingernails. Or maybe I was too overwhelmed by all the other things I could hear other than my parents' speculation; my dad had only just installed my auditory chips.

Now that I think about it, though, that kind of information, from prominent scientists like Valentine and Flore Blake, might have caused NeuroGo's stock price to take a precipitous tumble. Except by that time, Sallese was out as CEO and had sold off his shares. Hadn't he?

Frustrated, I move to a few crowdsourced reporting channels to see how others are reacting to Sallese's address. He repeated his call for "cooperation" from technocrats, hardly a witch hunt. Yet today at school, Bianca said her father wanted to leave the country. And Chen warned me that things were about to get a lot worse. Clearly they perceived a bigger threat.

"—not sure what started all this, but now the terminal is shut down," the Mainstreamer is saying as he presses his comband lens through a hole in a chain-link fence. "Airport administrators told a bunch of us that the flight, which was scheduled to land in Geneva tonight at four a.m. local time, was stopped on the runway and boarded just before takeoff due to a credible threat of terrorism. I don't know about you, but I think some people got hurt out there." The vid is being taken at Reagan National, and flashing lights shine off wet tarmac. The sleek silhouette of the hypersonic Air Suisse plane can be seen in the background, surrounded by emergency vehicles, including several ambulances.

I use my comband to try to contact Bianca, but she's off-line.

"My buddies Ryan and Yuli just took off to investigate reports of two other incidents, one at a cross-country skycar rental facility in the Anacostia Technology Zone, not far from the Fortin tower site, and another at a Potomac boathouse on Water Street. Roy Abdalla, the chief of the DC police, has already posted a vid telling us that these incidents were related to the investigation into the recent bombings, but he also cautioned that they're not gonna release more info until they get their marching orders from the FBI. Okay, he didn't say that exactly, but we all know the truth. If you upstanding citizens have any additional tips for us, ping our channel and we'll check it out. We're your eyes out here, so follow us to get the good stuff."

I flick the channel to silent. What do all of these locations have in common? The airport, a long-distance skycar rental facility, and a boathouse on the Potomac. The technorats are trying to flee the sinking ship while the captain cries terrorism. But who really poked holes in this boat? And what's to become of the poor terrified animals left aboard to drown?

I open my own channel, feeling reckless. I activate the camera while the words and thoughts are only half-formed. "See this cravat?" I say, fluttering my fingers beneath the droopy folds of lace at my throat.

"Verdict: devilishly disappointing. I've retied it *twelve* times now, and still I cannot get the silly thing to lie properly." I pause, trying to be clever since I haven't had time to dead drop new handwritten codes. "One would think I'd need a cathedral full of cannies just to fix it."

I'm not making any sense at all, but the National Cathedral is one of the meeting places we've used before, and I hope to god Chen is paying attention. I roll my eyes. "If any of you have suggestions, please tell me. I have friends who want to jump on this trend, but I can't help them right now. Not with what I'm working with."

I'm risking too much. I blow a kiss into the camera and end the vid.

Then I sit on the edge of my bed and imagine Marguerite watching, and what she would think. I wonder if she ever asks herself what *I* might think. I'm betting I know the answer. Shaking my head, I watch the comments flicker and pop into view on my screen.

DrywBG: Hang in there~but not literally, pls.

Ontop24923: You still look amazing don't change.

Lots of sympathy for me, poor little rich boy with a wardrobe issue. It's frankly unbelievable. But also, this:

Zerohour: I can help if you've got the raw materials.

There he is. I know it. Unable to sit still for another second, I walk over to the wall and lay my hand on it. "Sophia."
"Yes, Percy?"
"Is Yves available?"
"Logs show he is on-site and unassigned."
"Excellent. Tell him to meet me in the carport in ten minutes."
"Shall I alert your aunt to your departure?"

"You can tell her if you want, but she's already approved my use of a car, and she already knows why I need it."

"Of course, Percy."

I tear the cravat from my neck and toss it toward my closet. Then, struck by the need to be prepared for anything, I dig out my treasure box, open it, and grab yet another blank slip of precious paper and my father's pen. I have to assume all communications are being monitored, making this ancient practice one of the best ways to pass a message, so long as the recipient destroys It after reading. Electronic communications are too easily tracked, recorded, preserved, and I can't use my AI ghost program unless I'm actually inside the embassy—combands can be externally monitored and remotely capped. And I need to be more careful than that, immunity chip or no.

Not sure whether I'm playing a silly game or about to get myself involved in dangerous political intrigue, I leave my room and head for the carport.

Chapter Twelve

Marguerite

The mood in El's office, just off the Oval Office, is totally upbeat. We got to watch Uncle Wynn's speech live, and we know he nailed it. I can already tell from the hits and comments on the White House channel but also by general traffic and trends on the Mainstream. The number one search term from the past hour is "Gia Fortin terrorist" or something related, El announces.

"That's kind of a fun unintended consequence," he says with a chuckle.

"How is it 'fun,' exactly?" asks Audrey Savedra, our joyless veep. She's leaning against the wall, holding what appears to be a cup of coffee, looking sharp and pinched in her pantsuit. I'm assuming it is not by choice she's here tonight but instead that it's a matter of optics. "We aren't in favor of mob justice." She arches an eyebrow as she looks over me and El. "Unless I missed an important policy meeting."

"No, only the one where we had our humor chips upgraded," says El, walking over to her and offering her a glass of champagne, which she waves away. "Come on, Audrey. It's Gia's fault that the public hates her. Wondering if she's behind these attacks is more of a step than a leap."

"What's the difference, if there's no evidence to support either?" She stares at me as she says this, as if I'm the one responsible for any misunderstanding. "Communication is reality. You have to be responsible for what you put out there. You can't just pop off."

"Wait, me?" I ask. "I haven't ever popped off!"

"Funny, I thought that was how you got this gig in the first place."

"Madam Vice President, go easy on Mar, for pity's sake," says El, starting to sound annoyed. "And let her get ready for her one-on-one audience with the president."

Audrey's brown eyes widen. "*She* is meeting with—?"

"Yep." He walks over to a tray and then hands me a glass of sparkling juice. As I sip, he holds up a finger, then leans past one of the Secret Service cannies to make eye contact with Uncle Wynn. "You ready?" he asks, then nods.

He turns to me. "*You* ready?"

My palms are clammy against the slick sides of my glass. "I totally just realized he's the actual president."

El cracks up. "Just realized, Mar? Come on."

"I'm allowed to be starstruck."

"Sometimes I forget you're only seventeen."

"Now *you* come on," I say, laughing too. "You wouldn't have to do this much damage control for someone who was a responsible adult."

"Maybe, but we also wouldn't have captured ninety percent of the eighteen-to-twenty-four demographic. So here's to youth." He raises his glass full of champagne. Then he sets it on his desk. El never drinks.

The Secret Service cannies move aside, and I get a clear view of Uncle Wynn standing in front of his desk, talking to a few senators who supported him during the election. But when he sees me fidgeting in the doorway, he smiles. "Excuse me, gentlemen, ladies, I have an important meeting." More cannies usher out the politicians, and soon it's just me and the president.

Suddenly I remember that fake vid Bianca made. I remember the sounds and the sight of bare flesh in a backseat. The back of a head of silver-and-auburn hair. My feet in the air. My stomach turns.

He frowns when he sees the look on my face. "Hey, kiddo. You okay?"

"Yeah," I say, my voice weak.

His expression is all sympathy, all warmth. He opens his arms. "Come here."

I start to walk forward, and I hold my breath as he enfolds me in his bearlike body. The hug is firm but brief, and he steps back as if he senses it's not helping.

"Come sit down. There you go," he says as he guides me to one of the fancy couches in the room. I am sitting on history, and all I can think of is how embarrassed I am about that vid. I glance over my shoulder toward El's office to see him watching. He, too, gives me a sympathetic look, like he knows what's just happened. He mouths something I can't quite make out. I turn back around.

Uncle Wynn is sitting across from me, a good ten feet away. "El told me about that prank your classmate played."

"How did you know I was—"

"Oh, Marguerite. Give me some credit. I didn't get here by being a fool. And I want to tell you how sorry I am that you're getting beaten up this way because you fought for my campaign."

"I'm fine."

He nods. "I promise you, it's going to get better. Kids can be mean, as you know. But the best thing is just to kill 'em with kindness. I believe that. You can't fight mean with mean or hate with hate."

"I know." He's told me that many times, especially when I was ragging on Gia Fortin for getting nasty in the campaign.

"Petra always used to tell me that. I was more hotheaded when I was young." For a moment, a familiar grief darkens his expression after he mentions his late wife, but then he hooks an ankle over his knee and leans back. "Not that it isn't tempting sometimes to fight fire with fire."

"Like over the last few days?"

"You have no idea," he says wearily. "I'm so angry that all these people were killed on my watch. It's killing *me*. One of the worst things about it is that the ones who should care the most? They don't seem to care all that much."

"Gia Fortin?"

He tightens his mouth and looks out the window. "She's refusing to cooperate with the investigation, and her stonewalling sets a terrible example—the FBI's getting nowhere."

"El told me Dr. Barton attempted suicide just after she urged people to work with them."

"Yes, terrible. She was a patriot."

Was. "Her daughter Kyla goes to my school. She's really nice."

Uncle Wynn nods. "Her mother—she was one of the original creators of the Cerepin. Did you know that? Brilliant woman. Lots of opinions on how this tech should be used."

"Was Gia mad that she sided with you?"

"That woman is mad at anything that threatens her profits."

"El said before I came in here that Mainstream searches indicate people might think she's affiliated with terrorists. Like she paid them to blow up the Department of AIR."

Uncle Wynn casts an exasperated glance toward the door of El's office, now closed. "He shouldn't be spreading that around while the investigation is just starting. It makes people afraid, and fear makes them less likely to come forward."

"The vice president wasn't happy about that, either."

He grunts. "Well, Audrey isn't happy about much these days. She's realizing she's outnumbered. And she and El are like oil and water. She's a scientist by training. Methodical. Cautious. And El? He's energetic and loyal to a fault, but sometimes I think that boy shoots before pulling the gun from the holster."

I guess that would be what Audrey referred to as "popping off."

I sit up a little straighter. El and I are kindred spirits, in a way, so when Uncle Wynn says something like that, I don't feel good about it. "You're right. Surely Gia wouldn't do something that terrible."

He raises his eyebrows. "We don't know that she didn't. I'm just saying we shouldn't jump to conclusions, and we shouldn't encourage others to, either."

Now my cheeks are hot. Uncle Wynn smiles when I press my palms over them.

"El let me know that you've got a friend in Gia's daughter, Anna."

"She's not a friend, really, not yet, but I think she could be. She's been kind when she didn't have to be."

"Has El leaned on you to use that connection?"

I bite my lip.

"Just be a friend, Marguerite. If you just be yourself, she's going to understand that you wouldn't support an administration that wants to hurt people or destroy businesses. She'll know someone like you could never get behind something like that. Just be her friend."

He's so right. El had me trying to bring her around, but she'll see through that in an instant.

Uncle Wynn rolls his shoulders, looking a little haggard. "I'm certainly trying to be a friend to her mother. It ain't easy." He laughs. "Did you know we've known each other since business school?"

"Really? Wait, how come no one mentioned that before?"

"It was so long ago. But it's true. NeuroGo came out of a class project about products that could improve lives. And if you can believe it, that's when Gia came up with the concept for the Cerepin. Dr. Barton might have done a lot of the technical innovating along with her husband, but Gia had the idea for the original device. She even suggested we merge the two products—she wanted to use my idea for the neurostim in her device. A few years later she tried to acquire NeuroGo. Offered me four trillion! I didn't think it was a good idea."

"Why not?"

"We didn't share a vision. You shouldn't ever partner with someone if you don't share a vision. That's why we work so well together, Marguerite." He slaps his big hands onto his big knees. "Now, isn't it past your bedtime, young lady?"

"Seriously? I'm seventeen."

"It's a school night!"

"Not anymore. Classes are canceled."

His brow furrows. "Why? We've got things under control. Local officials in DC didn't issue an advisory on that."

"I don't know if it was the administrators so much. I think a lot of people were freaked out by the FBI request to interview so many technocrats, including a lot of my classmates and their families. They're especially freaked out that Cerepins are being used to track people." And they don't even know about Dr. Barton's attempted suicide.

The president rolls his eyes. "Technocrats strike again, I suppose. That's who runs the schools in DC."

"I think they're overreacting. If they'd just cooperate and get it over with, the investigation could progress smoothly."

"Mm-hmm." He stands up. "Fear is no friend to logic, that's for sure. The only people who need to be worried right now are the ones responsible for these bombings. *Those* people should be very nervous."

Something about the calm, matter-of-fact way he says it lets me know he's got this covered, and this familiar, soaring pride practically carries me back to the door of El's office. Wynn gives me another hug, and this time it isn't weird. The Secret Service cannies close the door behind me, and I realize I'm the only person in El's office. He's standing out in the hallway. I start to head out there, but then I realize he's talking to someone.

"Sounds like you got there just in time. Keep a tight leash on it, though. Otherwise we're gonna have a panic. It's bad enough already, and we need them to stay put until we get to them. Especially the big fish."

I stay very still, straining to hear who he's talking to, but the other person's voice is just a low buzz.

El chuckles, a grim sound I've heard many times. "Yeah. A real tragedy. It's almost as if those people have some major bad karma, am I right?"

Karma?

"No, don't move in until I make the call," he continues. "We'll let this settle down first. But let me know if they even twitch."

El looks over his shoulder, and I heave a smile onto my face and wave. He looks down at his comband, and I see a picture of a man wearing a suit and collar band. "Tell him I'll be there in an hour to see how everything's going." The comband goes blank. "Hey, you!" He turns to me, wearing a grin.

"Where are you going?"

"Aw, Mar, aren't I allowed to have a social life?"

"That didn't sound social." In fact, it sounded kinda ominous, in a way that's making my chest tight.

"I'm out of practice." He glances at the doorway to the Oval Office. "Done already?"

"I think the president was ready to go to bed."

"Can't blame him. Been a long couple of days. How about you? Ready to go home?"

"Sure, but can I ask who you were talking about? I heard you mention karma, and—"

"No fooling you, I guess." He sighs. "But look—we've talked about this—if it's classified, I have to follow protocol. What I can tell you is that I'm very happy with our progress tonight. And when the dust settles, I think you'll be happy, too. Now—go home, check on your mom, get some sleep, and maybe tomorrow, post a vid about the speech?"

"Sure." I'll have to do that before I go meet Anna. But I don't say that to El. I think Uncle Wynn had it right, what he said about just being a friend. I glance at the time. "Shoot. Yeah. I should get home. I wonder if Mom saw the speech."

"She did! She thought it went really well."

I shrug off the weirdness of knowing he talked to her before I got to. They're coworkers, after all. And if she's going to keep her job as his primary aide, she needs to be kept up to speed. "Thanks for filling her in, El. That's really cool of you."

"Anytime. You know I look out for you guys. Let me know if you need anything tonight, okay?" He herds me toward the lobby.

"I will. Thanks."

"Mar? One more thing."

I stop and turn. "What?"

El smiles. Rocks on his heels. "You're welcome."

I am up half the night, wrestling with unease that seems to have a black belt in jujitsu. It all centers around El, and part of it is what Uncle Wynn said—*Sometimes I think that boy shoots before pulling the gun from the holster.* Who was El talking to, and where was he going? Did it have to do with the Fortins, or with Kyla and her family, or maybe Bianca and hers? At three, I check on Mom, but she's fast asleep, so I catch a few hours before getting back up at eight. I post a vid, not even trying to conceal my pride at how well the president is handling this crisis. I tell people I spoke to him personally and how reassured I felt when he told me kindness is what's going to bring us victory. I can't bring myself to say anything about the investigation, though. Knowing what Kyla's mom did is bad enough, especially because they're keeping it secret, but what I overheard El saying last night just makes me feel icky. So it's a short vid, focused on having confidence in President Sallese. Vague but sincerely emotional, and honestly, sometimes that works best.

When I send the vid into the stream, the comments add up quickly. Most have no sympathy for technocrat Cerepin users and are angry that these hypocrites won't help the FBI investigate a terrorist attack—on the government's Department of AIR, no less. I wait for FragFlwr to visit and post his usual deflating gibes, but he's conspicuously absent again today. If he's a Cerepin user, then maybe he decided to lie low with the rest of them? But when I brought it up, he said I was making assumptions, which made it sound like he didn't have a Cerepin. Unusual for a technocrat, but . . . Wait. Wait. Percy doesn't have a Cerepin, either.

I click back and reread a few of my arguments with FragFlwr, who started needling me as soon as I formally joined the campaign. His tone is always the same—superior, condescending, and dismissive. He never engages in name-calling. He never gets mad when other commenters insult him. He's always detached, untouchable, amused.

My god. He's like Percy in troll form.

That jerkhole. It has to be him . . . doesn't it? He was all friendly to me yesterday, and all this time, he might have been trolling me. Or I'm just grasping. I need to figure this out.

While I'm churning, I get a text from Anna inviting me to meet her at a Leaf & Beam shop, and I decide to walk over instead of ride. It's only a mile or so, and the flying cars still scare me a little. They've been in use in a few cities on either coast since I was a kid—LA, San Francisco, Seattle, Boston, New York, and of course, our nation's capital—but in Houston, there was no money to set up the sky-system. We would have had to build up too much infrastructure. The closest we got was a cross-country skyport in the Woodlands, for people using the cruising versions of the cars as personal planes. But only rich people could do that instead of using mass transport, so I never thought I'd ride in one of them—until I got here.

The streets in this part of DC are clean, barely used, just a touch-down point for the cars before they rise with a soft whir into the air again. So different from the potholed streets of my hometown. Instead of looming high-rises, the houses here are narrow, old. They must have been built before the turn of the century, but they're cute and colorful, some of them painted bright yellow, pink, blue, purple. Never seen a purple house before. It has real flowers in a pot on the porch.

Not many people are out on the street, but maybe it's the hour. The ones I do pass hold their coats tight around their bodies. Some of them are muttering, the black nodules on their temples occasionally pulsing with blue or red light. I wonder, does it maybe signal an incoming com? Or maybe it's telling others that the user is connected to some other reality, a virtual one. I have no idea.

Anna is waiting outside the coffee shop. She's shivering in a metal chair at a metal table, her slender fingers curled around a genned recyclable cup. Another sits across from her on the table. She smiles when she sees me. "For you. I hope you like it with cream. They've switched to synthetic since I came here last. There's better coffee over in Georgetown, but this was halfway between our places."

"I don't mind synthetic anything. I didn't even taste real coffee until we moved here."

She gives me a quick smile and looks away. "Sorry. We're so spoiled."

Yes, they are. "How are things?"

"Want me to be honest?"

"Otherwise, what's the point of talking?"

She tilts her head as her eyes meet mine. Her stare is so eerie, like she's looking right at my brain. "We want to know what's going on. We can't reach the Bartons. They've effectively disappeared since Kyla's mom gave that press conference."

"They're grieving."

"Marguerite, let's get real. They'd respond to concerned coms from friends. No one's even seen them, and they don't seem to be home."

El and Uncle Wynn know where they are. They just won't tell me. But I wonder if my mom might, if I ask the right questions. "I'm not being stupid on purpose, Anna. Are you guys considering meeting with the FBI, cooperating with the investigation like Kyla's mom asked for?"

A line forms between Anna's eyebrows. "Look where cooperation got the Bartons—I'm really starting to think something's happened to them. My mom is doing her best to cooperate *without* surrendering her freedom."

"Okay, but that's not how it's playing, Anna. She looks like she's obstructing."

"She's reeling, Marguerite! She's trying to figure out how this could have happened, and she's trying to keep control of the situation."

"By hiding information?"

"Do you believe in the right to privacy? Because now that the government has created this supposed registry of Cerepin users, they can track our movements."

"But isn't that because Cerepins are built that way—so users can always be found and get help? Isn't that just a feature of the devices?"

"Do you think the government should have that information, though? And use it to track private citizens without any kind of warrant?"

"I-I—" I stammer. I don't actually know if they got warrants or not. "No, but I do want to know who's responsible for killing over eighty people."

"Would it surprise you to know that my mom wants that, too?"

"I'm starting to wonder."

"Would it further surprise you that she'd like to find a way to increase access to Cerepins while also respecting the rights of our shareholders and preserving her ability to innovate?"

I laugh. "Yeah, it would. It totally would." Because if she hasn't done it by now . . . when?

Anna shakes her head. "You make so many assumptions about us. You believe everything you're told."

"No, Anna, I believe what I saw with my own eyes, including my dad's dead body, and including the note he left explaining why he'd done it. Because he had no purpose. Because there was no reason for him to go on! He couldn't afford a Cerepin. He couldn't compete with AI!" My voice breaks and I bow my head.

She places her warm hand over mine, and I freeze. "I'm sorry," she whispers. "I don't want to fight with you. I think we have more in common than you think, but I know I don't understand what it's been like for you."

I raise my eyes and see that hers are filled with tears. "Wait, are you okay?"

Her face crumples and she sniffles. "I just never thought it would get this bad. My mom said it would, when Sallese won, but I—"

"He's a good man, Anna."

She shrugs. "I don't know him."

"And do you believe everything you're told by your mom?"

"That's fair, I guess. But I've seen things, too. I'm worried about my friends." She looks away, quickly wiping a tear from her cheek. "And my family."

I sit back, looking down at her hand, which is still squeezing mine. "What are you afraid of?"

She chuckles hoarsely. "Oh, that they'll swoop down on us in the night?"

A chill runs down my back as I remember the things I overheard El say. I bite my lip, and in that moment of indecision, I know what a true friend would do. "Are you guys thinking of getting out of here?"

"Define *here*."

Her tone tells me I just crossed a line. "I wasn't prying—I swear. You don't have to be in DC to answer the FBI's questions."

"Yesterday you told me there was no reason to pack up. Has something changed, Marguerite?"

We need them to stay put until we get to them. Especially the big fish.

"I don't know. I just . . . Maybe you guys should take a vacation?"

It is crazy to be thinking this way. But I can't rid myself of the thought, now that I've had it.

Anna holds her coffee just under her chin, inhaling the warmth. "Imagine how *that* would play."

I hold her gaze. "But you don't seem to feel *safe*. I wouldn't blame you if you and your family wanted to get out of the District for a while."

She scoffs. "Even if we wanted to, we can't."

"Why not?"

"Mom thinks we're being monitored and that they'd stop us if we tried. Especially after last night."

Let me know if they even twitch, El said. "What happened last night?"

"The raids . . ."

My heart is hammering. "I was at the White House. I don't—"

"FBI and police raided an airport, a boathouse, a rental carport. Terrorist threat, you get the picture?" All of a sudden, her face breaks into a surprised smile, and she waves at someone behind me. "Hey! What are you up to?"

I turn to see Percy Blake crossing the street, his long legs encased in stockings and knee breeches. His hair is all black now, not even a blond streak, slicked back on the sides and swooping back on the top.

"Fancy meeting you here," he says with a lethal grin.

"This isn't your neck of the woods, is it?" Anna asks. "I was just telling Marguerite that the best coffee is in your neighborhood."

He holds out his hands, nails freshly polished. "I was getting them done at this quaint little salon just up the block. *Actual* manicurists." He arches an eyebrow as he looks at me. "The breathing kind."

Looking for a distraction from the intensity of my and Anna's conversation, I pull out a chair at our table. "Do you want to join us?"

He looks at Anna, who has risen from her seat and is now standing between me and Percy. He reaches out and shakes her hand with both of his, then bows his head and brushes a kiss across her knuckles. As he straightens he murmurs something to her, very quietly.

Her shoulders go tense, and she looks down at the palm of her hand. "Oh my god, Marguerite. I totally forgot that I have to meet my brother and parents for lunch, and it's all the way across town. I just got the reminder." As she turns back to me, she taps her Cerepin nodule.

"That's okay," I say, looking between her and Percy and wondering what the heck just happened.

"I don't have a thing planned," says Percy. "Is your invitation to sit still open?" He eyes the chair I pulled out.

"Sure." My heart beats just a tad faster as I watch Anna fidgeting, putting her hand in her pocket before drawing it back out. "I guess I'll see you when classes start again?"

"Definitely," Anna says. "I'm sorry I have to fly."

Not ten seconds later, a car lands up the street and cruises over to her. She jumps inside and is gone.

"What just happened?" I ask.

"I'm sure her family needs her right now," Percy says breezily. "This week has been the devil for them."

"You have this way of saying things that makes everything sound so . . ."

"Glib? Trivial? Of no particular moment?"

"Yeah."

"By intention, I assure you. The insouciance of my speech is selected with utmost care."

"Don't some things need to be taken more seriously?"

The corner of his mouth curls and he looks up at the sky, watching the silent cars gliding above us, like birds reduced to squares, angles, trajectory. "Very *few* things, I have found. I'll save my energy for those."

"How about trolling Mainstreamers?"

His blue eyes slide over to me. "Trolling? That sounds vulgar. I've never trolled anyone in my life."

There isn't even the slightest trace of guilt in his eyes. "Okay, then. I'd like to know what the great Percy Blake finds worthy of his energy."

"But then you'd know me."

"Didn't you invite me to get to know you just yesterday?"

"Well. It was more of a challenge than an invitation."

"Would being known be all that bad?"

For a long moment, Percy is silent, simply staring at my face, maybe looking for a hint of disdain or sarcasm or who knows what. He wears a ghost of a smile. "Quite the contrary, Marguerite. I'm afraid I might like it much too much."

"You could try it," I say as my stomach swoops. "Thirty days or a full refund. Risk-free."

His laugh is sudden and surprised and alive. "I very much doubt *that*."

Chapter Thirteen

Percy

I replay my conversation with Marguerite as Yves slides his way through the sky over Anacostia. My heart rate is still over a hundred beats per minute when I think of the way she looked at me . . .

I force myself to halt the replay. They've just reopened air traffic in this zone, and I can see the deep hole in the earth where the Department of AIR once stood. It feels blasphemous to be fantasizing about kissing a girl while flying over a mass grave.

Chen coms me via Yves's secure connection, his words slightly slurred. "I feel compelled to warn you of the risk you're taking."

"Ukaiah reminded me that my parents were more than willing to take such risks."

"Yeah. Okay. She was right. But—"

Now I am fully in *this* moment, which only sends my heart rate higher. "I thought about this all last night. I think you and Ukaiah are right—the noose is tightening. I can't sit and watch it happen. I haven't been able to reach my friend Bianca since yesterday. She and her family were on that Air Suisse flight." Calling her a friend is a stretch, but she is one of the few people on this planet who I've allowed to get even remotely close to me.

"You're right on that count. After we spoke last night, I looked into what happened."

His regretful tone makes my stomach turn. "You have information?"

"Sorry, kid, but I think they're dead."

"Pardon me," I say, at my most polite. "But who exactly do you mean?"

"We've got a guy at the morgue. You know how they made a rule that a real person has to supervise cannies working with dead bodies?"

I swallow bitter saliva. "Chen . . ."

"There were twenty-three casualties from the raids last night. Twenty-three! Bodies still being identified. But my guy said that there was a middle-aged man and woman, genetic match to the Aebersolds."

"And?"

"Each of 'em had a hole in the temple."

"What kind of hole?"

Chen chuckles, raspy and low. "Right where their Cerepins woulda been."

"Someone pulled them?"

"Bullet hole, I meant. But in their autopsies, the cannies didn't report any debris in the brains like you'd expect if someone shot them in the head knob."

"So someone removed the 'Pins first. Then shot them."

"Looks like. Now, does that sound like the work of credible law enforcement to you?"

"What are the police saying?"

"Publicly? Nothing. Privately, they're even more tight-lipped."

"But we know it was the Aebersolds?"

"DNA don't lie, kid."

"What about Bianca? Her little sister, Reina? They were with her parents."

"Unknown. The government took a lot of 'em into custody, though. It was a big sweep. They were ready for them."

But maybe the kids were spared—except, Anna told me that she, Bianca, and Kyla were all on the list to be questioned, ostensibly because they were vocal members of the Young Technocrats during the campaign. I stare out the window at the smoking black crater. "Who knows about this?"

"My group. And now you, of course."

"There has to be evidence—vid on the Mainstream? You know some of these people had Cerepins. It couldn't have happened so quickly that they couldn't have let others know what was happening!"

"True. We've found traces of uploads on the Mainstream, but the vids have been scrubbed or overwritten."

"Government?"

"Who else, kid? You ain't the only one with ghosts."

"Good god," I whisper. Is this really possible? When Sallese was elected, the biggest fear was financial persecution of the technocrats—a socialized system for tech, the redistribution of wealth. No one thought they would pay in blood. In lives. Now Bianca's parents are dead, along with twenty-one other people. Cerepins pulled from their heads before someone used a bullet to fill the space. "That's probably what will happen to the Fortins if we fail. The only reason it hasn't is that they haven't tried to run."

Until now. Am I leading them into a trap?

"It could happen to *you* if they leave you hanging. Or worse, if they snitch. Think they'll do either?"

"Anna is a good person." I don't know the rest of her family well, but I assume they don't deserve to die. "I can't do nothing."

"Well, you're definitely doing something. I was just comming to tell you that we're all set on this end. We can get them to Canada."

"That's a long distance to travel."

"Ground transport's safest, kid. They're watching the sky."

"But a car, really?"

"Not a car, kid. You'll see."

Yves's voice interrupts after a brief buzz. "I'm sorry to cut in, sir, but we're about to land."

"Thank you, Yves."

"Be careful," says Chen.

"I thought you said cars with immunity chips were safe."

"Unless people stop playing by the rules."

"Sir," says Yves. "If your aunt pages me back to the embassy, I cannot refuse her order. She has the master code."

"Then let's hope she wants me to get laid as badly as I think she does," I mutter. I told her I was visiting Marguerite.

We descend to street level. The sun is setting, painting the sides of the mirrored high-rises with swirls of pink and orange. This is the true enclave of the technocrats, but we're going to drive right by—and hope that Anna did what I asked her to. I pull up my collar and tap my cheekbones, then my brow, summoning my internal prosthetics, which change the shape of my face just enough.

Yves is silent as he glides around a corner and rolls into a parking garage, passing a sign that says this space is designated for residents only. A scan slips over his metal skin, but here's the difference between Yves and a car without an immunity chip—this scan won't be able to tell how many warm bodies are inside Yves, because the chip disrupts all temperature and kinetic signals. The scan would also track Cerepin signals if the 'Pins were network connected, but thanks to the chip, it's a no go. It's illegal to fit most cars with such chips, but that's the benefit of having the protection of a foreign government.

I catch sight of Anna just as we enter the maze of closely parked autocannies. She and two other people, dressed in dark coats and wearing backpacks that make them look deformed, are standing near the elevator. "Open," I say, then jump out of the car.

When she sees me, Anna shakes her head. "What happened to your face?"

"No time," I say, pulling her backpack from her slender shoulders. "Get in the car."

Her mother, whom I easily recognize as Gia Fortin despite her thick black hair being pulled back into a ponytail and her sunglasses, touches my arm. "Anna said she goes to school with you. This is amazing, what you're doing for us."

"Please don't thank me until you're safe," I say. "Other technocrats in the city haven't fared well."

"Who?"

"The Aebersolds."

"Oh, god," she says in a choked voice. "Simon was a good friend. Is our president really doing this to us? All because of me?"

"Please consider pondering that from a place that's far from here."

She pushes the man beside her, a grim fellow I can only assume is Anna's father, toward the vehicle.

"We can't leave without him, Gia," he says.

"My son, Hammond," Gia explains. "He was supposed to be here, but he's always late." She bites her lip. "Should I stay, Griffin?" she asks the man.

"No, I will," Griffin Fortin says. "We can meet—"

"Percy," Anna calls, leaning out of Yves. "Your car is telling me that there are three vehicles designated as federal units that have just dropped out of skyspace and are heading in our direction."

"Neither of you will stay," I announce. "I'll take care of Hammond— but it's you they want." I herd Anna's parents into the back of Yves before jumping into the usually empty front seat. As it detects my weight, the control panel lights up.

"Human supplementation is activated, Percy," says Yves. "Federally designated vehicles two blocks and closing."

"Go!" I shout.

"Doors closing, seat belts activated," Yves says before accelerating so quickly that I am pressed into the seat. A harness snakes over my chest and clicks closed. He exits the parking garage at unusually high speed and executes a hairpin turn.

"We need to be going west," I tell him.

"My course is as you specified," he replies mildly. "With the order to avoid federally designated vehicles as the primary command, followed by the speed and directional priorities."

My fingers clench over the straps of my harness. "Then do whatever I told you, and I'll shut up."

Someone grabs my shoulder from the back. "Do you promise to find our son?" Anna's father asks.

"I promise. But he might be safer if you aren't with him." I hope Bianca is safe. As unpleasant as she was, I still don't want her to be dead. Maybe she's just being held for questioning?

I turn my attention back to our predicament as Yves rises into the sky at top speed. Below us I see the shimmering black snake that is the Potomac at night, the western boundary of the District. Once we get over that, Chen and his friends will be waiting to take over. We're only minutes away.

"The federal vehicles are joining us on this skypath, sir," Yves says. "And they're trying to open a channel for communication."

"Oh, god," Gia says in a choked voice. "I'm so sorry."

I glance behind me to see her clutching Anna, her face buried in her daughter's shoulder. Anna's fingers are clawed over her mother's head. Her eyes are riveted on mine. I lay my finger across my lips, asking for silence. Then I clench my jaw and face forward. "Accept the communiqué, but mask background noise and bio-signals."

"Certainly, sir," says Yves. "Diplomatic Vehicle Thirty-Two of the French Republic."

"Diplomatic Thirty-Two, is there a human on board?"

I tap the tiny nodule on my Adam's apple and begin to speak in a stream of perfect French, my voice an octave lower than it usually is. I explain that we are en route to an official meeting with a trade partner of the French government, an activity that is protected by rules surrounding unregulated commerce.

I looked all of this stuff up last night.

"Noted, Diplomatic Thirty-Two. We flagged you because you were detected at the Patrick Presidential Towers complex, which we have designated for increased security."

I clear my throat loudly and try my best to explain that my sojourn at that residential complex was of an entirely personal and deeply private nature, and further explain that this is the reason the French think of the Americans as prudish in the extreme, if they have indeed decided to monitor the boudoir activities of foreign diplomats. I can't help but add that such moral policing could interfere with the quality of the relationship between our two countries if I decided to report it to the American secretary of state. Next, I ask the fellow if he would like to give me his name and identification number so that I may include that in my report. It comes out in such a snobbish string of syllables that my American adversary merely stammers an apology and hangs up.

"Federally designated vehicles decelerating," Yves reports a minute later.

"That was kind of cool," says Anna. "I didn't know you could speak French."

I tap my Adam's apple and allow my voice to return to normal. "I can't. Not really."

"You have augmented vocals," Gia says, her tone full of wonder despite the extreme stress of the last few minutes. "Where did you get those?"

"My parents," I say quietly.

"His face is augmented, too," Anna tells her mother. "He doesn't usually look like this."

"To elude facial recognition?" Gia asks, looking at me with sharp interest. "That's impressive. Who installed it? I'd like to talk to them."

I stare straight ahead. I listen as Anna whispers to her mom not to ask me any more questions, that she'll tell her later. I don't know if she realizes I hear her. But Gia Fortin didn't get where she is by being meek.

"Anna told me your last name is Blake," Gia says. "Were your parents Valentine and Flore, by any chance?"

I don't answer, so she continues. "Your father was an outspoken critic of intracranial technology," she tells me.

"He was a brilliant technologist," I say, "as was my mother. I hardly think—"

"Oh, he was all for augmentations, which have understandably strict regulations," she says, and I can't quite translate her tone, despite my auditory chips. "But he insisted anything implanted in the brain should be used for what he called 'therapeutic purposes' only. He was totally against Cerepins, which he complained were a lot of risk just to have the Mainstream attached to your body permanently, a totally unfair characterization, by the way. He attended congressional hearings, demanding more rigorous rules about testing and developing the products. If he had his way, Cerepins would never have been available commercially."

"What about neurostims?" Anna asks.

"Those *do* have therapeutic uses," Gia says. "Wynn Sallese pushed hard to get them approved, and Valentine Blake demanded the raw data to perform his own independent analysis every time. He was a pest."

My fists clench.

Her chuckle is rueful—and oblivious. "Anyone and everyone who was working in intracranial tech at the time pretty much hated him." She sighs. "But we also respected him. I was so sorry to hear of their deaths. It was such a shock."

"Was it really?" I ask waspishly. "If he had so many enemies, that is."

"It just seemed like a terrible tragedy."

She probably celebrated when she heard the news.

"A *tragedy*? The murderer was wearing a neurostim device," I say. I don't understand why this was never a big deal to anyone but me. "And my parents were there to gather information on their use in treatment of addiction. After my parents were killed, neurostims continued to be marketed as a cure-all. For such a brilliant woman, you seem content to ignore the obvious reek of suspicion."

Anna clears her throat, but her mother merely gazes at me. "I was quite surprised when Anna told me you had enrolled at Clinton," she says, obviously caring little for the murders that brought me there. "We all knew Valentine and Flore had a son, of course. But we all heard about your accident—what was it, ten years ago? And afterward, your entire family all but vanished from the Mainstream. We assumed it was because you were . . . permanently disabled. Beyond the reach of modern medicine." Her eyes narrow. "But clearly you're quite the opposite—and it turns out you have a few interesting . . . qualities as well. Qualities that make me wonder what your father's agenda was all along."

When Yves announces that we've just crossed over the Potomac, I nearly cheer—this woman is yanking on my last nerve. "Get ready," I say as we begin to descend. "This is only the beginning of your journey."

"But you're headed back in, aren't you?" Anna asks.

"I am. It would be an international incident if I didn't."

"Please thank your aunt for us," Gia says.

"I will offer her your sincere gratitude." Aunt Rosalie would build her own guillotine and escort me straight to its bloody embrace if she had any idea of what I was up to.

"Landing," Yves says calmly. "Proceeding to the arrival point."

We touch down on a pitted road somewhere in Arlington, rolling past abandoned storefronts and walls covered in anti-technocrat and anti-canny graffiti. A few wary souls watch us from doorways and windows, but all they see is a sleek black flier with ebony windows. Even if they did have scanner tech, they wouldn't know who was inside.

"I'm not so sure about this," Gia says. "You know these people well?"

I peer out the window, and when I see what's waiting for us, I realize I really don't. Chen and Ukaiah aren't here, but the three people waiting in the garage bay are wearing Incomps—their heads seem slightly misshapen and are a mass of fused biocompatible plastic plates, data chips, and seemingly randomly placed LED lights. Gia lets out a squeak of horror when she catches sight of them. "This is a group of people who will always take the side of the private citizen over the corporate interest," I say.

Even in the dim light, I see the alarm on Gia's face. "And you're confident they'll help us? Because . . ." She gestures at the group as if they were a nest of vipers.

I chuckle. "Well. You're the disenfranchised one now, aren't you? Yves, open."

We step out of the car and are greeted by a terrible smell, along with what turns out to be two men and one woman. "We've got it all set," one of the men tells us after introducing himself as Jack. He gestures behind him at a freight truck. "Destination Toronto. Nonstop. It's ground all the way, which means a hundred percent automation."

"They'll have Bioscan machines at the border," says Griffin Fortin, looking alarmed. "We'll never make it through."

"We've thought of that. We selected the freight specifically for that purpose," says the woman, who has enviably prominent cheekbones that are discernible even through the mess of plastic and sensor wire beneath her eyes. "Live hogs."

Anna chuckles as her eyes meet mine. "That explains the stench."

"You'll have to completely disable your Cerepins, though," says the woman. "You can be tracked via their signals."

"It's a closed network," says Gia.

"Doesn't matter. Electromagnetic scanner could still pick up the energy, even if it can't translate the information. You have to go dark until you cross the border. Unless you want to get caught, that is."

Anna reaches up and taps her Cerepin nodule. "Come on, Mom. We can sleep the whole way."

"It's a twelve-hour drive," says the woman with the cheekbones.

"We'll be refreshed when we arrive," says Anna.

Her mother envelops her in a tight hug. "I don't know what I'd do without you," she says, her voice tight with tears. "And if Hammond doesn't make it . . ."

"He will," I tell them. "I'll make sure."

The woman ushers Anna and her parents toward the back of the freight transport, and Jack moves next to me.

"Are they really going to make it?" I ask.

"There's a pretty good chance," he says. "Ground transport is highly automated, since beating hearts tend to travel via skyway, and even the traffic patterns are handled by the regional computer systems. The interstate system and border are federal, of course, but this transport originated in Georgia and won't raise any red flags. They'd have to be willing to halt the whole system to even begin to search for the Fortins, and they wouldn't necessarily know exactly where to start. Assuming they get going in the next fifteen, because that's the scheduled end of this truck's recharging."

The third man in the group pulls a connector out of a port on the side of the truck and winds the thick cord around the dock, which was used for fire trucks long ago. "We've got a network up and down the East Coast and can program where certain transports are set to refuel," he says. "We also boosted the output so we got a full charge in eighty-six percent of the time."

I watch Anna disappear into the back of the truck with her family. "Farewell," I murmur.

Jack clears his throat. "So . . . I heard you say you got someone to go back for?"

"A young man. Hammond Fortin. He's only sixteen, though. It's possible that he won't hold any interest for the FBI now that his family is gone."

Jack's ruddy cheeks are almost purple beneath the plastic. "I don't know about that. Chen commed me a few minutes before you arrived. Said he needed to get a message to you but your coms were busy. He said it was urgent."

"Then why are you just telling me now?"

Jack lowers his voice. "Because I didn't want to make that family more anxious before we stick 'em in little transport boxes for the next twelve hours."

"Just tell me, Jack."

"Chen found your friend Bianca."

"Is she all right?"

"No, kid. She's not all right. She was one of the last corpses brought in. She'd been in one of the hangars at Reagan, I guess."

"Dead?"

"That's not all. Chen said there were signs of torture. Like they played with her for a few hours before killing her."

My gorge rises so fast that I have to clench my teeth to keep from gagging. "What?"

"Burn marks. Lungs half-full of water. I could go on, but you probably don't want me to."

"Why would they do that to her?" I whisper.

"Chen's morgue friend said it looked personal. Her Cerepin was ripped right outta her head."

Suddenly, Marguerite's words come back to me so forcefully that I nearly fall to my knees. *God, she's toxic. I'd like to rip that Cerepin right out of her head.* "She couldn't," I mouth, unable to draw breath. "She wouldn't."

I remember the look on her face, though, when she realized what Bianca had done to her. I remember her voice echoing out of that classroom as she talked to El, as she calls him. It took me five minutes to determine El to be Elwood Seidel, the president's chief of staff.

Wouldn't you love to take them down? El had asked.

At the moment? Hell yes, Marguerite had replied. *She's so freaking awful.*

But so is karma, Marguerite. And I have a feeling it's going to come back to bite Ms. Aebersold. Trust me on that. El had clearly relished the thought. And he had the power to make things happen.

Jack grabs my arm as I sway, torn between puking all over the floor and slamming my fist into the side of Yves. Marguerite used her connection to the Sallese administration to take out an entire family, to visit unimaginable pain on her enemies. And then she met Anna for coffee this morning, possibly contemplating the same end for her. She had looked me right in the face, and I had actually been thinking about kissing her.

"You okay, kid?"

I steady myself. "Of course."

"You're the color of grits."

"I don't even want to know what those are."

"Sorry about your friend. She's probably not the first or the last."

All in the name of law and order. Of justice. "We're not going to let them win. Can you arrange more transports like this one?"

He winces and rubs his hand over his greasy black hair. "How many you think you would need, exactly?"

"I don't know yet. But you'll hear from me."

He chuckles, reaches into his pocket, and pulls out a piece of paper—my father's stationery, with its primrose embossing—which I left at our dead-drop site before my brief encounter with Anna and Marguerite this morning. "Like this?" It contains the codes I put in my vids. "Boy, I hadn't seen paper in a hog's age."

"It only works if you actually destroy it when you receive it!"

He produces a chemical vaporizer from another pocket and inciner-ates the thing. We watch as black ashes fall to the ground. "There you go. Brilliant idea, by the way. We've got to stay off the grid or else we're gonna be the ones with water in our lungs."

"I'll leave the next codes for a meeting on that bench in Gingrich Park, and I'll trigger the next meeting the usual way. Just give me twenty-four hours. I'll let you know how many transports we need and for how many people."

"Okay . . . we'll do what we can."

"And tell Chen I want a present the next time I see him. He'll know what you mean."

Chapter Fourteen

Marguerite

I'm staring at the ceiling, listening to a crowdsourced channel speculating on what happened last night. A lot of people are trying to verify who was actually caught and whether they were really terrorists—or whether this was Uncle Wynn's administration taking out its enemies. The charge is so ridiculous, yet . . . it's stuck in my brain like a splinter.

"Marguerite, Elwood Seidel is at the door for you," says Helen, the voice of this brownstone.

A sudden chill runs through me. "Tell him I'll meet him in the living room."

I rise from my bed as I hear the door open, and find El in the hallway, just past the entrance to the living room, as if he was headed somewhere else. "Mom's sleeping," I say. "It's kind of late."

He glances at her door. "I didn't come here to see her."

I go into the living room and drop into a chair. All casual. "What's up?"

"We have to talk." He's making that face he makes when things aren't going right. Brows low, jaw clenched.

"I thought you'd be celebrating, now that so many terrorists have been caught."

"That was a huge step forward, for sure," he says, spreading his arms across the back of the couch. "Marguerite," he adds as his eyes lock with mine, "the Fortins have disappeared."

"But I just had coffee with Anna this morning." And then she ran off to meet her family . . . "Oh."

"You know something?"

I shake my head. "No, why would I?" Wow—did she actually listen to me?

"I thought you were making Anna Fortin your friend."

"I was. I had." But in the way Uncle Wynn suggested, not the way El did.

"Yes," El says, fiddling with his comband. "I guess you did."

He turns the screen so I can see it, but the image is sideways, and all I can make out is a blurred coffee cup. He taps the white blob of the cup, and a vid begins to play.

"Are you guys thinking of getting out of here?" I hear my own voice say.

"Define *here*." Anna's voice. This morning.

"I wasn't prying—I swear. You don't have to be in DC to answer the FBI's questions."

El pauses the vid. "Care to explain?"

"Do you?" My heart feels like it's about to explode out of my chest. "That's my screen! You capped my comband?" I'm almost shrieking.

"I have to know I can trust you, Mar," he says sadly. "And after I heard this, I wonder if I can."

"You snooped on my meeting, and you didn't tell me!"

"With good reason," he replies. "I had to know if you were loyal. Imagine how I felt as I listened to you tipping off the daughter of Gia Fortin, suggesting they leave the city."

"Oh my god, El," I say. "Can you blame me?"

"Yes," he snaps. "You seem to have forgotten what that family tried to do to us in the general election."

"You told me to be friends with her!"

"I *told* you to get her to cooperate," he says. "Not to suggest the whole family try to escape justice. They could be *terrorists*, Marguerite. You're aiding and abetting terrorists."

I sit back and stare. "El, you're scaring me."

"Am I? Good." He sets his elbows on his knees. "You need to understand a few realities. No one is going to get in my way. I am in this to win."

"Don't you mean *we*?" I ask weakly.

His stare is so steady that I wonder if he's even seeing me. "Our entire Department of AIR has been destroyed, including precious information and research, and it's increasingly obvious this was the work of technocrats bent on keeping us from regulating their business. The Fortins are almost certain to be involved—but suddenly they're gone. Because you tipped them off!"

"All I did was ask if they were considering leaving, because so many others were!"

"So many others *tried*, you mean. We caught all but a few of them."

"Terrorists. You're supposed to be tracking down *terrorists*. Not—"

"I don't need to explain to you of all people how the technocrats have terrorized and oppressed the American people. Look at Parnassus—they're responsible for what happened to your father, Marguerite. And Simon Aebersold was the captain of that ship."

I shudder. "Was?" I whisper.

"You were kind enough to warn me about Bianca Aebersold, so thanks for that one."

"What happened to them?"

"Like I told you, karma is a serious bitch. I offered Bianca your best regards before the end."

It feels as if every cell in my body has turned to ice. "El . . . what . . . ?"

"I took them down, just like you wanted me to."

"I never said I wanted that!"

El fiddles with his comband for a few seconds before replaying our voices from a previous com: "Lovely family, am I right? Wouldn't you love to take them down?" he had asked me.

"At the moment? Hell yes. She's so freaking awful," I had replied.

"Oh my god. What did you do?"

"*I* didn't do anything." He looks down at his comband. "That's what the FBI is for. They were cannies. No guilt. No hesitation. No empathy. Easier that way."

I think I'm going to be sick.

"This was for you, Marguerite. For you and Colette. People need to know that they can't do those things to you. I want them to *fear* us."

"They already did!"

"Not enough, though," he murmurs.

"You had her *killed*?"

"I ordered them to punish her first."

I am up and running for the toilet, my stomach heaving. I make it as far as the hallway before I lose it, and for the next few moments my body just takes over, wringing me out. As I lean on the doorjamb, I feel El behind me. His hands close over my shoulders, and I can't tell if he's steadying me or trying to keep me from escaping. "I made sure she knew it was because of you, Marguerite."

"Don't," I whisper.

"It's not like I enjoyed giving the order. But it was necessary—and right. I mean, I saw how she hurt you. I wanted to make sure we gave it back to her in spades." He lets me go. "And then, after all that, I find out you aren't on my side. I couldn't believe it. We were always on the same side."

Is that really how it was? My thoughts are unraveling.

"I'll clean this up," says Helen, sounding sympathetic. "Can I have Renata bring you a glass of water?"

"Yes, Helen," El says, all friendliness. "We'll stay in the living room."

A moment later, Renata, the house canny, strides in with water. I take it from her synthetic hands and avoid looking into her dead eyes. I close mine as she wipes my mouth with a cloth and retreats. "You're insane," I say to El when my voice returns. "Were you always this crazy, or did this just happen?"

"You know, it's easy for me to forget how young you are," El replies sadly. "And I know you haven't had as much support as you need, with your mother in such a vulnerable state."

"She will never forgive you when she finds out what you've done."

"Good thing you won't tell her," he says, and the intensity in his eyes burns right through me. "Because if you do, I'm afraid we'd have to reconsider your place in this administration."

I raise my head. "Uncle Wynn wouldn't let you."

"He trusts me to fix things for him. If he heard you'd decided to resign your post, I'm sure he'd be disappointed, but you can hardly expect him to show up on your doorstep."

"I'll talk to him myself."

"He's the president, Marguerite. You're a volatile teenager without a security clearance. Good luck with that."

"Mom has a security clearance."

"Only because of me. You think she would have passed the mental health examination if I hadn't spoken with the evaluator afterward?" He is standing not even three feet away. "Do you really want to ruin this for her by becoming a traitor? She's more fragile than you might think. I'd hate for her to suffer any more setbacks. She might not survive it."

I stare at his knees. "I can't believe I thought you were a good person."

"I genuinely care for Colette, Marguerite. I'm taking care of her in every way I can. I know what's best for her—and I'm going to protect her from everything. Including you, if I need to."

I force my voice to be quiet and even. "Then think about what she would want. She suffers when people get hurt. Like Dr. Barton—"

"She's still grieving. But now that she has purpose, she's getting over it—"

"*It* being my dad?"

"Don't try to turn this around. I made her my top aide and made sure she had all the benefits that go along with it. I talked the president into keeping you on after the campaign. I didn't have to do any of this, Marguerite. I did it for her. For you."

"Hoping you'd get the prize in the end," I mutter.

"*You're* the one who betrayed this administration, Marguerite. You betrayed our trust and our mission. But despite that, I'm going to give you a chance to redeem yourself."

My mind is spinning with how I'm going to get to Uncle Wynn. "I'm not doing anything for you."

"If you don't, you're going to find yourself with a one-way ticket back to Houston for a long visit with your friend. What was her name? Oh—Orianna. And it's really a shame, the infrastructure there in the Lone Star State. Did you read about that air-transport crash a few weeks ago? All because of a little glitch in the landing-guidance systems. Outdated, for sure. I hope you'd make it back safely, but really, it's a little chancy."

"Are you threatening me?"

"I'm just laying out the facts."

I cover my face with my hands, wishing I could rewind a few minutes, a few days, a few weeks. Maybe the entire last year. "What do you want?"

"I want you to use your powers for good. To set things right again."

"You want me to make a vid."

"Well, it's more specific than that. I want you to ask for help from your followers. There's someone we need to find."

"Gia?"

"I'm working on that. Someone else, though. The person—or people—who helped the Fortins escape DC."

My hands fall away from my face. "Escape DC? Are we living in a prison state now?"

"There's a state of emergency, and the police and FBI are indeed controlling transport in and out of the District to prevent terrorists from escaping justice."

"To prevent your political enemies from getting away, you mean."

"What's the difference, really?"

I just stare at him.

"Marguerite, these are the people who profit while their fellow Americans dwell in poverty. Our economy is in tatters while Asia and Europe thrive, and the technocrats have helped it happen."

"Seize their assets, then! Why kill them?"

"Live people talk and go to court and generally cause trouble. In your case, we'll use it to our benefit. We'd been watching the Fortins closely, and unlike several of their little technocrat friends, they'd made no moves to scurry away to Europe or South Korea. Still, we decided to pick up Gia for questioning in the bombing, figuring she might be more cooperative if she knew the fate of some of her closest conspirators. But when we arrived, the family was gone. All four of them." He gives me a stern look and glances down at his comband, the video he grabbed from my secretly capped device. "Thanks to you."

"I had nothing to do with their disappearance, El."

"Oh, I know that. You tipped them off, and then they found their own means of escape. But they had to have had help. Someone inside the city. This is where you come in. I want you to lure these people out."

"How?"

"Figure it out."

Or else hangs in the air.

El stands up abruptly and stretches. "I'd better get back to the White House." He follows the line of my gaze to my mom's room. "Be careful, little girl," he murmurs. "Never make the mistake of thinking you're more clever than I am."

I slowly rise from my own chair. "Just go, Elwood."

For a few seconds, he stands there, as if calculating which way he thinks I'm going to jump. Then his smile returns, and he reaches out and squeezes my shoulder. He heads into the hallway. I hear the door click open and shut. Only then do I begin to shake all over. On unsteady feet, I go to my mom's door and push it open. I can't believe she slept through all of that. As I walk in, Helen automatically illuminates the wall along the bed in blue light, allowing me to see her. Her black hair is fanned out across her pillow. A tiny, blinking red light within her locks draws my attention, and I walk over to the bed. She's wearing a neurostim device? She finally caved and got one. I guess I should be glad that she's getting some relief from her depression, but the sight of it makes me feel like I've lost yet another piece of her. I can't imagine losing more.

She stirs and opens her eyes. "Hey. Are you okay?"

I sit down on the edge of her bed. "Are you?"

She touches her neurostim and smiles.

Smiles. Everything inside me goes quiet with amazement.

But then she says, "I'm great. El found me a doctor, and I got it put on this afternoon. Easy and painless."

El. Suddenly the sight of the tiny red light at her nape makes me want to puke again. "I'm glad you're feeling better," I manage to say.

"This isn't one of the cheap ones." She rubs her eyes. "It's amazing, being here, isn't it? I still can't believe it."

"Don't you ever miss home?" Because right now, I feel the walls of this place closing in.

Her smile evaporates. "The place that killed your dad? I'll be grateful if I never have to set foot in Texas again."

"I didn't know you felt that way."

"I'm sorry, baby. I know you still have friends there. But for me . . . that place is poison." She pulls me down and hugs me. "You saved me, you know. I never really thanked you. But if it weren't for your vids and everything you've done? I don't know that I would have survived. You rescued us from that place, and look where we are. I know it's not perfect, but compared to anywhere else . . ."

She releases me and I sit up. "I'm glad you're feeling better," I say, standing and walking to the door. "Sorry for waking you up."

"Maybe you should get some sleep yourself. You don't want to be too tired for school."

"Right. Good night." I slip into the hallway and close the door before she can say another word. I feel like I'm going to explode. Every single thought I have is a dead end. Elwood Seidel has walled all of them off and booby-trapped them on top of it. And I let him. I *helped* him.

If it weren't for me, Bianca might still be alive. At worst, she would have died quickly. I have blood on my hands. El was right about one thing—I have to make amends.

But I have to do it carefully, or else I'm going to become his next victim.

Chapter Fifteen

Percy

The FBI agents arrive at the embassy early, as Auntie and I are at breakfast. She is imperious as she tells our butler to seat them in the parlor. "They say one of our diplomatic fleet was engaged in suspicious activity last night," she says as she accepts a third demitasse of espresso.

I bow my head and laugh.

"Percy?"

"You did tell me I could have the use of a car to go visit *mon amour*."

"You believe it is *you* they would like to talk to?"

I fan my face as if embarrassed. "Must I explain my romantic rendezvous to the United States government? How gauche."

"Indeed. But you can't be too careful at this time, *mon petit chou*. Sallese and his minions have embarked upon their own reign of terror. If he would talk to me, I would remind him of how history has treated such misadventures. The French understand such things."

"I'll be more careful."

She frowns as she hears footsteps in the entryway. "Perhaps you should find other ways to meet with your lovely lady, Percy."

I slump and let my voice roughen. "She is the bright spot in my life, Auntie. When I'm with her, the burden of my grief lifts for a few sweet moments. I feel *normal*."

When I raise my eyes to hers, I see that she's fighting tears. "Oh, my darling boy," she says huskily. "Love is the highest calling." She rises, dabbing her eyes with her napkin and patting my arm. "I will send these silly, prudish fellows on their way. We will not allow anything to interfere with affairs of the heart."

I place my hand over hers. "I am eternally grateful, Auntie."

She kisses the top of my head and disappears into the hallway. I stare down at my half-eaten croissant and consider what the hell I've done.

As far as I know, the Fortins should be nearly to the Canadian border by now—minus their son, Hammond. I'm headed to school shortly to see if the fellow shows up, because I need to find him and get him out.

Bianca is dead. She was a petty, mean girl. For that, she deserved social humiliation, perhaps. I would have believed that to be just. Instead, she's in a morgue somewhere, wearing all the gruesome evidence of the last few painful hours of her life.

And I just told my aunt I was carrying on a passionate affair with the girl who is responsible for Bianca's death. I push my plate away and jump to my feet.

"Percy, would you like to have your breakfast wrapped and warmed for the ride to school?"

"No, I'm not hungry, Sophia. Thank you." I stalk down the hall to my room, my heart rate rising over a hundred beats per minute, my teeth clenched around the rage. I had thought that the most important thing I could do was to find out what really happened to my parents, but now I know I have to set that aside, for now at least. My parents are dead. There are people like them, living people, who are in danger. I approach my desk screen, thinking about the vid I'm going to create this afternoon—and I see that my darling little murderess, Marguerite, has created a new vid of her own. I motion for the vid to play and let her rise up in all her glory to hover in the air above the desktop.

"A few days ago," she says, her brown eyes full of fire, her stare boring a hole in my heart, "over eighty people were killed in a terrorist attack. No one else should die."

Here, she chokes up a bit. As if she actually cares.

"No one," she says again. "Should. Die. I know all of you out there feel the same. No matter how you feel about the technocrats, no matter what's going on in your daily lives, I know you recognize that all of us are human beings. With families. With children."

A tear streaks down her face. Damn. She is good.

She draws in a shuddery breath as I sink into my chair and let my gaze trace her features, marveling at how fine-boned she is, wondering how much pressure I'd need to use to crush her windpipe, to give her even a taste of what Bianca must have experienced in those hours of utter agony and terror.

"I know at least one of you out there is taking matters into your own hands. Is it you?"

I swear, she's looking right at me.

Why is it that I am imagining kissing her and choking her at the same time?

"Percy, your biostats register an extreme stress response. Your heart rate is one hundred—"

"Seventy-eight beats per minute, Sophia. *Yes.* I *know.* Privacy." My voice echoes off her painted plaster skin.

"Yes, Percy."

Marguerite continues. "But is helping terrorists really the way to get justice? Is that brave? Wouldn't it be braver to let the authorities who risk their lives to keep us safe do their work?"

Watching her is the strangest experience. Her eyes are intent. Full of secrets and promises. Her mouth is full of lies. I can't decide where to focus. She is more skilled than I gave her credit for. I can't believe she's doing this, and doing it so well, even though I shouldn't be at all surprised.

"I know most of you have no idea what I'm talking about, but if you do, talk to me," she says. "I'll listen. I want to understand. I know I'm just a kid." Now she tilts her head, her eyes glittering with tears and dangerous sincerity. "But I believe in equality. In the right of every American to live and work and have a shot at a happy life. I still believe that. Maybe you believe that, too? Maybe that's why you're doing what you're doing?"

She smiles, suddenly, and her cheeks become the most delectable shade of pink. "Washington is such a strange place, you know? I don't really belong here, but I came because I wanted to help. And that's why I'm staying. I want to help."

The way she says those final words . . .

The vid ends, and I freeze the final image. Marguerite is trying to draw me out. Well. She has no idea it's me she's trying to lure, but still. She is a weapon of the government, and like she betrayed Bianca, like she would have betrayed Anna had I not intervened, I know she will betray me if given the chance, and possibly my aunt by extension.

"I won't let you, darling," I murmur. I open my private portal and log in, using the AI ghost program Chen gave me to render the connection untraceable. "But you're welcome to try."

I type a few words and smile grimly as they appear below her vid, the last in a column of comments.

FragFlwr: Catch me if you can.

The herd has thinned. As I disembark from the embassy vehicle (not Yves, though I've told him to be on standby, with my aunt's approval) I can already see that so many of my classmates are either gone—fled with their families, perhaps sweating bullets in their respective luxury apartments—or dead. It's impossible to know which, because a quick check of the school's social network shows that nearly all of them are off-line, and the Mainstream crowdsourced news reports nothing except speculation. Auntie told me that in the past there were actual news organizations with professional news reporters. Now, we have a host of aggressive freelance amateurs who are usually strikingly good at showing the world things other people would prefer us not to see. But in this case? Almost nothing. Just the vids from a distance at the airport and nothing from the other raids.

I walk toward the wheelboard rack, where Hammond is usually slouched with his friends, all of whom are in dire need of more frequent showers. Today there are only two boys there, and neither of them is Anna's younger brother. "Greetings," I say.

They give me the look I am so used to receiving, one that says they think little of my airy walk and immaculately styled and utterly classic ensemble. I smooth down a fold of my cravat and smile at them. "I'm wondering if either of you chaps have laid eyes on Hammond Fortin in the last day or two."

The shorter of the pair is Winston, and he gives his taller friend a shifty look. "Why do you want to know?"

"I lost a wager, sadly. I need to know how he would like to receive the funds."

The tall friend, a junior named Finn Cuellar, is square-jawed and muscular and perspiring despite the chilly winter breeze. "Haven't talked to him."

"Hmm." Both of them look nervous. "I suppose he might have caught the same cold that's going around." My gaze sweeps the front of the school, where students are being scanned for contraband. A row of Secret Service cannies stands by. More than last time.

Finn coughs deliberately into his shoulder. "I'm feeling a little sick myself."

"Maybe it's the French stench," Winston says, his lip curling.

"What a deft little rhyme, darling," I say. "But there's no need for it."

"Why? My mom's being followed by the freaking FBI, and you just zip in here, carefree, because you live at the French embassy! You have no idea what this is like." His eyes are red, I realize. This overgrown boy has been crying. "She made me come here because she thought I'd be safer. In case they raid our *house*."

His mother is the recently unseated secretary of AIR, as I recall. "You do have my sympathy," I say, glancing around and tapping my auditory projector to prevent any nearby cannies or sets of augmented ears from catching my next few words. "And I might have a friend who can help."

I thought of this in the car on the flight over. Quick as I can, I reach into my pocket and pull out a square of the embossed paper. "Destroy this contact method after you memorize it," I say as I lean forward and shake his hand, keeping the scrap of paper pressed between our palms.

Looking startled, Winston tries to pull out of my grip as Finn looks on with wide eyes. But as so many others do, Winston underestimates my strength, and I keep a grip on him. "Read it in a place where there are no eyes on you, then destroy it. Swear."

"You're hurting me, man," Winston whines.

"Swear," I say. "Your life, and the lives of your family, might depend on it."

He goes still. "Okay. I swear."

I don't let go quite yet. "And if you tell a soul that I'm the one who gave you this information, I will happily break every bone in your body. Understand it would be easy for me. Much easier than you might expect."

His eyes go wide as I squeeze a little more and then abruptly let go.

"Hey," says Finn. "What about my family? Both my parents have been told to report to FBI headquarters. My dad says Sallese is probably going to have them arrested just because they work at Parnassus. Neither of them even expects to come home."

"Tell your family they have friends on the outside. They will hear from someone."

"My girlfriend, Hannah—her dad is the CFO at Parnassus," Finn continues. "He's been called in for questioning, too."

"Their situation will be looked into."

Honestly, I'm making stuff up now. I'm making promises I might not be able to keep. But I swear, I'm going to try. "But I need to hear from Hammond. My friend is interested in helping him."

"I can get a message to him," says Winston, his fist clenched around the paper, one that contains the contact information for one of my aliases. "He's gone dark because he's scared he's next. They disappeared his whole family last night, man! He woulda been caught, too, if he hadn't been late."

"He can see his family again if he trusts me," I say.

"Wait, they're okay?"

I nod. "I think—"

"Percy!"

I freeze at the sound of her voice, and Finn and Winston flinch. A quick glance over my shoulder reveals Marguerite, her wavy hair pulled back, her brown eyes warm, standing on the curb. Her skin is paler than usual, but she's no less beautiful for it.

I give her a fluttering finger wave before turning back to Winston and Finn.

Finn looks incredulous. "You've got to be kidding me. You can't be friends with her after everything that's happened. She's in bed with the devil."

"How well I know it," I murmur. "But never show your hand, gentlemen." I lock eyes briefly with Winston and he nods, looking scared but determined. "And I'll talk to both of you soon."

I turn to Marguerite, who is approaching with an open look on her face. She cranes her neck to see Winston and Finn behind me, so I walk toward her, giving them a chance to disappear. I give her an elaborate bow and straighten to find her smiling. "Here we are, back in the halls of learning," she says.

I offer her my arm, and she bites her lip. Then she takes it, and I put my hand over hers. I lead her toward the security cannies at the door. "I see we have more blessed protection from on high today." I incline my head toward the Secret Service machinemen. "Or you do, at least."

She smiles at them, but I swear it looks forced. "Oh, yes, the president wanted to make sure we were all safe." Her voice . . . has she been crying? Or is it an extremely accomplished act?

"I wonder what Bianca would say, were she here?" I ask, keeping my tone light. "Would *she* feel safe?"

She gives me a startled look. "Why do you say that?"

"Merely wondering. It's a moot point. I suppose she's sipping bubbly in a chalet somewhere. After her vid escapade, I'm sure you don't miss her."

Now Marguerite's staring at the ground. "I . . . ," she begins, then clears her throat. "I hope she's somewhere peaceful."

The urge to wrap my hands around her throat is on me again.

"Ow," she says, pulling her arm away.

It seems I was squeezing her hand a bit too hard. Sometimes my body does operate outside of my control. "Apologies," I say. "I'm always a bit nervous around these scanner creatures, you know."

"Why?"

Because I am a trove of secrets wrapped in a cloak of skin. I raise a conspiratorial eyebrow at her. "Because who knows when they'll discover the contraband in my pockets."

"Contraband?"

I lean closer, close enough to smell mint on her breath. "Never say I'm not a sinner."

Her gaze is on my mouth, and my body is confused. I have to remind myself that if she has the chance, she'll offer my head to Sallese, most likely separately from the rest of me.

"What kind of sins?" she whispers.

"The kind that can't be revealed at school."

"Then you shouldn't have anything to fear."

"I never said I was afraid."

"You don't say much at all," she says. "At least, not much that's real. You hide behind this mask you wear, Percy. I'm interested in what's underneath."

Oh, I bet. "We all wear masks, darling. Sometimes the loveliest hide a rotten core."

Her smile flickers. "Are you saying I—?"

"You? But why would you assume I'm speaking of you? Are those lightning reflexes triggered by a guilty conscience?"

"What would I be guilty for?" But she betrays herself—there's a shine of emotion in those eyes.

"You tell me," I murmur.

"You really know how to turn things around on people. Just another way to hide?"

"And now we've completed our circle around the dance floor. Care for another round?"

She laughs. "I'm not sure I can keep up with you."

"No one can."

She pauses before we reach security and gives me a shrewd look. "You must be very connected, I'm thinking. Living at the French embassy, being a star of the Mainstream, friends with Anna Fortin."

We face each other and hold out our arms as the security cannies do their work. Because my paper isn't metal or heat-producing, they ignore it. "True, true, and true," I say. "Your point being?"

"I was just thinking . . . I'd like to meet more people. And with Anna gone . . ."

My, my. Marguerite is *sleuthing*. And she wants me to help her do Sallese's dirty work. "You've developed a sudden interest in making friends? I was under the impression that you thought all of us were irredeemable techno*crites*."

"Hey. You *have* seen my vids," she says.

"Perhaps one or two. I had to see what the fuss was about."

"Have you ever commented, maybe?"

"Commented on *politics*? Why would I?"

She's smiling now. Fetching. Flirting. Trying to draw me in. "Because you enjoy needling me."

I give her a smile of my own. "That's quite a weapon you've got there."

Her face falls. "It's not a weapon."

"Isn't it? My dear girl, tell the truth. You'd like to see some of us get our comeuppance. In fact, what was it that you said, that you'd like to rip Bianca's Cerepin from her pretty skull?"

"Why are you saying this to me?" she asks quietly. "Have you heard something?"

"There are rumors," I whisper. "And I'm wondering if they're true."

Marguerite Singer has the most expressive face. In the seconds before she pulls away, I see surprise and fear and hope—then fear again . . . and then nothing. "I wouldn't believe anything you see on the Mainstream," she says breezily. "I mean, just this morning, I heard the strangest thing myself. I read a post on some board where someone claiming to be a skyway auditor reported that the Fortins might have left the city in a vehicle with a diplomatic chip."

"I wonder if the FBI read that very same posting," I mutter.

"Sorry?"

"Nothing. You were saying?"

"I just thought it was wild. I haven't seen or heard from Anna since yesterday at coffee. This morning I read that they escaped in an embassy car, evading the FBI, who wanted them for questioning."

"And as you say, the Mainstream is not always a credible place—"

"What if the person who helped them worked for an embassy?"

She's just a step too close. "That's an interesting theory," I say. "I don't doubt the Sallese administration is looking into it."

"I'm thinking that person should be very careful."

I pause at the base of the stairs and look down at her. "Is that what you think, darling?"

"I would warn the person myself if I knew who they were. I care about Anna. I don't want to see anyone get hurt."

I lean over her hand and kiss the soft skin between her knuckles. She smells divine to my heightened senses, and she gasps audibly as my lips make contact, but no matter. She's also my enemy. "Then perhaps you should close your eyes, Marguerite. Because I have a feeling your side is playing for keeps."

Chapter Sixteen

Marguerite

But I don't close my eyes. Instead I stare down at the ruby flower fastening his elaborate French cuffs. I can't figure him out. For a second, I thought he might help me. He lives at one of the embassies, after all. He could find out information. Then I'm reminded of what he really cares about: presence, not politics. "Those are pretty," I say, nodding at the cuff link.

"A family heirloom on my father's side. That's a kind of English primrose, from the old family crest."

A family *crest*? "I sort of wish I could step into your world for a while," I say, trying to keep my tone light.

"You know what they say about grass," he says with a charming smile, releasing my hand. "Shall we head to homeroom?"

He is remote and polite as we head up the stairs, which is a better reaction than I get from most. I should feel better that at least one person is being nice to me, but in some ways, this is worse, because even though he's standing next to me, he seems miles away. I sit silent in my half-empty homeroom and am actually relieved when it's time to slip into a cubicle and interact with Aristotle, who invites me to discuss how our current economic situation parallels that of eighteenth-century

France and how it diverges. When the AI's done with me, I slink out the front and hop into the waiting car.

"How was your day, Marguerite?" Jenny inquires.

"Weird," I mutter. Even though I was braced for drama when I got to DC, I had no idea how cracked it was going to get. Now most of my classmates are afraid to even show up—or they've already bailed with their families.

Oh, and the president's chief of staff is a psychopath.

And one of my classmates is dead because I trusted him. Maybe more than one. Kyla is still MIA.

I haven't eaten since last night. My stomach is too wobbly, too prone to turning inside out every time I think of Bianca. I stare at the rain-flecked windows and do my best to think about what El has asked of me—I'm supposed to help him catch the person or people who helped Anna and her family escape, but what I'd really like to do is help that person out. If I do, though, I'm dead, and my mom . . . I'm completely trapped. I need to check my channel once I have some privacy. I haven't seen any of the comments or reaction to my last vid. I can barely remember what I said, only that my heart was pounding the entire time I was streaming it. I need to take a look, though. I need to think about how to handle—

El is standing in the doorway of the brownstone as I get out of the car. "Welcome home," he says.

"Where's Mom?"

He grins. "Making cookies."

"Don't you have a job? Doesn't she?"

"We're heading back to the White House shortly. I just wanted us to be home to greet you after your school day."

"Right. What's happened now?"

"Your vid happened, Marguerite. Now please get in here instead of standing on the sidewalk in the rain."

As I tromp up the stairs, I see his eyes are bright, and my heart sinks. "Did Christmas arrive early?"

"You could say that." He gestures me into the sitting room.

"Marguerite?" Mom calls from the kitchen, from which wafts the scent of chocolate chips. She's actually baking? "How was your day?"

"Fine, Mom. How are you feeling?"

"Better!" She comes into the room carrying a plate of cookies, which she sets on the coffee table nearest me. "Have one—they're still warm."

I take one because she looks better than she has in months.

She sees me watching her, and her fingers rise to her nape, where the neurostim is blinking. "It's really helping."

"I can see that," I say, feeling melted chocolate coat my fingertips. I shove the cookie in my mouth just for something to do.

Her comband buzzes, and when she looks down at it, she starts. "Oh! That's Mazin. I need to—"

"Go ahead," says El. He looks over at me as she bustles from the room. "The president's new scheduling secretary. Chose him myself."

Like he's warning me not to even try to get around him. "So," El begins, taking a cookie of his own and sitting down across from me. "Clever angle of attack on that vid this morning, Mar. For a moment, I couldn't figure out if you were working with me—or against me."

"I meant to do that. I wanted to draw them out, not drive them away. How am I supposed to help you catch these people if I can't get them to interact with me?"

"Exactly. That's what I realized, too." He takes a bite of his cookie, which leaves a smear of chocolate on his lip. "Because you succeeded, young lady. You succeeded."

"I did?"

"See for yourself." He moves the cookie plate off the table and waves his hand over it, waking the screen up.

Obediently, I lean over and let it scan my face, which brings up my channel. I activate the vid, and while it plays, I read the comments. A chill runs through me as I read FragFlwr: Catch me if you can.

"Oh my god."

"Who woulda thunk it?" El says gleefully.

My heart is trying to escape my rib cage by way of my throat. How could he be so stupid and obvious? Or . . . maybe this is proof it isn't him? God, I don't know how to handle this. "How do you know he—or *she*—isn't just trolling?" I ask, trying to keep the tremble from my voice. "That's kind of what he does."

"Because we put a trace on it."

"And?"

He chuckles as he sits back. "It's untraceable."

I squint at him. "How is that even possible?"

"We're trying to figure that out, but in the meantime, doesn't it make sense? Who has an untraceable account? I'll tell you who—someone who is capable of smuggling the most high-profile family in DC out from under our noses. Except . . . you got him to talk to you."

"Sort of? I mean, not really. He's been trolling my channel for months, always leaving snide little remarks, accusing me of being a puppet and stuff like that. More like he was trying to make me look bad."

"I'm not so sure. Maybe this person was trying to lure you out."

"Yeah, but a comment war doesn't help the cause!"

"I know, but this is different. If this person really is involved, we need you to get in the mix with him."

"Or her. It might be a her."

"Whatever."

"Why do I need to get into any mix at all? Seems like you already think this is the smuggler."

"Yes," El says, his feigned patience sounding a lot like Aristotle. "But the security around that account is tricky. It'll be tough to pinpoint where the user is unless you're interacting with him at the time."

"Seriously?"

El shrugs. "Our technical team told me this morning that it was the only way, because unless there's an active signal, the account doesn't even seem to exist. It's like dark matter. Just a blank."

"Nothing is blank on the Mainstream!"

"Right, not as it's happening. But this account must have some sort of piggyback AI ghost that automatically erases its electronic trace as soon as the person has signed off."

"But what about the ghost itself?"

He smiles. "Good girl. That's what we're trying to trace now. But we need you to get us more data so we can nail this guy."

"To the cross?" I mumble. Because I'm guessing what happened to Bianca is nothing compared to what he'll have done to FragFlwr.

El's brow furrows. "Don't be snide. Just respond to his comment. Try to start a conversation. I've got someone from the tech team on standby now, so do it at a time that makes sense and see if you can really get an interaction going."

My terror is so heavy that I'm suddenly exhausted from carrying it. "Where are we going with this, El? You can catch this one person, maybe, but you can't put every technocrat in jail. You can't kill them all just because they piss you off."

"Piss me off? That's what you think this is about?"

"All I know is that the president told me he didn't want more people to die."

"But these are terrorists, Marguerite." He says it so calmly. Like it's obvious on whatever twisted planet he's living on.

"Is Kyla Barton a terrorist? She was nice to me, El. She was sweet. And her mom *helped* you guys."

El snarls, his mouth ugly on his narrow face. Maybe it always has been. "Collateral damage is an inevitable part of war."

"What the heck?"

"If you don't think we're at war, you haven't been paying attention."

"Collateral damage? They're people, El! Did you kill Kyla's family, too?" I stare at him. "Are you going to kill me, even if I help you? Are you going to kill my mom?"

"Your stupid friend's not dead, Marguerite! Jeez! What kind of monster do you think I am?"

"Really? Kyla's okay?"

"It's classified, but you're smart, aren't you? You know there will be serious consequences if you betray me again. If I let you see her, will that help?"

Knowing Kyla's all right won't erase the guilt I feel over Bianca, but now that Anna's gone and Percy may or may not be El's next target, it might help me figure out what's going on and what I should do. "Yes, it would help, and the deal is understood. Plus, I have nowhere to run. And even if I did, my mom . . ."

"Okay, okay. I'll take you to her myself. But after you see that she's alive and well, you're going to go after FragFlwr for me. With every ounce of cleverness in that pretty little head of yours."

"Anything you say," I reply. "You're the boss."

He nods solemnly. "I'm glad you've figured that out."

Chapter Seventeen

Percy

It's dark in this alley, though thanks to dear old Dad I can see clearly. I meant to get here earlier, but I had to have a leisurely dinner with Auntie, and I had to convince her I'd be with my imaginary girlfriend tonight. She hasn't made the connection between my nightly forays and the rumors that technocrats are being smuggled out of Washington, and I make sure to distract her every time she gets close.

There are no streetlights on in this part of town, which is adjacent to the tightly guarded zone where the Fortins and many other technocrats live. Especially tightly guarded tonight, as it turns out, because federal cars have ringed the zone. The place is being cut off, isolated. I wouldn't be surprised if they blocked transmission of signals soon—it's getting that extreme. Yet no one is talking about it on the Mainstream, which makes me think the channels are being monitored and wiped by federal agents.

This is not freedom. It's not justice, either.

It's also going to become increasingly tough to get anyone out of this city, even with an unmarked embassy car. The authorities are on the lookout for a vehicle with a diplomatic chip, and even though I'm in Jacques tonight while Yves gets his ID switched out to a larger vehicle, shedding his previously surveilled metal skin at my request, it's still a risk. But I have every reason to believe that my quarry tonight isn't in that little closely watched enclave.

A shadowy form hovers in a doorway up ahead. His back is lit from behind with a faint blue glow, a metallic sort of light that practically hums along the fibers of my nerves, sending sparks up off the wires. I shiver and straighten my jacket.

The sign above the doorway just reads "Game."

"We're full tonight," he says, turning my way. His Cerepin nodule blinks quickly, red and blue.

"I'm just looking for a friend."

"Aren't we all?"

"Mine is in a bit of trouble."

He scowls. "Police came by this morning."

My heart rate rises precipitously. "Did they find what they were looking for?"

He thinks I can't see his face. He thinks the dark will hide the glint of suspicion and interest in his eyes as he takes in my hair, my clothes, my face. He's trying to use the facial recognition feature of his Cerepin, but my facial implants are activated and he won't find a thing. They make me look different enough—and they never take on the same shape twice. "Name?" he asks, squinting at me. The system rarely fails. "Who're you with? You a cop?"

"I go to school with him," I say, because this fellow knows who he's protecting. Winston gave me the tip after our Aristotle lessons this morning, scrawled in his blood on the very scrap of paper I had given him earlier.

I forgot that no one carries pens or even owns them. Without paper, there's no reason. Winston shoved me in the chest, and when I looked down, the paper was half sticking out of my lapel. I slid it the rest of the way in and smiled at him. "Keep your promise, or I'll run you over with my dad's car, freak," he said in a low voice and pushed past me.

For a lad who can't keep his collar even remotely clean, it was actually fairly respectable subterfuge.

On the scrap was only one word. I flick my gaze up to the sign over the door. "A friend of his sent me. I'm here to help."

"Right."

"You know at least one family has made it out of the city?"

The guy pulls his shoulders up to his ears and glances around. I hold up my hands. "I assure you, no one is listening." I have my auditory shield activated.

"Believe whatever you want, but I'm just gonna pretend you didn't say that."

This is taking too long. "I'm going to come in and speak to Hammond. Don't try to stop me."

The guy's brow furrows. "I don't want any trouble. I'm just . . ."

"He's paying you to protect him. How much will his family pay to have him back, do you think?"

Again the guy looks around. "I could be recording you, buddy. You realize that?"

"No, you can't," I say, annoyance creeping into my voice. In addition to my auditory shield, I'm wearing my patches. All he'll capture is himself, talking to a ghost, with only white noise for sound. "Now. How would you like to be remembered?" I take a step forward.

He takes a step back. "Fine! Whatever. Come on in."

He stomps up the two steps and through the door to Game. I follow him between two walls of aquariums that hold those glowing canny fish that became so popular as pets after dogs and cats were banned, first from the District and then from several other states. There's only a narrow aisle between the bubbling tanks, and at the end of it is a door. "Name's Hash," the guy says.

"Nice to meet you."

He gives me a peeved look. "I'm trying to be nice."

"You're trying to get my name."

Hash opens the door. "This way."

I am suddenly on guard. My muscles draw tight. My lungs expand to oxygenate my blood. Adrenaline makes my limbs tingle. I feel electric. We head down the steps to a hallway lined with open doors leading to rooms where people sit in reclining chairs, their eyes open and staring at the ceiling while the tiny lights on their Cerepins flash.

"They can play the game here without sending signals all over the city. Data stays in this room. Server's on-site, and their 'Pins can be switched to hard connections." He peers at my temples. "You don't have one?"

"I'm a rebel."

He grunts as we reach the last door on the left. "Hey. Hammond. Friend to see you."

"What?" yelps Hammond. I step into the room to find him sitting up on one of those reclining chairs, ready to bolt.

"Calm yourself," I say, and he does a double take and leaps off the chair to press himself up against the wall, as if that's going to help him.

"Who are you? Do I know you?"

I've distorted both my voice and my face, so I simply say, "A friend. Your family misses you very much, Hammond. Let me take you to some people who can help reunite you with them."

"Why should I trust you?"

"If you don't, the feds or the police will find you sooner rather than later. They're tightening their grip on the city with every passing hour, and the government doesn't seem to be much for due process these days."

He looks confused, and I see that his Cerepin is dark—normally it would define terms he doesn't know, but . . . "They're not going to be careful with you, Hammond. You won't get a lawyer or a trial. They want your mother, and they'll use you to get her. They'll do whatever it takes."

"That's why I'm here, hiding! They left me behind!"

"You were late, as I recall."

His eyes go wide, and Hash looks at me with respect. "You're the one," he says.

I gaze at him steadily.

"I won't tell," Hash says quickly. "I think you're a hero. Everybody here does. But—"

"Just help me get Hammond to safety."

A sharp beep from Hash's Cerepin jolts me. "It's the cops," he says. "Their scanners set off my early warning. They said they'd be coming back with a warrant. You guys better clear out. I need to go warn the others who've been hiding here."

I grab Hammond by the grimy collar of his otherwise expensive crew neck. "Which way?"

Hash points to the door across the hall. "That connects to the next building, and there's a back exit. But there's surveillance."

Which means they'll pick up Hammond, but not me. Hash's Cerepin beeps louder. "They're at the door. If I don't get up there, they're gonna come in hard."

I can hear the shuffle of their feet and one asking if they should use their canny's battering ram. "Go," I say, and Hash jogs back the way we came, banging on doors and issuing terse commands to run. I drag Hammond in the other direction, happy for the head start. "This would be easier if you'd move your own legs."

"I'm trying!" He claws at my hand, and when I look, I realize I've actually lifted him up off the ground. His toes are scraping the cement floor as he dangles. I drop him quickly and blink at my hand. He's not a small kid. Am I actually that strong?

"This way." I peel silver patches off my shoulders and slap them onto his as we slip through the door and run along one hallway, then another, until we reach a staircase that leads up. We're far enough from the entryway of Game that I can't hear Hash's voice, which is good.

"What are these?" Hammond asks, cringing as I press a patch to the top of his head.

"It will keep you from getting picked up by the surveillance. We're going to move you out of the city tonight. Some of my friends are waiting across the Potomac to get you to safety. Your family already made the same journey."

"So you know they're alive?"

"That's what I'm told." Apparently Gia contacted Chen from Toronto to let him know they had all made it—and wanting to know where her son was.

"Are they mad at me?" he asks quietly.

"I'm sure all will be forgiven once you're reunited."

"You remind me of someone," he says. "I can't think of who."

"Don't trouble yourself about it." I pull him to a stop in front of a metal door marked "Exit." I place the remaining strips on his body, making sure he'll be concealed from any cam chips on the outside of the building.

"These will really hide me?"

"From everything except actual people."

"But what about you?"

"I'm going to be right by your side. All the cams will see is an extremely good-looking man out for a jog."

He eyes my black shoes, black pants, black shirt. "A jog? But you look like—"

"Hammond," I say, snapping him to attention. "Just get in the car when I tell you to."

Before he can say *what car*, I'm tapping the signal into my comband. It's set to the secure channel owned by the French diplomatic corps and will be sent to all the cars, but it's just a nonsensical pattern of taps, and only Jacques will know it means to follow the signal to my location.

"Three minutes, sir," says a soft voice emanating from my screen.

"How come you don't have a Cerepin?" Hammond asks.

"Just keep yours off until you're in Toronto, all right? They can use any signal to track you, no matter what setting it's on." I push open the door. Flashing blue lights warn me of cops on the street out front, but we're shielded by the building. Only problem: if any of them have a Cerepin and are hooked into the DC infrastructure network, they can access the surveillance—

"Freeze!" shouts a cop, who has come around the corner about one block up and is now sprinting along the narrow lane between fences.

Hammond does—until I poke him in the ass to get him moving. He runs in the direction I steer, climbing clumsily over a chain-link fence that I hurdle a moment later. "Whoa," he says, panting as we sprint up the lane.

Jacques drops out of the sky and lands at the end of the block. His rear passenger door slides open. I give Hammond a little shove in front of me as I feel the charge of the cop's neural disruptor crackle several yards behind me. Fear lights up my brain.

"I said *freeze*," the cop yells as Hammond dives into Jacques—and as the neural disruptor balls scream past me, each trying to snag skin and bone with its singeing barbs. My ears fill with a sizzling hiss. I can feel the electricity—it makes my limbs vibrate. I stumble.

"Go," I shout to Jacques.

He rises into the sky, and I spin around in time to narrowly dodge another neural disruptor strike. Before the cop can aim again, I knock the weapon from his hands, throwing it into a puddle of muddy water on the other side of the fence, then go over the chain-link fence myself, stumbling again on the other side.

"I'll shoot!" the cop yells, but he's not fast enough. Even trembling and with my vision alight with white sparks, I'm as fast as my parents made me to be. I sprint two blocks before remembering that every surveillance chip in the area is recording my every move. But they can't hear what I say or detect the secure diplomatic channel, so as I run, I page Yves.

"Yes, sir?"

"Pick me up at the edge of the old navy yard. You can follow the signal."

"Your aunt would like to know when you'll be home."

I wince at the crackling pain along my ribs, and that's when I realize one of those blasted barbed balls from the neural disruptor has snagged me. I rip it out and sag with relief as the tingling stops, but as I try to run again, I can barely get two steps in before I stagger. The burst of electricity has probably fried one or two of my augmentation chips.

Without the chips that connect in a network, carrying signals from my brain to my muscles better than any nerve could, I would be paralyzed from the neck down. I can't get hit again.

But my hearing is fine, and I know the cops are only a few blocks away. I pull a cap from my pocket—one with a lovely blond ponytail attached—and cram it over my head. Then I shed my black shirt and toss it into the overgrown, weedy yard of the nearest seemingly abandoned building. Shivering in my undershirt, I tap my cheekbones, temples, and forehead to cause the implants to shift once more, changing my appearance, and I alter my gait, an act that is much harder than it usually is. The urge to limp is rather strong.

My heart is hammering at 190 beats per minute. Near the maximum.

I reach a populated intersection before the cruisers roll past, though, and I quickly switch my direction so it looks like I'm walking toward them instead of away. I squint as their scanner beams slide over my face, but I don't turn my head. That would be suspicious. I already know they won't find a match, no matter how many angles they captured back near Game.

As soon as they continue on without stopping, I let myself limp. The pain radiates out from the little neural disruptor spine wound and crackles across my ribs, and it's unpleasant to draw breath. I haven't been in pain like this for a long, long time.

Pain is good, Percy. It means you're alive. It means you can feel things again. It means you're getting better. My mother's voice is soft and sad.

"P!" says a voice emanating from my comband. "You there?" It's Chen, still sounding a little slurred.

"Yes—where are you?"

"Arlington, with your new ride. Ukaiah's loading up the kid for the next transport. But Jacques said you ordered him to leave you behind. I expected to see you."

"Had a brush with the police."

"You okay? You don't sound like yourself."

"Voice modification."

"You hurt?"

I grit my teeth. "No." As quickly as I can, I make my way to the edge of the old navy yard.

"Okay. Okay. You did good, P. But I think things are about to get dire, man. Ukaiah and I ordered two more transports for Friday. Can you supply the persecuted souls?"

"I'll do my best." I press my hand over my ribs. "But now we're going to talk about my birthday present."

He lets out a heavy sigh, but pain has stripped me of my patience. "I want it," I snap. "I have to know everything. Tonight I lifted a boy who weighs nearly as much as I do off his feet with one hand. I ran as fast as a canny. I am driving this vehicle without a license, Chen. Do you want to be responsible when I get into a wreck?"

"That's exactly what I'm afraid of," he mutters.

"I need every tool in this body at my disposal if you want me to take these kinds of risks and actually survive them."

"Funny you say that . . ." He's quiet for a few long seconds. "But I guess that's fair," he finally adds. "I just have to think about how we're gonna do this."

"Figure it out. Now. Because I'm heading your way."

Chapter Eighteen

Marguerite

My mom coms just as El and I are leaving the apartment. Weirdly, she doesn't buzz *me*—it's El's band that hums and shows her face. *I'm your daughter,* I want to scream. But technically, El is her boss. Her sadistic boss.

"Hey," he says. "How's the big guy?"

"Waiting for some good news," she says.

"And how are you?" he asks, giving me a sidelong glance.

"I'm doing great, El. I have more energy than I have in ages. Thank you. I mean it."

His grin loses any shred of cynicism. "Anything, Colette—you're paying me back with that smile."

I feel sick again.

"Marguerite and I are actually headed to Bethesda. Want to come?"

"Is this what we talked about?" Mom asks.

"You know," El says. "I think we can trust Marguerite to handle the information maturely."

"I'll meet you there, then," Mom says. "I need to deliver that one last briefing you sent me."

"Perfect. Maybe we can get dinner after?"

"Sounds good!" She hangs up.

"I'll tell you what," says El. "Those neurostims are a godsend." He squeezes my upper arm as we approach the waiting car. "Maybe you should get one. You seem kind of anxious lately."

"No thanks." I've decided they totally creep me out.

"Well, look what it's done for your mom. She's her old self again, am I right?"

"You didn't know her old self."

"Go ahead and stay grumpy—even though I'm giving you something you asked for in seeing your friend." He scoffs. Then he gestures for me to get into the car. "Kids these days. No gratitude."

The flight to Bethesda lasts only a few minutes because there's no traffic at the altitude reserved for official White House vehicles, but the whole time, El is barking at people on his staff about scheduling and Mainstream messaging. As always, he's the consummate micromanager, and he still seems to think we're running a campaign, with the way he's so concerned about how the president is polling this week after the terror attack. Even though I used to love going back and forth with El about strategy, right now I'm too stressed.

Also, murderer. I'm sitting next to a murderer.

When we touch down and roll to a stop in front of the hospital, we're greeted by six Secret Service agents, none of which are human. They lead us to an elevator that takes us down instead of up, and when the doors open, we're on some kind of sublevel. "Dr. Barton is in this room down here," my mom says. "The doctors are feeling optimistic!"

I let out a breath. Mom sounds more optimistic, too. She was so broken up about what had happened. "Is she awake?"

"No, but she's responding to sensory input like bright light and temperature changes."

I frown. That doesn't really sound very promising to me, but I'm not going to say that to her. She's smiling. "What about Kyla?"

"That's who we're here to see," says El. "Just like I promised." His eyes lock with mine. "I always keep my promises."

I shudder. My mom puts her arm around me. "Are you cold, Marguerite?"

I lean into her. "Just a little."

Mom chuckles and looks over at El. "She grew up in the tropics, compared to here. Especially in winter."

"Do you miss it, Marguerite?" El asks, sounding innocent as a baby.

"Sometimes," I say honestly.

"But not enough to want to go back, right?" asks Mom.

The look on her face makes me want to cry. "No," I mumble. "Here is good."

She grins and gives me a hug.

El steps around us and goes to talk to a medical canny who looks so eerily human that it isn't until I see the overhead light reflect off his synthetic skin that I know he's AI. El confers with the intelligent machine, then beckons to me and my mom.

"How's she doing?" Mom asks.

"Better!" El announces. "I think she's ready for visitors, and Mar can be her first one. See? Trust. I know I can trust you."

Mom turns to me, her fingers rising to her nape to touch the controls on her neurostim device. It reminds me of Orianna back home, except she always seems more sleepy, almost stoned. Mom looks bright-eyed, even a little wired. "This is a big responsibility, Marguerite."

"I don't get it. It's not like Kyla tried to kill herself. I don't understand what you guys are trying to do—or hide. Why are you keeping her here, period?"

"Well," says El. "We removed her Cerepin."

"What?" I say it so loud that the medical canny actually shushes me, telling me I have exceeded the acceptable decibel level in this particular hallway.

El holds his hands up, gesturing for me to calm down. "It was the best thing for her."

"To silence her, you mean?" Because if she still had one, she might find a way to communicate with the outside world—Cerepins make that easy, instant, and invisible. Without it, she's isolated.

Mom's eyes go wide. "How could you even suggest that?"

I clear my throat. "I just meant—did she consent to that?"

El gives my mom a quick smile. "Of course she did. She just wanted some peace and quiet in her own head."

Another chill. "Okay, so you took her Cerepin out. But if she's okay, then why are you keeping her in the hospital? Does she not have anywhere else to go? Where's her little brother?"

"We found him a good caregiver while we help figure out a more permanent plan," Mom says. "This poor family has been through so much."

"I love your empathy, Colette," El says to her.

I barely stop myself from making a gagging face. "Can I go in?"

"Sure thing." El waves at the medical canny, who passes his (or its, more accurately) hand over the scanner in the door, which slides open immediately. "Go ahead. Fifteen minutes, how about?"

I walk by him into a big hospital room with a sitting area. Curled up in one of the chairs, staring at a comband streaming some anime movie, is Kyla. Her hair has been neatly styled and braided at the top, curling around her shoulders. Though from the way her hands shake, I'm guessing she didn't do it herself. "Hi, Kyla," I say quietly.

She turns her head and looks up at me, revealing the bandage at her temple. Her eyes fill with confusion first, then a flash of recognition, and finally, pain. Before saying a word, she reaches up to the nape of her neck. I see a small flash of blue and red within the coils of her hair, and then her eyelids flutter.

"Are you all right?" I ask.

"Fine," she says, all mellowed out. She goes back to watching the movie.

I sit there and watch her. "Everyone is so worried about you. No one knew what had happened to you!"

"I'm totally fine, all things considered. No one needed to worry."

"But Kyla, your parents . . ."

She's staring intently at her comband. "I know. It sucks."

It . . . *sucks*? "Um . . . have you been able to see your mom in the last few days?"

"Yeah. I think so."

"You don't know?" This is not the Kyla I met on my first day of school. She cared more about me, at the time still a hostile stranger, than she seems to about her mom now. I stand up and go over to her, then place my hand over the screen.

"Hey!" she says, though there's not much anger or annoyance there. "I was watching that."

"Have they given you drugs or something?"

"No. Nothing."

"What's the neurostim for?"

"They thought it would make me feel better. I've been through a lot."

"And the Cerepin?"

Her fingers twitch as she gently touches the bandage over her temple. "It had to be done. I needed quiet."

My eyebrows rise. "You couldn't just set it to blank?"

"No. It was still too much."

"Okaaay. When are they going to let you out of here?"

"When they can be sure I'll function properly."

Sounds like canny speak. "You're not a machine, Kyla."

"I wish I was," she whispers. Then she pokes at her neurostim and sighs as it zaps whatever part of her brain is making her sad. I don't actually know what it's doing, but that's certainly how it looks, because she smiles at me as her hand drops to her lap. "How have you been?"

My laugh is as dry as West Texas. "I'm just doing my thing. Posting vids."

She looks down at her comband. "You're famous. Even the famous think you're famous."

"What?"

She shrugs. "Percy. He's been fascinated by you since you joined the campaign. I was jealous. He had notifications on your vids and everything."

"But I thought he didn't care about politics."

"Not sure if he does. But he certainly did seem obsessed with your vids."

"I . . . okay." Another hint that he might be the troll—the one who El is determined to catch. "He cares about you, too, Kyla."

"I'm fine. I don't know why anyone needs to worry."

It's eerie, the way her voice is so flat. "Are you going to come back to school?"

"When I'm ready. The doctors will decide." She goes back to watching her comband.

This time I don't stop her. I stand up and take a few steps backward, and she doesn't even look up as I walk from the room. Mom and El are waiting for me when I come out. "That was quick! How is she?" Mom asks.

El sees my face and gives me a warning look. "Mar?"

"She's . . . not quite herself."

Mom frowns, but El just nods. "We gave her a neurostim to help her recover, but it's going to take a little time for her to be up and running."

Mom looks relieved. "She needs any kind of boost she can get." She turns her smile on me. "I'm so glad you got to see her."

"Yeah," I say. "Me too." Am I?

"Great! Now, let's go get some dinner," says El. "I got us reservations at Kintiko, and we've just got time to eat before I have to go brief the president."

He offers us each an arm. Mom takes his right. He looks down at me. "A deal's a deal, Marguerite. Let's go eat, then you have work to do."

I owe him FragFlwr's head on a plate.

I swallow back the urge to start screaming, and take his arm.

Chapter Nineteen

Percy

I badly need a medical time-out, and I'm desperate to know what my father wanted Chen to give me, but just as we end our connection, Chen drops another bomb—he tells me he's come into possession of a vid so secret that people would kill to get it back, so sensitive that he's scared to transport it from its chip back into the District for fear of detection. I have to go back to Arlington.

Yves, looking all muscular in his new SUV body, picks me up at the navy yard and glides across the Potomac. He touches down without incident in the parking lot of a restaurant, then drives along a narrow residential street before turning onto a dead-end road. Marguerite is right about one thing—outside the few affluent technocrat enclaves, the country is in dreadful need of a makeover. Most of these homes look abandoned. Not shabby chic, just shabby. As I start to get out of Yves, he tells me Jacques is on a suicide mission.

"What does that even mean?"

"He monitored police channels and detected a police officer offering an accurate description of his exterior as well as his license ID."

"But . . . suicide?" Odd. I'm not sure I ever thought of him as living, which now seems unfair.

"Jacques thought it prudent to crash nose down into a field from five thousand feet instead of allowing police officers to apprehend him. The debris will consist of small pieces, and because of the height from which he fell, much of it will be embedded in the dirt. It will take the law enforcement cannies an extended period to find the fragments necessary to identify his remains." Yves is quiet for a moment. "His consciousness can be replicated using the server at the embassy, though without experiential memory," he informs me. "There is no need to feel sad or guilty."

I feel neither. At least, I don't think I do. I'm in too much pain to ponder it right now, and I want to get back to the embassy, where I can examine myself in peace and privacy, rearrange my face to its default configuration, and take a nice, long bath. God, I could really use a bath. And a manicure. "Tell him thank you—"

"He's already gone, sir."

"Very well." I pause before closing the car door. "Not feeling suicidal yourself, are you, Yves?"

"If necessary, I will do the same, though I believe the ambassador will be not be pleased to lose two of her fleet in the same brief time interval. She may pull us in for triple-S scans before she allows you to ride in one of us again."

I chuckle. The triple-S—Safety, Sanity, and Stability—is an analysis program provided by canny manufacturers. We all know AI can be a bit fragile when it isn't operated within its parameters, like an airplane flying out of its flight envelope. My father used to joke with me and tell me he was going to give me a triple-S if I didn't listen to my mother.

My mother never thought it was funny.

I shake off the memory of both of them and the resulting ache in my chest. My steps are quiet on the driveway, and Yves's headlights illuminate the leaning front porch of the house. I wave my hand for him to turn them off, and the path forward is plunged into darkness that doesn't affect me at all.

Chen is peering at me through one of the glass cutouts in the front door, his expression tight. Well, half of it. The left side of his mouth is drooping. He opens the door quickly as I mount the porch steps and ushers me into the small entryway. Ukaiah is next to him. Their helmet devices hum and click. Ukaiah's cheek is twitching compulsively, and I wonder if she had that tic the last time we met or if it's new.

"We think the FBI is doing flyovers, but there was some sort of explosion about twenty minutes ago that drew them back across the Potomac."

Probably Jacques, completing his final self-assigned mission. "So we have a little time."

Chen nods. "I know you want the goods, but I have to show you this. Just got it this afternoon from my buddy who works at Bethesda."

"You have far more friends than I might have guessed," I say to him.

"You'd be surprised how many of us there are," Ukaiah says, walking toward the gloomy kitchen with rust-stained sinks and mouse droppings along the baseboards. I haven't heard the house itself say a word, so it's either too old to have a consciousness or it's been disabled by my two hacker friends—or looters desperate to make a bit of coin. "We just want to live without government oppression and control."

"So who did you vote for?"

They both look at me as if I'm insane. "What makes you think we'd vote for either?" Ukaiah asks.

"Sallese certainly seems dangerous."

"Oh, he could be," says Ukaiah, giving Chen a meaningful look that I don't have time to parse right now. "But Zao was just as bad in his own way, working with Congress to outlaw new tech that couldn't be controlled by his friends like Gia Fortin and Simon Aebersold. Yolanda Reynolds was more of the same, a technocrat through and through. She might've won, too, I think, but then her campaign ran up against a few factors they couldn't control."

Both of them laugh. They might be talking about Marguerite. Anyone on the Mainstream knew that with a massive war chest and the help of every tech corporation in America, Reynolds was coasting until Marguerite burst onto the scene, full of grief and passion and a demand that her leaders do better for people. The Sallese campaign knew emotional genius when they saw it, and it was all downhill for the technocrats after that. Marguerite raised a tsunami of pent-up rage, and Sallese is a very good surfer.

"But now you're on the side of the technocrats?" I ask. "Despite their corruption?"

"We're on the side of *freedom*," says Chen. "And that's why we have to show you this."

He reaches up to the side of his head and pulls a wire from it. The silvery filament unspools as he offers one end to me. "We plug this into your comband, and you can see what I see. We have to hardwire it—too dangerous to let those electrons loose."

Ukaiah shudders next to me. "I don't envy you," she says to Chen. "I wouldn't want to watch it twice. Poor girl."

I hesitate before accepting the wire. "Bianca? If this is a vid of her final moments, I don't want to—"

"What, you think I'm into torture porn or something? Why would we show you that?" Chen looks outraged as I take the end of the wire from him and plug it into the port on my comband. "No, I think this might be actionable. If we're not too late."

I stop breathing as my screen flickers and comes to life with the vid Chen begins to stream. It's from a surveillance chip located in the upper corner of what looks like a hospital room. There's a bed against the wall. There are wrist and ankle restraints dangling from the metal railings along its sides. But that's not what makes me want to slam my fist through a wall.

It's Kyla. Her eyes are wide, and her pretty face is twisted in an agony of sorrow. "You can't do this," she shrieks as three scrub-clad medical cannies close in. They are smooth and certain, none of the little twitches and pauses that make humans human. Kyla's hands are up, trying to hold them at bay. "I didn't agree to this! My mom wouldn't want you to do this! Please!"

Her back bumps against the bed railing. She's sobbing now, and she sounds terrified.

"When was this taken?" I bark.

"Two days ago," Chen says, but I barely hear him over Kyla's screaming. The med cannies are on her now, wrestling her onto the bed, prying her fingers from the railing, blocking her kicks. She wails as they fasten the wrist and ankle cuffs. They speak in soft tones to her, telling her that she's going to feel better soon, that everything is going to be all right. They are following an empathy and reassurance protocol.

They tell her all is well as they wheel her out of the room, but Kyla, smart and sensitive as she is, knows better.

"What did they do to her?" I ask quietly.

"My source is a janitor. Hasn't been able to get back in to see her, because he was told to take a week of paid vacation. He said all the human staff were. Security is tighter than anything we've seen, because of the administration's involvement. But there's something weird going on over there. The doc who gave that press conference asking technocrats of interest to come forward? We've got vid of her, too."

"In the hospital?"

He shakes his head. "No, this was her public statement. Something odd about it. Hang on." His fingers dance over the surface of the helmet, over the various sensors wired into his skull. "Here it is."

I look down at my screen again. There's Dr. Barton, who has Kyla's high cheekbones, standing at a podium with the president and his staff behind her. One of them I recognize—a fellow with graying hair and a narrow face. I've seen him in campaign vids, always standing next to Marguerite and a dark-haired woman who I assume is her mother, given their similarities.

"That's Elwood Seidel," Chen says when he follows the focus of my gaze. "He's now—"

"The president's chief of staff," I supply. "He managed Sallese's campaign. They go way back."

Elwood is standing to Dr. Barton's left. She's announcing her intention to work with the Sallese administration in order to find the people responsible for killing her husband. She's urging Gia Fortin to cooperate with the investigation in the name of all those who were killed, including Dr. Barton's husband, also a researcher.

"We thought it was really strange that Wendy Barton was willing to toss her former boss under the bus like that," Ukaiah says between cheek twitches. "By all accounts, they were friends."

"So we analyzed this vid really closely," says Chen. "And look." He pokes his finger at my screen. "See? Look at the back of her neck. It's coming up in a few seconds. Easy to miss."

"Her hair covers her—"

"*Look.* It's here in three . . . two . . . one . . ."

I look at the back of her neck, covered by her black hair, but still, for a brief second, I see a little flash of blue. "Pause it. Can you enlarge that, or is it locked?"

All official vids are, to prevent tampering. But Ukaiah grins. "Locked. It's as if you don't know us at all. Hang on." Chen fiddles with his Incomp.

The focus zooms in on the back of Dr. Barton's neck. I squint at it, grateful for my augmented vision. "What is that?"

"Come on, P. You know exactly what it is."

I raise my head. "A neurostim device? Why would she of all people be wearing one?"

"That's the question of the hour, isn't it?" Chen says. "But Elwood Seidel knows it's there. We used gaze triangulation. He looks right at it four times during this vid. Bet he gave the order to have it installed."

"Without her consent?"

Chen arches an eyebrow. "Isn't that the question?"

"Does the president look at it, too?"

"Not even once," says Ukaiah.

I focus on Elwood Seidel's face with new interest. First Bianca, and now this. "What's your read on him? Is he a henchman or a weasel?"

"He's someone to watch out for, is what he is," says Ukaiah.

"We used to call him the puppet master," says Chen. "He knows how to get things done, even if he's not the one doing them."

"Puppet master." What does that make Marguerite? "And speaking of, I believe you've been pulling on my strings just a shade too long."

"Told you," says Ukaiah with a low laugh. "It's not like he was going to forget."

Chen gives her an irritated look, I think. It's a little hard to tell, because of the thing on his face and the sagging lip. "I've got ethical qualms."

"Ethical qualms? So you're willing to violate a sacred trust bestowed on you by a dead man? You're willing to keep information from me when you claim to be a champion of freedom and choice? You're willing to—"

"Fine," he says loudly. "But tell me this, P—have you ever activated your integrated neural menu?"

"Once."

"Did you happen to notice anything . . . incomplete about it?"

(option disabled)

"What do you have for me?"

He swallows, and his shoulder jerks up and down a few times, no doubt another tic caused by one of the wires he's implanted inside his own brain. "A few weeks after he died, I got a package, like I told you when we first met." He limps out of the room and returns with a small plastic case. He presses his thumb to it—the thing must have been coded to his DNA. My father must have trusted him.

Chen's hand trembles a bit as he lifts two pieces of blank paper from the case. "One is coded to me. The other . . . that's for you. But read this first." He brushes his finger over the embossed flower on the top of one of the sheets of paper. Writing appears on it as he hands it to me.

Chen,

If you're reading this, the worst has happened, and I must ask you for a favor I'll never be able to repay. You have always been the most perceptive and thoughtful of my staff, and I will always be grateful that you came to me with your suspicions instead of making them public.

"I had helped him debug a piece of unbelievably complicated nano-cyte code. Really cutting-edge stuff," Chen says. "And I made some educated guesses based on what I was seeing. We all knew he and Flore had a sick kid at home. We all knew no one had ever caught a glimpse of you. But the code . . ."

"It was for me. For something they were doing to me."

"He admitted as much. He knew the government child-protection agency would swoop in and take you if I made a call. But he told me that he knew he could give you a better life than you would ever have if he and Flore didn't take these risks." He blows out an unsteady breath through the sagging part of his mouth. "Talk about an ethical dilemma . . . but in the end, I knew how brilliant he and your mom were. And I also knew they were good people."

I go back to reading the note.

Percy already has all the building blocks he needs. But there are certain things we wanted to keep locked until he is old enough to make sound decisions. I had hoped that Flore and I would be here to guide him through it, but I also wanted to make sure we didn't leave him completely alone in this if we couldn't. So—here is what I ask: Watch over him from a distance. Reach out to him when you feel the time is right. And when he reaches the age of eighteen, give him the second page of this document. It's already coded just for him. And please let him read this.

Below this is a description of all the things they did to me. It is more than I ever guessed. The way the parts of my body are held together, the way the things that live inside me communicate, the options I have (and don't have) to control them. And below that . . .

A chill goes through me, as it always does when I read my own name in my father's handwriting.

Percy, I wish I could have made a vid to explain all this to you, but it's too dangerous. Paper is the only thing that can't be hacked. It's time for you to make your own choices. The second page will tell you the rest. It is for your eyes only.

"Can I have the room?" I ask softly.

"We don't think there's any going back after you do this," says Chen, sharing a worried look with Ukaiah. "You might want to be double sure."

"Please."

They leave.

I sit on a rickety kitchen chair at the rickety kitchen table, and I activate the second page with a brush of my own DNA.

I read my father's instructions. His admonitions and warnings. His belief that I must be able to control my fate.

And then I scan the code that enables me to do just that.

When it's done, I clear the paper. My hands are steady as I tear the now-blank page into tiny pieces and wash them down the kitchen sink. When I join Chen and Ukaiah in the dank living room, they look at me as if I'm a dead man walking.

It's possible they're right. I just don't know yet. "I thank you for the gift." I smile at them and offer a deep bow and a flourish of my hand. As I straighten, I ask, "So Kyla and Dr. Barton are at Bethesda Medical Center?"

They both seem to understand that we are not going to discuss what I just did, not now, not ever. Ukaiah's cheek twitches as she says, "Remember what we said about it being well guarded?"

"What if I could get around that?"

The two hackers eye each other, then Chen nods. "We'd do whatever we can to help you get them to safety."

My comband vibrates. "Sir," says Yves. "Your aunt has commed twice. She's heard about Jacques and is calling the entire fleet back to the embassy."

"On my way," I say, then pull a different piece of paper from my pocket—the one on which I've written the codes that will signal the time and place and nature of our next meeting. I hand it to Chen and walk toward the door. "Keep an eye on my channel. We'll reconvene once I have the necessary information."

"This isn't going to be easy, kid. Picking up fugitives on street corners is not exactly the same thing as stealing a patient from a facility guarded six ways to Sunday by the Secret Service. I don't care who you are or what you've got on board—you're still made of flesh and bone. You can't force your way in."

"Oh, I have no intention of using force."

That's because I have *every* intention of using Marguerite Singer.

Chapter Twenty

Marguerite

Catch me if you can.

Is this a game to him?

Or maybe it's a trick—a way to keep us tied up in knots, trying to find the account and its user, while he goes off in another direction?

Is this Percy? If so, does he have any idea how dangerous this is?

I want to help either way, whether this is a stranger who hates me or . . . the strange boy from school who probably also hates me. Because in a short time, the technocrats who appeared enemies now seem largely innocent of everything except privilege and obliviousness, or at the very least of the murders I know at least one person on our side is capable of. It doesn't change a thing about what I believe—all Americans deserve access to the same technology and education and jobs, things I will never stop fighting for. But the battle can't be won when El is on the field. He seems too willing to destroy our humanity just to score a victory—and that's something I can't live with.

Leaning over my desk screen, I call up the comment reply box and tell it to send a private message to FragFlwr. "Taking this into the back room," I say, watching my words appear in the message area. "Because I'd like to have an honest conversation. Send."

There. FragFlwr has come at me before, challenging me to take a hard look at the Sallese campaign and what it really stood for, questioning whether Uncle Wynn himself was a good man. It was always easy to brush off as technocratic paranoia, especially because by that time I'd gotten to know Uncle Wynn. "Good man" doesn't do him justice— "great man" is closer to the truth.

I frown. I still believe in Uncle Wynn, but I don't understand how he'd let someone like El become so powerful. Especially because I know he has concerns about El. He told me himself. Has he always doubted him, or is El only now getting careless and letting his true self show through? My head hurts with these questions. Because if El was evil all along, he had us *all* fooled.

My eyes flick to the message area again. FragFlwr's icon is dark, offline. And apparently untraceable as a result. I'm supposed to signal the tech team on my comband the moment FragFlwr appears in this space, because El said that a troll this sophisticated might be able to detect if they had tracers in place and waiting beforehand. I don't understand how any of this is done, only that El has the team on call and working directly for him.

I wonder if Uncle Wynn knows about *any* of this. Including about Kyla and her mom.

There's still a sick, uneasy feeling in my stomach, left over from my visit with Kyla, if I can really call it that. I'm not even sure she was really there, and I'm not sure how to help her. Was it the removal of her Cerepin that caused her to be so spaced out? Or . . .

On impulse, I wake my comband and com Orianna. There's a long pause, and just before I'm about to give up, her face appears.

"Hey, girl!" Her voice is mellow, bemused. "Didn't expect to hear from you so soon."

"Hey," I say, peering at her face. She looks sleepy, but it's kind of late. "How are things?"

She shrugs. "Same, I guess."

"How's your family?"

"Living. Surviving."

I frown. "School?"

"Oh—I didn't tell you? Dropped out."

"What?" My voice is so loud that she jerks and blinks, then reaches up to press her neurostim device. It forcibly reminds me of Kyla this afternoon, doing the same. "You seriously quit school?"

"It was a mutual breakup, I think."

"You were doing so well, though!" My dad used to rave about her essays. I can't believe this.

"You don't know what it's like, Mar. It's just going in, sitting in this little cubicle . . ."

"I've met Aristotle. I get it. But—"

"Just doesn't seem worth getting out of bed for, you know?"

"No, I don't," I snap. "I'm here fighting for a future for everybody, and you're just giving up?" I brace myself—when Orianna gets pissed off, it's epic.

She just chuckles, low and heavy. "Oh, god, Mar, dramatic much? You're *fighting*? Come on. You're making a few vids and riding around with the prez in his limo."

"It's more than that!"

"Mm-hmm. Sounds real rough." She yawns.

I lean close to the screen, ready to tell her all my fears, but then I remember that El has capped my device—he could be listening *right now*. So I force a smile. "I just meant that you're too smart to drop out."

She leans back, her hair spreading across her pillow. "Nah. I'm too tired not to. Honestly, we've got the subsidy since Mom and Dad were laid off. We have food, and sure, it's all genned, but I forget what anything else tastes like." Her eyelids flutter, like she's about to drift off.

It's so unlike her. I mean, yes, it's sort of late, but I've commed her at one in the morning before, and she's like a live wire. "Have you had a Bioscan lately?"

She grunts. "Just when I had my neurostim attached."

"And?"

Orianna starts like she'd begun to drift off. "Oh. I'm fine. Just stressed out and depressed like everyone else. But now we all have these babies . . ." She reaches up and pokes at her device again, then lets her head fall onto the pillow. Her screen is half-covered because her arm is propped against her body. "You'd think we'd be down each other's throats, since we're all here all day. But we get along great."

"Orianna, do you feel . . . normal? You seem kind of wacked out."

"I feel fine. So much better. I was a total ball of stress before. Now I don't worry about anything."

"Yeah, but you're not *doing* anything, either."

For the second time, just out of habit, I get ready for a sassy comeback or a snarky insult, but all I get is a soft snore.

"Orianna?"

She doesn't answer. Her breaths come slow and heavy. Her arm flops to the mattress, and her screen goes dark.

Something's gone wrong with my best friend, and I can't help but think that if I had been there, she'd still be in school, determined to make it. I had no idea things had gotten so hard for her. And now I'm not sure I'll be able to help, because I might not even be able to save myself.

A neurostim could probably take all this fear away. But the more I see the effects of these devices close-up, the more I wonder what else it would steal from me in the process.

I glance down at my comband and then at my desk. El may have capped my band, but he intentionally didn't cap my desk for fear that the surveillance would be detected by FragFlwr. I send my comband into hibernation, then unstrap it and carry it into the living room, where I lay it on the couch. Then I return to my room, rubbing at the warm imprint of the screen on my arm. "Look up neurostim devices," I tell the desk screen.

I flip through the results, most of which are related to Uncle Wynn's old company, NeuroGo. "The neurostimulant device has now been approved as a treatment for depression, anxiety, panic attacks, pain, muscle spasms, and vocal and behavioral tics," an article from about three years ago claims. "New findings on the use of these devices in the treatment of chemical addiction, including alcohol and opioid abuse, are forthcoming." I tap on a channel link that carries me to a few vid articles, one about how Uncle Wynn was selling NeuroGo, fueling speculation that he was going to run for president, and another about how some scientists who specialized in the interface between humans and machines were advocating for more controlled studies of the effects of these devices on certain parts of the brain before they were sold to the general public. Apparently, a few were concerned about some of the claims that these things were healthy.

Most of the scientific blah-blah is over my head, and I start to skim, but then my gaze jerks to a stop, frozen on one name.

Blake.

It's not a totally uncommon name, I guess, but when I drill down by swiping at that name, a picture appears. A man in his thirties or forties, maybe. Blond hair. Light eyes.

He and his son have the same nose, long and thin. His name is Valentine Blake. He was a technocrat. Educated at Caltech, he was the founder of the Blake Consortium, which is focused on development of these things called "self-organizing nanocytes" that would treat various diseases that can't be cured by the standard gene therapies, as well as catastrophic injuries.

Or rather, it *was* focused on those things. I hit the post that tells me the consortium's government funding was pulled just over two years ago, along with a quote from Dr. Blake saying that his company was being targeted by larger businesses with political connections. He says he can't be intimidated into silence, though. That he won't stop raising questions about neurostim devices in particular, because they're being marketed to vulnerable people—and being advertised as healthy and harmless when they could be used in all sorts of dangerous ways. He sounds paranoid and angry.

And then I come to a vid about his murder.

A Mainstreamer stands just inside a set of glass doors as rain pours outside. The location beacon on the vid indicates it's being taken at the New Hope Addiction Clinic. The Mainstreamer turns the lens toward the inside of the clinic, and I gasp. Two people lie on the floor, side by side, their bodies covered in bloody sheets. A thin, tall man in a white coat leans over them while several others mill behind him, and then turns and sees the Mainstreamer. She sounds out of breath as she bursts into the rainy street and says, "Two people were just freaking murdered in there! I saw the guy run out of that clinic and had to go check it out, and then I picked up the com for police on my wireless scan!" Sirens are audible in the background, and the Mainstreamer runs to a car and jumps in. The vid ends.

It's been viewed only a few thousand times, and there are only a few comments below it, one chastising the Mainstreamer for posting something so vulgar and graphic, which is common for any vid like this but sort of silly considering what else is out there. The commenter is probably a senior citizen longing for the "good old days" when government was still trying to control what could be posted on the stream. One of the comments on this bloody vid is what brought this up in my search—a user named Triplechen identifies the victims as Valentine and Flore Blake and says there is no way this was a random attack. Heart skipping, I tap on that username to find out who Triplechen is . . . and discover that the account has been terminated. Another dead end.

More searching consumes the next hour or so. Valentine and Flore Blake were both widely recognized and respected scientists, which makes me wonder what Percy's IQ must be even though he enjoys pretending his head is full of fluff. I find a post mentioning their wedding twenty years ago, and then a few posts and vids featuring an adorable blond boy with flashing blue eyes and a mischievous smile. In one, he's climbing in a play park, and his mother is filming while she calls for him to get down before he falls. Instead of listening to her, he hangs by one hand and laughs. I watch another of him blowing out candles on his seventh birthday, just a skinny, smiling boy with two parents who obviously doted on him. Already he's showing his love for fashion, opening a present with sparkly fingernails. The gift is a canny bird that talks and flies, and he seems delighted. I look for other vids to see an older version of him, but that one was the last that was posted. Almost eleven years ago. After that—until he was about fifteen and started posting his fashion vids, there are no pictures, no mentions by name, no posts. It's like he didn't exist during the years in between.

"He's not your focus right now," I mutter to myself. I was trying to understand more about neurostims, and his dad came up as suspicious of them, demanding more research be done to make sure they didn't have long-term negative effects. Until he was murdered in a clinic that treated addiction. Silenced, according to at least one person.

I trace my search flow back until I find the picture of Dr. Blake. He's looking right at the camera and has his curled fingers under his chin like he's pondering something deep. A bit of red near the cuff of his sleeve catches my eye. "Zoom," I murmur, and the screen obediently closes in on what I'm staring at.

A flower with ruby petals. An English primrose.

A *flower*.

Oh, god. The final link is forged in my mind so suddenly that it's like plugging into a power source. The current jolts my body. The Fortins escaped in a car with a diplomatic chip. Percy lives with his aunt at the French embassy. And now: Fragflwr. Fragile flower?

Catch me if you can.

I knew he was hiding something, but until now I didn't quite believe he was capable of this. But now there is no doubt. He's definitely the one El is looking for.

The screen throbs red, indicating that I've got a message waiting. "Accept," I say breathlessly, and my message space appears.

FragFlwr: Love that you brought me into private space, Marguerite. This is so intimate.

I stare at the words, wondering what tone to adopt. Percy is risking his life to get technocrats out of El's reach. I don't want to signal that I know who he is. I don't want to do anything to tip El off. Before I get a chance to come up with my reply, he continues.

FragFlwr: It's just you . . . me . . . and whatever government hacker you com to trace my account.

"I haven't," I say, watching my words appear in the boxed-in space.

FragFlwr: But you will. Fair warning: I'll know when you alert them.

"Why did you challenge me to catch you? What was that for?" I ask.

FragFlwr: Aren't you eager for revenge? It must have galled you when the Fortins escaped. You've been after Gia for some time.

"That doesn't mean I want her and her family killed!"

FragFlwr: Like what happened to the Aebersolds? Your father committed suicide after Aristotle, produced by Parnassus, resulted in him being laid off. You must have savored what happened to them.

"You're wrong," I say thickly. "You couldn't be more wrong."

FragFlwr: Did you give the order for his daughter Bianca to be tortured, or did you simply enjoy hearing about it afterward?

I close my eyes as tears start to form. I suspected he hated me, but this is proof. "You don't know me. At all. If you did, you'd know I would never have wanted her to die."

FragFlwr: Didn't you say more than once that you wanted
to take her down?

"She did something terrible to me, okay? And yeah, I was mad about it! Really mad. But in the same way anyone would be! When I found out that's what happened, I . . ." My voice fades away. I am on dangerous ground. The minute I call in El's hackers, they'll read every word of this, and so will he. Nothing is secret.

FragFlwr: Why should I believe you?

"It doesn't matter if you do or if you don't."

FragFlwr: What if it does?

"You already think the worst of me. You always have."

For a whole minute at least, the message space following his user-name is blank, waiting for him to reply. *Is it really you?* I want to ask. *And if it is . . .*

FragFlwr: We all have our reasons for embracing a cause.
You embraced yours, and I have mine.

"We both want justice," I say. "Not bloodshed. You have to believe me." I bite my lip, then recklessly blurt out, "I warned Anna to get out of DC. She was my friend. I wanted her to escape. You can ask her."

El already knows, and if Uncle Wynn ever reads this transcript, even if I'm dead and gone, at least he'll know I followed his advice. And if he asks me about it, I'll play it off—I'm just trying to draw FragFlwr in, right?

Yes, I am. Except I'm not.

FragFlwr: Maybe I will.

"Can you get in touch with the Fortins?"

FragFlwr: Why? Do you have a message for your vanquished enemy?

"Tell Anna that I enjoyed our coffee, and I wish we'd had more time to get to know each other."

FragFlwr: How sweet. Is your finger hovering over the button, darling?

I stare at the endearment, every cell in my body vibrating. Because if I wasn't sure before, I am now. He's being cocky, and if he's not careful, he's going to give himself away.

"It's not a button."

I hold my finger over the icon, knowing what I just said was either obvious in its stupidity or stupid in its obviousness. But in the time it takes me to decide, FragFlwr's name goes dark. He's gone.

Chapter Twenty-One

Percy

It's not a button.

I log out instantaneously, after which I get the notification from the AI ghost that any trace of FragFlwr has been scattered randomly across the Mainstream in pieces of data so small that even if they're detected, they'll be indecipherable. More importantly, my link into the Mainstream can't be traced back here to the embassy, both because of the security and because of how I get around it. I learned this particular trick a year ago from Chen, and so far, it's been quite useful.

Never more so than now, as I lean over my desk and let her words brand my brain. *It's not a button.*

She was telling me she's being watched, that she had to call the hackers in to find me. I run my hand over my mouth, my perfect teeth and perfect lips. I've learned a few things in the last several minutes. First, the new guard in the White House is just as oppressive as I thought, just as desperate to find and crush any person who defies their vision of order. So desperate that they'll use a teenager as a puppet. But then again, I already knew that.

The question is whether the teenager in question is a willing creature—or just a victim waiting in the wings.

From the moment Marguerite burst onto the scene a year ago, I watched her. I was already tracking the campaign, because I had suspected for months that Wynn Sallese or one of his minions had something to do with my parents' deaths. If neurostim devices had ever been proven harmful after Sallese had pushed them so hard for so long, his political aspirations would have died on the vine—he'd have been just another corrupt businessman who made money on the backs of the masses, who were already suffering with the economic downturn and the rise of the tech market overseas. Sallese capitalized on Americans' fear of foreign goods and especially foreign tech, and made his company synonymous with patriotism and freedom from all that ails you.

Watching him, it's hard to believe he's evil. He truly seems to care. He's a man I could like if not for my past, my parents. I've always understood why Marguerite, so raw, so real, believed in him. But something there is not right, and it killed me to watch this girl capture heart after heart and lay them at the feet of the man who might have benefited most from the death of the two people who created me and then re-created me.

It's true that I've taunted her. I wanted her to question why she was doing all this—for attention? To distract herself from her grief? As a ticket out of Houston, well known as one of the most dangerous and depressed urban centers left in America? But she is a true believer.

Or she was. Now I'm not sure. Her last vid reeked of manipulation, but it wasn't clear whether she was pulling the strings or being yanked around.

I can't trust her.

I want to trust her.

Anna wanted to trust her, too. Or so Marguerite claims.

If Marguerite *is* on my side . . . she is in more danger than anyone else but me. And she is also more dangerous than anyone else but me.

Still, could she get me in to see Kyla? Well, not me, FragFlwr. Me, Percy Blake. Fashionista. Fool. "Definitely fool," I mutter.

"Percy," says Sophia. "Your aunt requests entrance."

I wipe the screen black. "Tell her to please come in."

"Percy?" calls Aunt Rosalie from the hall.

"Welcome, Auntie," I say as she comes into the room, a crocheted shawl draped over her shoulders.

"Oh, Percy, you look pinched, dear."

My hands move quickly over my face, reassuring myself that I've returned my features to default. "I'll wear a moisturizing mask to bed," I tell her with a wave of my hand.

She sits down in a chair close to the window. "I thought there might be tension with your young lady friend."

I turn to her as she pats her silver hair, pushing a stray strand back into place. "The course of young love never runs easy," I say, "but is there a more specific reason why you suspect such a thing?"

"Ah, well. I investigated who among your classmates carries this name. Marguerite."

Our eyes meet. "And you found her."

"She is lovely, Percy, but she is also one of President Sallese's most vocal attack dogs!"

"Now, I don't find 'attack dog' quite fair. She's a normal girl of steadfast opinions who is having some trouble settling in."

"Trouble of her own making!" Auntie humphs. "She is absolutely not good enough for you. I am of a mind to revoke your car privileges."

I square my shoulders. "Do that, and you will have lost a nephew."

She presses her lips together and looks toward the window. "Not for the first time," she murmurs. "Would you really break my heart like that on purpose?"

"Only if you break mine first."

"But Percy, she is dangerous. You put yourself in the crosshairs of Sallese and his administration by becoming involved with his little plaything. What if they find out who you are? What if they knew you are the son of Valentine and Flore Blake?"

I sigh and undo my cravat. "I'm obviously harmless. I'm not uploading vids on molecular structures, Auntie. Besides, they must already know. You don't think they dug deep inside our most private lives before Marguerite Singer came to school? Would Sallese trust his plaything, as you call her, to a group of unvetted technocrat hooligans? Whoever enrolled her at Clinton knew what he was doing."

She looks conflicted. "No, I suppose not. But still, this girl is trouble. She is on the wrong side."

"Are you supposed to be on a side, Auntie? Isn't your job as ambassador to—"

"To pursue and protect the interests of the French people in the United States." Her voice is losing its rounded softness. "After the recent detentions without due process of several citizens, and with the American government refusing to answer for its actions, Madam President is considering withdrawing all diplomatic personnel from this country until such time that the United States reinstates liberty and freedom."

"You mean closing the embassy?"

"For a time."

"Wouldn't that make things worse? If this government is becoming a fascist dictatorship, it seems like they need to be watched."

"We are not here for *them*, and now I am becoming worried for us. All embassy personnel are currently the focus of an investigation into our fleet, prompted by losing Jacques last night, I imagine. They have requested permission to scan the AI in the vehicles." Her stare is steady on me, as if she is giving me information only because she is seeking some in return. "I can't protect you from them as well as I'd like, not while we are on American soil."

"I can't leave, Auntie."

"Why? Don't tell me it is this girl. French girls are much more refined, and those interested in *politique* engage in a more dignified manner."

"Is it wrong to want justice for the citizens?" I ask. "One could argue that dignity is just what Marguerite is pursuing. This administration came riding into power on the swell of a populist wave, Auntie, made up of Americans who felt deprived of their dignity and basic rights as human beings. Who are we to judge the hoi polloi that have been ruled by the technocrat elites and have seen few benefits from such rule?"

"And so their solution is to send the nobility to *Madame la Guillotine*? Is that what your Marguerite believes? She has a French name, but does she know French history? Do you?"

"I know enough, Auntie. Maman made sure of it."

She mutters something easily detectable as religious even without a translator chip. "Then you know that things could get a lot worse before they get better. Such a reign of terror goes wide and deep before it burns itself out."

"History doesn't have to repeat itself. That was hundreds of years ago. The world was a different place." Even as I say it, I'm not overly sure, though. The way Bianca was treated was utterly savage. Cutting off her head might have been a more merciful death.

"You are not this silly," she says, and now her voice is sharp, reminding me of her power—including over me until I turn eighteen. "The director of national intelligence himself made the request today. If I allow the CIA to investigate our diplomatic fleet, what will they find?"

"You won't."

"You are depending on that, aren't you?"

I clench my teeth and stand up quickly. "When will Madam President make her decision?"

"She is trying to reach out to President Sallese directly. If he does not respond favorably with an explanation as to what is happening here, she will make the call."

"I just need a week."

"For what, exactly?"

"For you to trust me."

She folds her arms over her chest. "You are asking for much from me."

"Your trust is out of my reach?"

She curses in French, but her eyes glitter with tears. Her Cerepin flashes blue and then green. "Do you know how much you remind me of your father? Not all the time. But right now, certainly. He was a pigheaded and thoroughly confounding man. Flore was the only one he seemed to allow inside his head."

Mentioning my parents like this, with those tears on her face . . . it's threatening to undo me. "I've heard all this before."

"Have you?" she says sadly. "Have I also told you that they were the only ones who believed you'd survive to see your eighth birthday?"

The memory of my father leaning over me comes sudden and hard, pushing everything else to the side for the moment. "Tell me."

Because they never did. They never talked about what I had been. They only focused on what I was becoming.

"You were a beautiful little boy. We all thought you were perfect. Flore was overcome with happiness, and Valentine with pride. The best of two brilliant people. And there you were."

You're still Maman's perfect boy. I still remember her voice, soaked in sorrow. I can't see her face, though.

"I will never forget the moment Flore commed me. I couldn't understand her, the sobs. She was crying too hard. Finally I understood there had been an accident."

I look down at myself. "The last thing I remember is my seventh birthday party." And after that . . . I have only pieces. Flashes of strange, insistent memory. His face. Her hands. Quiet voices. The bright slash of a laser. And pain. So much pain.

"They withdrew from public life to care for you."

"What happened to me? I know I fell, but how?"

"You tumbled over a balcony, darling. Afterward, Flore told me you were trying to fetch your pet bird, which had gotten stuck in a tree whose branches stretched toward the house. The creature—a delicate little thing—had been a birthday present." Her face crumples. "From me."

"You can't blame yourself." I remember the canny bird. I remember its tiny, beady eyes, full of secrets. I remember its wings and wishing I could fly.

"Of course I do. But your mother blamed herself. She turned away for an instant, and you fell more than ten meters to the ground and shattered like an egg. She was afraid Valentine would never forgive her." She pulls a handkerchief from the neckline of her dress and dabs at her nose. "She told me that though your spinal cord could be regrown, it wasn't enough. Because the damage to your brain was permanent."

"Well, obviously—"

"Obviously your parents were more resourceful than most." Now she looks troubled as her gaze roams my face and body. "Your parents left a will with very specific instructions. They wanted you to make decisions about your own health. Perhaps because so many choices were taken away."

They left me with specific instructions, too. I think of my father's letter, the one he gave me on my sixteenth birthday, just a week before he was killed. "They must have known they were in danger."

"Your father might have been a technocrat, but never was he a slave to corporate interests like this Sallese," Aunt Rosalie says. "Near the end, he felt as if they were trying to take everything from him. He feared for you and your mother." She blots her eyes with the lacy scrap of cloth. "And he was right. If Flore hadn't been so stubborn, she'd still be alive. But she wanted to go with him that morning. She wanted to help."

I have never asked her before, not directly. But it's time. "You don't believe the attack on them was random, do you?"

She presses her lips together. "I have been afraid to talk about this with you, for fear of losing you as well. But now I'll lose you either way, won't I?"

I sit down next to her. "Not if you help me. Tell me what you know."

"I don't know that much. Flore did tell me they believed that NeuroGo was paying doctors to falsify and fabricate data to support positive claims about the neurostims." She gives me a dark look. "There is a reason such devices are banned in Europe, Brazil, and South Africa. Most other countries believe they are too dangerous—for the brain, yes, but also because the things are vulnerable to hackers, who might seize control of the signals remotely. Unfortunately, the foreign ban on this technology may have only opened the market for NeuroGo."

"If the connection is NeuroGo, does that mean you think Sallese is responsible for the murder of my parents?" I ask. "The timing seems remarkably advantageous for him. First Derek Kasabian disappeared, and I'm sure you know that Weisskopf has vanished now as well."

"I didn't know you heard." Auntie frowns. "But the detectives never found a clear link. The connection to a larger conspiracy was never proven."

"That doesn't mean Sallese didn't want to protect his reputation as he ran for president or that someone else didn't do it for him."

"I know that, too." She touches my arm. "But we have no evidence for this, and he is now the most powerful man in this country. America might be a backward, depressed place, but when it sneezes, the world still catches cold. It is best to let this upheaval work itself out while we watch from Paris."

It doesn't feel right, but arguing more is only likely to cement her position. "I will go with you if Madam President recalls you—I give you my word—but first I have some things I need to resolve, and to do that, I need a car. Marguerite and I have unfinished business."

She laughs, then sighs. "Remember to think with your head, Percy."

I strut over to my closet, where I begin to thumb through my evening jackets while trying not to wince at the lingering pain along my ribs. "And my heart, Auntie? What about my heart?"

"Protect it, my love. It might be more vulnerable than you think."

Chapter
Twenty-Two

Marguerite

I push the icon. Instantly, the screen goes gray, and I slide back from it as if it's contaminated. What if he left traces of his path behind? What if they're able to find him? By the time my comband vibrates a few minutes later, cold sweat has broken out on my forehead.

"What's wrong, Mar?" El asks drily. "Seen a ghost? Wrestling with demons? Both at once?"

I hate him. "I did what you asked."

"Did you? Hans just informed me that you only signaled him *after* Frag had signed off."

"Frag told me he'd be able to tell when the scan started," I babble. "I was hoping Hans could get something if I did it quickly enough right after?"

El has his face close to the screen, so it's the only thing I see. "Nice try."

I roll my eyes. "No matter what I do, it's never good enough."

"Just do exactly what I say. Frag is willing to engage with you, Marguerite. That makes you valuable. I took a quick read of your transcript, and really, it's masterful."

I start to relax, but then he says, "Until that last tip-off, of course."

"What?"

"Don't play dumb with me. I know you better than that."

"It's not like I'm used to all this coded covert master-spy crap, El."

"Mm-hmm. I've watched you win over skeptical crowds just by sensing the vibes in the room, the looks on a few key faces. You know how to do this."

"Okay," I say. "But how about this—by tipping him off, I've made him trust me more. Because I don't think he believes I'm stupid, either. I'm counting on it, in fact."

Oh, god. I'm just making this up right now. What I need is El to trust me, because that might be the only way to gain access to the president—and that's the only way to stop what's happening.

El is watching me intently. "You think he'll seek you out again."

"I do. Especially if your hacker guy can't trace him. He'll feel safe. And more confident." Then I'll see him in school, and maybe together we can get out of this. Assuming I can get *him* to trust me. I'm not doing so well on that front these days.

El smiles. "That sounds like it could work. I'll give you another day to make contact again."

"Just a day?"

"Things are moving quickly. We're trying to nail down all our assets and contain this before Americans start to lose confidence in their new president. They expect results quickly, and we need to give it to them. Fortunately, we got a big break about an hour ago. A lead in the bombings."

"Really? And?"

"Uh-uh. That's classified." His look is classic El. He was just waiting for me to ask so he could put me in my place.

"You're hilarious. I know you want to tell me something, just to keep me hanging. I'll wait." Because he's not the only one who knows things.

"Fine. There's a hacking collective here in DC that caused all sorts of trouble for the Zao administration. As they left office, they gave us their notes on these hooligans."

"Really? Something we actually agreed on?"

"Apparently these folks were so much trouble that the Zao administration wanted to see them caught no matter what. They gave us info just on principle."

"You think these hackers had something to do with the bombings."

"They think they're more clever than they actually are, and one of them flew a little too close to the sun."

"What is that supposed to mean?"

"Oh, we dug deep on some personnel files at a few local facilities after some info leaked that we felt was best kept out of the public eye."

"You caught someone who was going to tell on your agents for torturing innocent girls?" Even saying it makes me sick.

"You make it sound much worse than it was."

"Somehow I doubt that."

"Anyway. We figured out that one of these guys was once a roommate of a man named Martin Chen. And Chen, well."

Cold chills run down my back. Triplechen. He said the deaths of Percy's parents weren't random.

"Well what?" I'm proud of how calm I sound.

"Just rest assured that we're going to catch the culprits of the worst terrorist attacks in DC history. They were almost certainly paid by Gia to do this. We're going to hang these guys."

"I feel safer already," I mutter.

"We still need to find out who's smuggling them out of DC, though. The embassy car . . ." His expression shifts from eager to calculating. "So, I was reviewing files on your classmates, and I found an interesting connection."

My heart rate skyrockets. "Oh, do tell," I say, all boredom and annoyance.

"Percival Valentine Blake. His aunt is the French ambassador. Know him?"

"Of course I know him. He's hard to miss." If El catches me in a single lie, Percy's dead, so I need to tell as much truth as possible.

"He's an orphan—did you know that?"

"Yup. Common knowledge."

"His dad was a piece of work, I can tell you. The guy did his best to take down both Fortin and NeuroGo. He had no problem trying to deny lifesaving neurostim treatment to millions of Americans."

I stare into El's eyes. "Until he was murdered."

El smiles. "Yeah, that was a tragedy. But it wasn't the first to befall this family. Percy was."

"Well, he's kind of an idiot, but that's hardly what I would call a tragedy."

"No, that's more of a miracle, actually. See, that kid should have died a long time ago."

"What are you talking about?"

And El can see that he's hooked me. "The Blakes' only son suffered a terrible fall when he was seven years old. And the kid wasn't seen or heard from again . . . until he enrolled at your school. Interesting, am I right? Despite the fact that his hospital records show—"

"Those are private!"

"Matter of national security. I got a warrant."

"Yeah, I'm sure."

"Anyway, his hospital records show that his spinal cord was severed and he had severe brain damage. The kind that doesn't mend. Then his parents took him home—they were offered hospice care for the child, but they didn't accept it. And then, almost a decade later, here's this kid."

This doesn't make any sense. Percy has no visible scars, no problems moving around. His brain seems to work just fine . . . mostly. "Why are you telling me all this?"

"Don't you think it's odd, Mar? Especially since his parents were specialists in use of augmentation chips and nanotech—most of which have been banned for private use because of the risks involved? If they used that stuff on their kid, that's just cruel. And illegal."

"Even if they saved his life?"

"Not if he's carrying illegal tech." El smiles. "Maybe we need to take a closer look at him. Lives at the embassy, with access to embassy vehicles. Had parents who pretty much hated everything our president stands for. Do you think—"

My laugh is loud and harsh. "Oh my god. You don't know Percy at all." I flick my finger against the corner of my screen, and the image splits. I switch on sharing so El can see what I'm doing. "The Fashionista File," I say, and Percy's channel comes up. I scroll to an image of Percy wearing some sort of dress and tell the vid to play.

Percy, sporting platinum hair with a sparkling crimson streak, leans toward the lens, blue eyes glittering, as he puts on a thick layer of lush red lipstick. "Feels divine," he says. "How do I look? This shade is Red Death. Kiss me and it might be the last thing you ever do." He grins and steps back, revealing once again the dress that's draped over his long, lean body. I know very well that this frivolous stuff doesn't mean he's not a freaking dangerous super spy, but I'm fairly sure it'll take El longer to figure that out. I let the vid keep playing. "Now, I'm wearing Johann Richter tonight, because I was feeling saucy, and no one does minx better than Johann. Boys, if you haven't tried his line of frocks, you really must. The cut is perfect for us gents." Percy whirls around, letting the skirt billow around his shaven legs, and then curtsies for his audience.

El laughs. "I don't even know what to say."

I pause the vid, relief making my limbs loose. "Percy is the most empty-headed, shallow person I've ever met. If he's got some kind of illegal augmentation, it's probably his fashion sense. You can see he's got nearly ten million subscribers to his channel. He posts every day and spends more time on his makeup and nails than his schoolwork.

The day of the bombing, he went and got his hair done. Check out the timing on the vid."

"All right, all right. I'll keep looking. It just seemed like too much of a coincidence."

"Feel free to watch more of his vids if you want some tips on how to apply highlighter to bring out your cheekbones or cover up your under-eye circles."

He's still chuckling. "Oh, I've missed this, Mar. I miss you. I want things to be better between us. Your mom would like that. It'll make it easier."

"Make what easier?"

His face grows solemn again. "I'm just going to come out and say it: I'm in love with her. But you already knew that."

Now my muscles are knotting in rebellion. "She's vulnerable, El. Not ready—"

"She's better, and you know it. And she's realizing she has feelings for me, too."

No. No. "Um . . . she's never really . . ."

"You've been preoccupied with your own stuff, Mar. Your mom is coming alive again, and I'm going to make her very happy. I hope you'll be a part of that."

Truthfully, she does seem better. But the thought of her and El together makes me sick. "I'll com tomorrow for an update on your progress," El is saying. "So you'd better post a vid or something to lure the guy in. And this time, try to call in Hans a little earlier. He said all he needs is a full second of connection."

"I'll keep that in mind."

"You'd better, Mar. Don't break my heart, now."

"Nah. That's my mom's job."

He coughs like I've just hit him in the chest. "Not funny. At all. You planning on tanking my prospects just to get back at me for leaning on you?"

"Leaning on me? *That's* what you're calling this? Now I totally understand how you sleep at night."

But El is totally somber now. "Mar, really. Don't make me do something I'd forever regret."

Somehow, this statement is the most terrifying of the night. I hang up. Then I bury my head in my pillow and scream.

Before I leave for school, I creep into Mom's room to say good-bye. She rouses as I kiss her cheek. "Leaving already?"

"It's after eight."

Her eyelids flutter. "Oh, god, I've overslept."

"Mom, does that neurostim make you sleepy?"

She sits up slowly. "It definitely *helps* me sleep. I never told you, but I've had such insomnia for the last year. I was really a zombie."

She didn't have to tell me. I knew. "So you think you're just catching up?"

She nods. "El said I could come in later this week as I got used to it, but I don't want people to think I can't handle the job. I need to help El plan the president's victory tour for this spring. It'll take a lot of coordination."

"Victory tour?"

"Yeah. When we have the concessions from private industry and increases in production for Cerepins in particular, he's going to tour the US to present it, including introducing programs to install both Cerepins and neurostims at the same time, assuming we get approval for that. We think his numbers will go even higher."

"But with all this terrorism stuff, how . . . ?"

"Now that Gia Fortin is a fugitive and her stock has fallen, we've called on Congress to bail it out. But we'll also need industry leadership and expertise to put the company on the right track again."

"Would NeuroGo fit the bill?"

She peers at my face. "Why do you say it like that? Are you all right?"

My comband vibrates. "Yeah—hey, the car is here for me. I'll see you later."

As I walk out of the room, she's reaching up to press the stim device. To put her back to sleep, to calm her nerves, to make all the grief go away . . . I have no idea. All I know is that it bothers me in a way the sight of those things never did before. I thought they were a good thing, but these days I really wonder.

Wondering about neurostims was what Percy's parents were doing when they were killed.

I grab a breakfast bar from Renata on my way out and force it down as I sit in Jenny's backseat. A few crumbs land on my comband, and I don't even bother to wipe them off. My screen has become a leash. For so long, I thought it was a private thing, an extension of my body, and now it feels like El's fingers are wrapped around my arm in a punishing grip. I stare at it as the car glides toward school, wondering how El managed to cap it and if his hacker team is listening right now. It might be conveying every single thing I hear and say to El. It's so easy to forget that. I did last night for a few minutes as I spoke to Orianna, as I watched her fade in and out. I did just now as I asked my mom about NeuroGo. I'm giving El every reason to come after me. I'm being stupid.

If I'm not careful, I'm going to get someone else in trouble.

As we land, my mind whirls with possible scenarios. If I do something suspicious, El will pick it up. If I'm not careful with what I say, El will hear every word. And who knows where else he has eyes. The first things I see as I get out of the car are the school's security cannies—flanked by Secret Service cannies. These are supposedly here for my protection, but they offer El and anyone else who's helping him a 360, all-day view of exactly what I'm doing and who I'm talking to.

Any hope I had of talking to Percy, warning him, helping him . . . all of that fades away as I realize the best thing I can do for him is to ignore him completely.

Maybe I'm imagining it, but the Secret Service cannies seem to be watching me with particular interest this morning. One of them says, in a synthetic-gentle voice, "You are safe, Marguerite."

I laugh as tears fill my eyes. "Thanks."

There are even fewer students here than yesterday. It looks like two-thirds of my classmates have stayed home. The ones here look like they were forced by their parents, because they all wear these sullen expressions that harden to hatred when they see me. But none of them say a word. Which is wise. I'm basically radioactive.

Percy is already at the top of the stairs, talking to a few girls. He's holding himself differently today, less straight, one arm pressed to his ribs. His gaze flicks over to me and away, then returns and holds as I mount the stairs. I press my comband to my side and bite my lip. I wish we could communicate by telepathy or something, because I have no idea what he's thinking. His look is less flamboyant than usual, black pants, a gray turtleneck sweater, boots with heavy soles. His fingernails are black and so is his hair. I am struck again by how perfect his skin is. He's wearing makeup, foundation and eyeliner, more than usual, but I can see the sweat glistening at his temples as I draw near. Is he nervous? Why is he standing like that?

I avert my gaze quickly. I have no idea whether one of the Secret Service cannies is streaming this to El or whether he's listening and watching via my screen. I wish I could take it off and fling it over the edge of the banister, but no doubt that would result in more scrutiny. I wish I could talk to Percy, but I can't. I just can't. There's no way to do it without putting him in more danger.

I head to homeroom and sit through Mr. Cordoza bravely discussing freedom of movement and association in our society. His comments are pointed, and he's clearly trying to spur a discussion, but everybody looks like their mouths are sewn shut, including Percy. Including me—I'm terrified that if El hears this, he's going to punish my teacher. Bring him in for questioning and disappear him forever.

Finally, Mr. Cordoza gives up with a sigh. "I get it, guys," he says wearily. "This is a tough time. Good luck with your Aristotle sessions."

We all shuffle to our darkened cubicles to commune with the AI that killed my dad. I've just put on my goggles when the booth starts to emit a strange static sound, white noise on steroids. As I start to pull my goggles up to see what's happening, something scratchy and rough slides into the back of my collar. I go stiff as I feel a warm body behind me and someone pulls one of my earpods out. A deep, rustling voice speaks into my ear. "Destroy after reading."

With that, the person steps through the curtains that partition the booth, and the white noise dies. My goggles are flashing, and I cram them back on again. Aristotle is waiting, and I tell him I want to start with the history lecture. I am once again pleasantly surprised by how steady my voice sounds, though if El can access my biometrics, he'll see my heart rate is off the charts. I laugh to myself and say to Aristotle, "You were glitching there for a second."

He ignores me and keeps up his lecture, and I set my comband to capture it. El deserves to listen to this pretend teacher droning on and on about the French Revolution.

With the screen pointed away, I reach up and pull the scratchy thing from my collar. I yawn, pretending to stretch, with the scrap of scratchy material crumpled in my fist. Then I let my hand drop beneath the table. I push my goggles up again and look down at the object sitting on my palm.

I know what this is—Dad had a whole box of it, mementos from the past.

It's paper. I run my thumb over its surface. It's thicker than I thought it would be. There's a raised pattern on it, something I'm dying to examine in the light. Instead, I clutch it tightly, palm sweating, until we reach a pause in the lecture. "Aristotle, I need to go to the bathroom."

"You may have five minutes, Marguerite."

My legs shaky, I leave the goggles behind and head for the bathroom. There's no one in here, and I duck into a stall. Praying El will turn off when he realizes this is the real deal, I sit down and pee. And as I do, I carefully aim the screen away from my body, and with my other hand, I pull the paper from my pocket and look down at it.

Sit on my left side at lunch.

That is all it says, written in block letters by hand. I've never seen handwriting in person before. The corner of the scrap has a symbol pressed into it.

A flower.

It all makes sense, the cuff links, the username, this symbol. It really is him. He's trusting me with his life, and I think he knows that.

I let the paper drop into the toilet and flush it down.

The next hour or so passes in a haze. Aristotle is bland as always, but I swear I detect a note of disappointment in his voice when I get every single question he asks completely wrong. I walk to lunch feeling dizzy and uncertain. His left side? Why? And isn't he afraid of being spotted? Maybe he doesn't know my screen is capped, that every word he says can be recorded and parsed, analyzed and compared to any other data source they have. That his face, if I happen to aim the screen at it, will also be scanned and image matched. It's not just my screen, either—the Secret Service cannies will surely be watching. There is no privacy.

For a few anxious moments after I enter the cafeteria, I consider sitting somewhere else, off in a corner by myself. But when I look around, I don't see a single canny. Percy sits at a table near the windows. Deciding that I'd rather not be alone, determined to keep the conversation completely stupid and light, I grab a sandwich, swipe it across my screen to pay, then head over there and plop down.

As I do, he raises his left arm and lets it fall in eerily exact parallel with my right, the one with the screen. I don't know how he does it, but by the time my arm settles on the table, his screen is pressed to mine. He reaches over and casually taps a button on his, and I feel the seal that's created through rubber edges perfectly aligned. I stare down at it and then look up at him.

He grins. "You can talk normally."

I shake my head. Muted by fear.

His eyes are so, so blue. "All your minders will see is a normal view of the cafeteria, and all they will hear is a silly conversation about whether the meat in my sandwich is real or genned."

"How—?"

"Bianca wasn't the only one who was excellent at fabbing vids. Who do you think taught her?" His smile has gone, though. The tension is right there, at the corners of his eyes.

"The cannies, though," I whisper.

"Gone to investigate a suspicious package near the garbage incinerator at the back of the school."

"They have ways . . ."

"They haven't caught me yet." The back of his left hand brushes against the back of my right. Our arms are practically glued together. The cold metal of the ring on his middle finger makes me realize there's a flower there, too.

I direct my gaze out the window. "I couldn't live with myself if I'm the reason you get caught."

"What's one more life on your conscience?"

"Please," I say, nearly choking on my sorrow and shame. "You have to know—"

His other hand covers mine. "I'm coming around." He lets me go. "Will you forgive me?"

"For what?"

"For being the gadfly on your channel. For making things even harder."

"Only if you forgive me for being completely blind. I feel so stupid. I believed it all."

"What do you believe now?"

"That people deserve to know what's happening. I'm not sure if the president actually knows, to be honest."

Percy's smooth brow furrows. "Are you sure? He's a savvy man, Marguerite."

"But it's his chief of staff, Elwood Seidel, who's pulling the strings now. He won't even let me get to the president, which makes me think Uncle Wynn doesn't know what El has done."

Percy regards me for several long seconds. "You're sure?"

"El's been with him for years. He's the filter for information, for staff, for messaging. And I don't think the president approves of everything he's done. El's the one who . . . who . . ."

"Bianca."

"Yeah," I whisper. "He used me as an excuse. I swear I didn't want her to *die*."

"Where do you stand with him?"

"On very shaky ground."

"And why are you sitting here with me?"

"I shouldn't be. He asked me about you this morning. He knows about your parents. He told me about your accident. He . . . thinks they did something to you."

Percy laughs. "Why am I not in custody, then?"

"Because I showed him a vid of you dancing around in a dress and trying on lipstick."

"Old prejudices die hard, I suppose." He leans closer, smelling of flowers and electrical fire.

"You need him to believe you're harmless. If he thinks you're a threat, it'll be bad."

He purses his lips. "Are you trying to *save* me, Marguerite?"

Anger heats my cheeks. "Are you trying to get caught?"

"Heaven forfend. I'd hate to miss the rollout of Johann Richter's new spring line."

"Be serious, Percy!"

"I'm deadly serious." And suddenly, he looks it. "Will you do as I say? Will you trust me?"

"You're the only person I trust right now," I murmur as a Secret Service canny strides into the room. My voice drops to a whisper again. "El is planning more arrests for tonight—he's after some hacker group led by a guy named Martin Chen. I don't want anyone else to get hurt."

Percy freezes for a second, but only a second. Then his smile returns. "Enjoy your lunch, darling. For the record, I still think the meat is genned. But I have no complaints."

He has disconnected our screens. And now he's walking away, his steps relaxed but not quite normal. His arm is still wrapped protectively over his ribs. It reminds me that he is just a boy, just a human, and we're up against an entire government controlled by a conniving, sadistic traitor. The fear returns, spreading through me like a bloom of poison.

But I'm not going to give up. I'm going to see this through to the end, no matter where it takes me.

Chapter
Twenty-Three

Percy

I don't check until I'm in the car and on the way back to the embassy, but it has meant fighting temptation every second. Once I'm inside Charles, though, I can't hold out any longer. I activate my comband and see what I've got—and what I've got is more temptation. I've cloned Marguerite's device, so I have access to everything. I can already see that it's been capped by someone who knows only slightly less than I do, maybe the hacker who so clumsily left his or her gummy fingerprints all over Marguerite's message space on her channel.

This is all right, though. It could be useful.

I can also see the coms she's made, the posts, her search items. I could check to see if she's looked me up.

I will not do any of these things. From what I can see, Marguerite is living her life under an electron microscope. Whether she knows it or not, she hasn't had secrets for an age, except those locked in the maze of her own mind. But anything she's done, said aloud, or seen, this device has recorded it. Someone has drilled himself a peephole, and he's watching her like the festering pile of faux humanity he is.

Time to look up Elwood Seidel.

Marguerite believes in Wynn Sallese. I'm not sure I do, but after watching him I understand why she does. But Elwood? He's the one who had Bianca murdered, and that means I need to know more about him.

I turn my clone version of Marguerite's device to dormant and then I switch to my own secure channel. With the further layers of shielding security inside this embassy vehicle, I have no fear of detection. I look up Elwood Seidel, and I see he's originally from Mississippi. His parents ran an online venture selling chain-saw wood sculptures (I will admit I had to look up what exactly that was), which seems to have gone out of business when he was a teenager. He attended state school and majored in business, worked as an account manager at a few companies, and then, about ten years ago, was hired by NeuroGo in their business-expansion department—in charge of finding new markets and uses for the neurostims. When Wynn Sallese left the company three years ago, El went with him. And when Wynn sold his entire interest in the company . . . El did nothing of the kind. At least, not that I can find. He must still hold NeuroGo stock. A lot of it.

Interesting.

More research simply reveals what Marguerite disclosed, that El is the one who discovered her, that he was the architect of Wynn Sallese's surprisingly and devastatingly successful populist campaign. Marguerite was not the only Mainstreamer he hired, but she was the most effective, the least scripted, the youngest, the one who seemed to have the least to gain. The most genuine. Today in her eyes, I saw her idealism crumbling, crushed by terror.

I'm about to put her in more danger, but I think, with luck, she'll be instrumental to my own plan.

She's probably in the car on the way home from school, just as I am. I go back to my clone and use its internal signature to send her a system notification, an invitation to run a malware scan. It will provide the cover I need—while it's running, nothing will be captured. She activates it immediately, which makes me smile. As soon as it starts, I send a shot-message programmed with a six-second erase path.

38°56'22"N 77°3'52"W

9pm

Wondering if I'm about to cement my future in hell, I return to my most immediate concern: I have tried to ignore my injury, hoping it would simply go away with a bit of time, but my ribs still feel as if they're about to splinter. And I'm having trouble breathing. I slathered on my foundation this morning to cover up the pallor, but now I'm sweating through makeup that was supposed to be bulletproof, literally. I'm going to contact the cosmetics company and let them know there's a nasty vid in their future if they don't improve their formula and be more honest in their claims. Ugh.

I lean back against the seat. What I need is a medical scan, but my parents told me I should never get one. They said medical records are never completely private and that sooner or later a scan would draw attention that I wouldn't want. They made me promise, just like they made me promise not to get a Cerepin, because connecting myself to a network would have major consequences. It all seemed paranoid then, but after reading my father's note last night, I understand what would happen.

Good thing he gave me the tools to fix myself. It's time to give that a try.

Charles lands and rolls into the embassy carport. As I make my way past the fleet, I lean on Yves's hood. "I'll need you again tonight."

His headlights flash.

I walk to my room, carefully minding my gait. But once I'm inside and have my privacy settings on, I collapse into my chair. It's possible I would heal with time, but time is something Kyla and Winston and Finn and every other technocrat in the city do not have. I need to be strong enough to finish this. Groaning, I limp over to my closet and dig out the paper with the menu access code my father left me.

I press my thumb to the flower at the top twice to skip past his handwritten words to get to the code that unlocks my internal memory. Swaying, I focus on the words that appear to float a few feet in front of my face:

<u>Health and Safety:</u>

Bioscan
Site management
System update
Self-destruct

All my options are enabled. Lovely. When I chuckle, it hurts enough to make me wince. I blink a few times, adjusting my vision as I read. Here goes nothing.

"Bioscan."

It's like electric ants crawling all over my body. I stand stiff, unable to move even though I want to sink to the floor. The sensation is everywhere at once, from the bottoms of my feet to my balls, for god's sake, my chest, my face, behind my eyes, in my armpits, along my screaming ribs.

Synaptic chip malfunction in the 5th intercostal nerve due to electrical input that exceeds system parameters, says the message that pops up a moment later. Do you accept this diagnosis?

"What the hell else am I supposed to do?"

If you refuse to accept the diagnosis, the program will close.

"No, don't do that. I need help."

For help, select site management and follow the prompts.

"Site management," I say, melting into a chair now that the paralyzing scan is complete.

Another menu pops up.

Site Management:

Nerve block
Disengage affected augmentation chip(s)
Initiate nanorepair

I consider my options. Nerve block seems like it will stop the pain, but I consider pain valuable information. And I'd be terrified of turning off any of my augmentations, even though I don't know what all of them do. With them, I can control my body. I know what's going on with it. I know how to change the way it moves and looks. Without the augmentations, I will fall apart, possibly literally.

"Initiate nanorepair," I say.

Please remain stationary until the process is complete, say the words that hang just in front of me. Initiating.

I yelp as a grinding pain bursts into my awareness in an area just to the right of my spine, in the middle of my back.

Please remain stationary flashes pink then red in front of my eyes, warning me. I grit my teeth and do my best not to writhe. It's not easy, because lord, the pain. The cure is worse than the disease. The agony crawls along my rib cage, and I realize that my initial pain is gone!

But only because it's been dwarfed by the fire engulfing my entire chest.

Please remain stationary is just solid crimson now, blocking my view of the room.

Then this programming equivalent of the devil helpfully provides me with a timeline for my suffering, and I watch the minutes count down.

"Percy, I am sensing that you are distressed," says Sophia.

"For god's sake, shut up," I say from between clenched teeth.

"The ambassador would like to know if you would like to join her for dinner."

"Yesss," I hiss.

"Are you in need of assist—"

"Privacy," I shout.

"I could lower the temperature of the room. You are generating sufficient body heat to cause the ambient temperature to exceed specified parameters."

"Damn the specified parameters," I snap.

A cloudy drop of sweat lands on the front of my gray sweater. Now the cosmetics company is in for it. I mentally compose a vid trashing their new product line while the nanocreatures I had no idea I was harboring work to repair the nerve damage caused by that neural disruptor barb from last night. This is going to be a diva rant of epic proportions, if I do say so. Right now I'm wishing I could set fire to the cosmetic company headquarters. Sweat runs in rivulets down my face. It's stinging my eyes, and the only thing that's not blurry is the words being projected against my lenses.

"Fine," I say peevishly. "Lower the temperature. And then leave me alone."

The pain disperses quickly as the final ten seconds count down. When the clock disappears, I slide from my chair and land in a limp, sweaty heap on the floor.

Nanorepair complete, my internal system helpfully informs me. **Synaptic functioning restored.**

I close my eyes in exhaustion as the words fade. I'm not sure if I'm glad I did that or deeply sorry. Since I can breathe normally now, I suppose it was a good decision. I wonder what else those nanocytes can do. If I have to be injured to find out, perhaps it's a question best left by the wayside.

I have enough to worry about. This morning, Winston told me he and his family will be ready to go tonight, but Marguerite told me Elwood was planning to initiate more arrests. So much for due process and democracy.

I take a quick shower and check my comband as I towel off. No messages, but that means little, because no one I need to hear from would be stupid enough to send me anything over standard channels. Not even a coded message. Not now. I wonder if Chen knows he's been made.

I need to warn him.

Quickly, I use the towel to turn my black hair into a wild mess, and then I lean over my desk screen. The effect is ghoulish. I'm shirtless, and there are circles under my eyes. Perfect. I grab the bottle of damnable foundation and hold it next to my pale face, then I start to stream.

"Do you see this, fans and friends and followers? Do you see it? This is the substance that has utterly ruined my day. Revgen's Bulletproof Perfection, in Fair, though I'm guessing every other shade is just as impotent. A warning to any and all. This product claims to protect your skin. It claims to be bulletproof, but all I can tell you about that is after wearing this for a few hours, I wanted to shoot myself in the face! Avoid it at all costs. Be careful not to accidentally pick it up. Because you will get *burned*."

I am nearly yelling at this point, eyes bulging. I must look completely unhinged. I feel a little sorry for Revgen, because they've provided me with the perfect cover, just not the kind they were shooting for.

Oh. I'm still thinking in vid mode. I send my vid into the stream and sit back down to wait for comments.

Scrolling, scrolling. The comments say I look great without makeup, offer suggestions for a different foundation, and then this:

Haruki656: Epic rant, P. Maybe you should start wearing a mask, though? I would if I had an ugly mug like yours. JK

"Very funny." At least I know he's okay. He's gotten the message. The rest will have to wait until tonight.

"Percy, the ambassador has a message for you. The president of France has recalled all diplomatic personnel to Paris. Your aunt wishes to discuss this with you at dinner. She said to bring an open mind."

"Tell her I'll try to find one at a discount."

"As you wish, sir."

"Someone should activate your humor setting, Sophia."

"It is activated, sir." There's a pause. "Ha."

"Oh, lord help me. I'm starting to like you."

"Don't worry, sir. It won't last. You'll be telling me to self-destruct before you know it."

"Go convey my message, you saucy minx. And stop being so deadly on the nose."

I have to do this tonight. I've already got most of the pieces in place. I just need to follow the steps. It might kill two birds with one stone, or more accurately, save both. But it will require every single detail to go perfectly right between now and then.

I can only hope it's not too late for all of us.

I happen to be very good at details. While Yves transports me to the meeting place, I tuck the most important one into a storage compartment between the seats. "Depending on how things go, I need you to take this to a friend after we're done tonight," I tell him.

"Yes, sir. May I ask whether you mean if things go right or if they go wrong?"

"It's going to look like both, depending on where you're standing." I tell him exactly what I need him to do.

He acknowledges the orders as he starts to descend, then says, "There are twelve federal cars in the neighborhood below us."

"We're meeting the passengers at a mass-gen facility."

"When we get close enough, they'll detect my signal block and know this is a diplomatic car. They're on the lookout for us."

"Then we'll have to be quick, old man."

"I am neither old nor a man."

"Just go with it."

He is silent for a moment, then: "What you're doing is quite risky, isn't it?"

"Nothing worthwhile isn't."

"I'm not sure the ambassador agrees. She told me to make sure that you return with all limbs intact and lipstick on your collar."

"My own or my lady friend's?"

"I didn't ask for specification."

I smile as we start to descend—I can see Winston peering out the window of the facility, a place where people without home fabgens can download and gen their garments. It's closed now, and Winston figured it was a good place to lie low until we got here. Winston's father knows the owner and got the code.

But as we pull up to the curb and Yves informs me that the federal cars closing in are equipped with restriction broadcasting that blocks AI-piloted vehicles from exceeding the speed and altitude limit, I begin to wonder. Yves throws open his back door, and I gesture frantically for Winston, his father, his mother, and his two little sisters to jump in. They cram themselves in the back, looking frazzled and terrified. "It's been quiet," Winston says between pants.

Yves slams his door shut and hurls us into motion. "Two blocks and closing. It's possible they were waiting for us."

"Get into the sky," I say, peering at the view offered by the rear camera.

"There's a sky access strip three blocks ahead."

"Be there now," I say, because Mrs. Hethermill screams and then her little girls do the same as three federal cars turn the corner.

"They've activated the speed restriction, sir."

I curse. "Manual override."

Then I place my hands on the panel in front of me, which lights up at my touch. I've never driven a car before, but in theory, I know how it's done. Speed restrictions can be defied only in manual mode. I tap my left index finger, and we all lurch forward as I bring us to a sudden halt.

"Wrong button," shouts Winston.

"Obviously," I say, tapping my left ring finger this time. Yves shoots forward just as the federal cars draw even. My heart rate is 159 beats per minute and rising quickly. My respiration is even but rapid. My palms are sweating as I twist my right hand to steer.

"Oh, god, they're going to shoot us," Winston's mother wails.

"Please shut up, Mrs. Hethermill," I say loudly. "You're scaring your children." I torque my right hand, and Yves neatly executes a sharp right turn, then accelerates with a press of my ring finger as we barrel down a hill.

The federal agents begin to fire magnetic disruptors at the wheels. "Air," I say to Yves. "I don't care what you have to do."

"Flight button," he says. "Left thumb."

With a jab of my thumb, we are launched into the air at a strange angle. I right us with a jerk of my hand, just in time to avoid colliding with the side of a building.

"They're in the air behind us," says Mr. Hethermill, who sounds only slightly less shrill than his wife. "If they catch us—"

"None of that talk." I dive back toward the ground again in a move that makes my stomach swoop.

"You're exceeding my safety parameters, sir."

"Well," I say. "I guess this is the day for that."

We land hard back on the road again, and I accelerate into a tunnel with six lanes and scattered traffic.

"There will be agents waiting on the other side, sir."

"Yes." I jab the flight control and rise high enough to fly over cars— but I have to swerve to avoid a mass transport gliding along in the center lane. The Hethermills all scream in unison. "Winston, this is a new side of you," I say as I turn Yves around in the air and shoot back the wrong way. I don't even know how I'm doing this, but it's rather fun. Yves is beautifully responsive, like an extension of me. I feel his machine soul humming beneath my hands as we bullet through the tunnel over oncoming traffic and zoom over the tops of two federal cars grounded at the entrance.

They can't turn fast enough to follow us. But then Yves flashes a proximity warning.

"Three federal agents closing from above."

"Can you go any faster, Yves?"

"I am already exceeding my—"

"Exceed them a bit more, dammit," I shout.

Yves compliantly accelerates and the proximity warnings go silent, but I know the fed cars won't give up or go away. They practically saw me load this family into the car. This family with the teenage boy and the two tiny girls in the back, the ones with the red tearstained faces that peer at me with pleading eyes every time my gaze slides past the backseat cams.

I imagine them with water in their lungs and scorch marks on their bodies. That is the kind of evil we're dealing with. The kind that stabs an innocent couple to death. I know who my target is now. I'm going to see this through.

Those are my crimson, throbbing thoughts as I soar through the sky over DC, barely avoiding several law-abiding cars operating well within the parameters of safety.

Here's the thing—it's hard to beat someone who's not. The fed agents are depending on their perfectly programmed AI-piloted vehicles to catch up with me, but I'm flying very much like a human right now—emotional, risky, and flawed. Almost fatally. When I clip the side of a flying transport and send us spiraling toward earth, I yell, "Yves, take over!"

It's the only reason we don't crash. He swoops low over the Potomac and streaks into Arlington. "They've lost visual, but they'll detect me when they fly over," he tells me. I understand what that means—he doesn't want to lead them to the rendezvous point.

"Got it." I use Yves's diplomatic line to send a quick message to Chen, who tells me he can be at a meeting place within five minutes. "Yves, stop here."

He does. I turn to the terrified family in the back. "Get out now, and get into that abandoned library. See it?" I point across the street. "Someone will be here to pick you up shortly."

"But they'll come after us," snaps Mr. Hethermill. He looks indignant, like I've given him bad service at a restaurant instead of saving his life.

"No they won't. Now. Get. Out."

Yves's door pops open.

"Do as he says, Dad," says Winston. He looks at me, and I see his fear but also respect. "Thanks, man. Sorry I called you a freak."

The entire Hethermill family tumbles out of the car, and as soon as they do, Yves asks me what I want to do.

"Into the air, old man," I say. "We're the distraction."

"This will present a significant risk to your health and well-being, sir."

"It's not as risky as staying still."

Yves ascends so rapidly that my ears pop, but even so, I'm tapping my face, activating the implants beneath the skin of my brow, cheekbones, jaw, and nose. Then I hit the spot on my Adam's apple that controls my voice. *"Ah voilà,"* I boom. "Tenor to bass in an instant."

"Should I ask why you need that kind of disguise?"

"Best not to. Now, I need you to go have a conversation with a certain girl." I pat the compartment between the seats. "You know what to do."

"I do. But sir . . ."

"This is where we part, Yves. At this point, there's no other way." I take off my comband, activate the clone of Marguerite's device, and set it on the seat next to me. "Use this and find its twin. It's going to be on her wrist." I give him the coordinates where she should be in about . . . "You have less than an hour."

"May I ask what you'll be doing, sir?"

"Me?" I draw in a deep breath as we dive quickly, shooting past two federal units that were about to cross the Potomac. "I'm going to topple the empire."

Chapter
Twenty-Four

Marguerite

The taxi drops me off at Hazen Park, the spot indicated by the coordinates Percy sent. Mom was still at the White House when I left, so I asked Renata to tell her I am meeting a friend for a late-night slice of pizza. It sounds so random, but I also streamed a vid earlier this evening talking about how I needed to experience life as a normal teenager, especially when it was this stressful. I'm hoping she sees that and lets me have a few hours. More likely, El will see it and know I'm up to something.

I know how I'll spin it—I'm trying to catch FragFlwr. I'm trying to lure him in.

And I am, sort of. I swear, this afternoon, when he was so close to me . . . we had a moment. I don't know what to make of it, but I know I want a chance to figure it out.

I'm trying not to let doubts about it creep in, but Percy is an amazing actor, too. He's serious and heroic, but he wears the mask of a fool more often than not, a brilliant disguise. And he's documented his life, top to bottom, in those vids. I know he streams them to hundreds of thousands of fans in the United States and to millions of people all over the world who've got the tech to watch him, but in reality, I don't think anyone knows the first thing about where he really came from or what happened to him. Or if they do, they're not saying.

And here I am, shivering in my newly genned coat, obediently standing in the exact spot he told me to, at the exact time. I've been thinking about this nonstop since I got his message. I'm guessing I'm a decoy. I glance down at my comband. El is probably listening and watching. Percy is probably up to something tonight, maybe trying to get more technocrats out of DC, and El told me he had more arrests planned. But if he thought he could capture FragFlwr, wouldn't he divert resources to do that? Wouldn't that give Percy a little time and space to rescue whoever needs it?

Then again, the federal government has a lot of resources.

A single headlight pierces the darkness ahead of me, roaring like nothing I've ever heard. I gape at the oncoming vehicle as it speeds toward me, and when I realize we're on a collision course, I stumble back over the curb to get out of its way. It comes to an abrupt stop in front of me, burping mechanically. It looks like a motorcycle, but it's leaner and belches smoke. Its rider removes a bulky helmet to reveal— another helmet?

"Marguerite?"

"Yeah?"

"Ukaiah." The woman offers me the helmet not fused to her skin, and I take it because I'm not sure what else to do. "Get on."

"Um. Where are we going?"

The helmet that's still on her head is flickering with lights, and her brown skin is slightly puckered in the places where the helmet fits most tightly. Her face is twitching, too. "Away from here. Company's coming." When I don't move, she adds, "Percy sent me."

As if on cue, a siren sounds off, a few blocks away. I get on the bike and cram the helmet over my hair, then wrap my arms around the woman's waist. She's solid and strong, but her head is shaped so strangely that I lean back away from it. I'm afraid that if I bonked against it, it would hurt her.

It seems to be bolted onto her skull.

With a twist of her wrists, she revs the noisy, smelly engine. It must run on gasoline, which means it's illegal—but also that it's too old to be part of the DC tracking grid. "It's okay, stare all you want," she says as she steers the bike over the curb and turns us toward a dirt trail leading into the woods.

"Sorry?"

"My head. Stare all you want."

"I wasn't—"

"I've got eyes back there, girl."

I notice the two red blinking lights on the back of her helmet or whatever it is. It looks like a Cerepin that mutated and grew all over her head.

"It's an Incomp."

"A *what*?"

"Internal computer. I told Chen people would think it stands for 'incompetent.' I guess I enjoy being underestimated, though." With that, she opens her fingers and we lurch forward. I hold on so tight that I'm surprised she can breathe.

Inside the helmet, I hear her voice, echoing and tinny. "Can you hear me?"

"Yeah," I say.

"We can talk without your capped screen overhearing for the moment."

"Where are we going?"

She accelerates, sending us charging down the trail. "Away from the DC police."

I look over my shoulder to see one police car and then another pull to a stop at the place I was standing just a minute ago. As Ukaiah turns to stay on the trail, a bunch of canny officers get out—it's easy to tell because they move eerily fast.

"At least we got 'em out of their cars, am I right?" she asks.

"They can probably run as fast on foot."

"Oh, I know they can."

"So you knew they were coming?"

"Didn't you?"

"I knew it. I'm a decoy."

"Not exactly." She sends us roaring up a hill, and then we're in the air for a few seconds before crashing down on the other side of a small brook.

My butt rises off the seat, and I yelp as it slams back down. "Then what am I doing here?"

"Saving the world?"

I groan.

"Okay, okay, just the country. Isn't that what you've been trying to do all along? Start a revolution?"

"Maybe, but this—"

"Is the real revolt. It starts tonight. Assuming we actually survive." She swerves as I catch sight of a canny officer's illuminated skin streaking through the woods only a few hundred feet from us.

"Where's Percy?"

"Percy got the Hethermills out, but he's still trying to keep the feds off their tail. Right now he's doing that by putting them on his."

"Oh, god."

"Yeah. We're gonna try to help him, but he might be on his own. And Chen says that might not be a good thing."

"Why not?"

Ukaiah pulls a device that looks like a neural disruptor from her belt and aims it at the canny running next to us. "Because Percy is more dangerous than anyone on this planet." She shoots at the canny, and the thing goes down like it's just a hunk of lead.

"What was that?"

"Localized EMP. Turns the lights out real quick." She shoots one on our other side without even slowing down. "I invented it myself."

We race along with woods on either side. Ukaiah takes down three more cannies and dodges a few others. We nearly crash into a fallen tree as she tries to take out a canny right behind us. "Do you want me to try and shoot it?" I ask, my heart in my throat.

"Nah. No offense, but if you aim that thing the wrong way and hit me, I'm probably dead."

I take in her deformed head-helmet Incomp, which actually seems kind of like an *Ex*comp, if you ask me. "Okay."

"Take off your comband. It's time to give them something else to chase for a second."

With my arms still around her waist, I unstrap the screen. El will know, but I guess that's part of the game. "What do you want me to do with it?"

"Toss it. Go ahead."

I do, and the canny just behind us veers off to retrieve it, which allows us to extend our lead.

"About time for you to hitch a ride with someone else," Ukaiah announces. "Ready?" We're traveling at high speed along a trail, and the headlight illuminates a car as it hovers about twenty feet in the air ahead of us.

"What about you?"

"I'm going to give them something to chase. You just . . . let gravity do its thing. Good luck."

Footsteps behind me tell me a canny is closing in. I scream as I feel something brush my back. Ukaiah tenses and then slams her palm down on the control panel.

The engine goes silent even as I feel a startling whir between my calves. We take off and climb into the air to the tune of my startled shriek. I lose my grip on Ukaiah as she rockets vertically into the sky above the trees, and then I'm falling, clawing at the air, trying to get a foothold in the clouds, knowing I'm about to die.

I hit sooner than I expect, and bounce. The world turns sideways and a voice says, "Welcome, Marguerite."

I glance around me. I just fell through the open back door of a car, apparently, and landed on the curtain air bags deployed on its other door. The car rights itself and closes the door. I take off my helmet and peer through the windshield. Ukaiah is a speck in the sky, heading away from us. "What-what-what—"

"My name is Yves."

"And you just caught me midair."

"I thought it was a rather skillful maneuver."

"No kidding," I say, panting and holding on to the seat as Yves banks into a sharp left turn, heading back into DC.

"There's someone who wants to talk to you, Marguerite."

"Percy?"

"No," says another voice emanating from the speakers. It sounds weirdly electronic and distorted. He hasn't engaged vid, so all I've got is sound. "My name is Chen."

"Oh my god. You're the one El thinks is a terrorist."

Chen laughs. "I'm the one he'd like to finger as a terrorist," he corrects. "Because it would be pretty convenient for him, don't you think? Take out the hacker who's about to expose him by framing the guy for a crime he probably committed himself?"

A chill runs through me. "You think El is responsible for the bombings?"

"Think about it, kid."

Suddenly, it all makes sense. El was at the Department of AIR that morning. He could have even planted the device himself! He put Uncle Wynn in a terrible position but ultimately got rid of Fortin Tech, clearing the way to serve his own financial and political interests. And while the president was encouraging me to be a true friend, El was setting everything up to destroy anyone who got in his way. "But if he's willing to do that . . . you have to be careful, because he's coming after you."

"It was only a matter of time," he says. "Because I'll never shut up. And now we need to talk about Percy, because he's going to need your help. We're all going to need your help."

"What can I do?"

"First, you need to understand him for this to make sense. Percy isn't normal."

I laugh, and it ends in a scream as Yves touches down and starts to race along a residential street. "Yeah, I already knew that."

"That's not what I mean. You know his parents were killed."

"I saw the vid taken right after their murders," I say. "I read your comment. That was you, wasn't it?"

"Not one of the smartest things I've done, making that comment. It's what drove me underground. But that was an emotional day for me. The Blakes were my heroes. I was a junior associate at the Blake Consortium before it lost its funding."

"Did you know his parents well?"

"They were pretty secretive, but I knew what they stood for. I only found out later what they were protecting."

"And that was . . . ?"

"Percy. But Blake must have trusted me—after he and his wife died, I received a little trail of breadcrumbs that led me to the treasure—his notes. Basically, his last will and testament. One of his requests was that I take care of his son, and so I have. The only way I know how."

"What do you mean, 'take care of him'? Why would Percy need that? He has family, and he lives at the French embassy."

"Yes, but even Rosalie doesn't actually know him. She doesn't know what he is."

"So what is he?" My heart is beating so fast.

"Well, before the what, the why. Percy nearly died. Valentine's files said that his skull was smashed in a fall, along with a few dozen other bones in his body. He was injured so badly that he was never going to walk or talk again, even with the best medical care. His parents took him home from the hospital, and that was that."

"But he looks so . . ."

"Perfect? Do you have any idea how brilliant his parents were? And what kind of resources they had access to? They basically turned him into their guinea pig, and before you get all high and mighty about that, remember the alternative would have been Percy the cucumber."

"Why did they do all of this in secret?"

"The government was coming after the consortium. Zao wanted to clear the way for places like Fortin and, believe it or not, NeuroGo. If Blake had revealed what he was doing to his own son, they would have used it as an excuse to crush him, discredit him, and then steal from him. In the end, they did anyway, but the secrecy probably bought him a few years. It was only the Blakes' sense of justice that did them in, you know. They could have sat back and let those neurostims go unchallenged, but that wasn't who they were. And by that time Percy was healthy again. He could protect himself. He was just never meant to be alone at such a young age. And I'm afraid I've made it worse."

"What did you do?" I mutter, pressing my forehead to the seat. Immediately, it grows cool against my skin, as Yves responds to my biostats.

"Percy is half canny, Marguerite," Chen continues. "At least half. He's still discovering the full range of stuff he can do. He has almost complete conscious awareness and control over most of his biological systems. He is as fast as a canny. He can hear and see just like they can. He can morph his appearance at will to avoid facial recognition, and he can change the way his body moves to evade gait analyzers. His body is full of self-organizing nanocytes, and they are part of a self-monitoring system, but he can also control them manually either by accessing the implanted augmentation chips just under his skin or through use of a neurologically integrated menu. But he's not connected to any network, so there is no trace of him except what he decides to show to the world. And he's more clever than even I gave him credit for. Possibly more suicidal, too."

I raise my head. "Suicidal? He doesn't seem depressed at all!"

"No, the opposite. I believe he's overly rational." Chen sighs. "Percy is equipped with a self-destruct mechanism. I know that must sound crazy, but I'm sure his dad just wanted him to be able to control his fate."

"And he can just trigger this thing at any time?"

"As far as I know. And tonight, he's taken off by himself, and he's playing his own game. But I'm also pretty sure he's going to let himself be captured."

"Why, when he knows what El might do to him?"

"Because he also knows El is connected to his parents' deaths. Figure it out."

"He's going on a suicide mission. And he's hoping he can take El with him," I say, my lips growing numb with horror.

"There you go. And it's my fault, and if he succeeds, I will live with that for the rest of my life, which might not be very long, because I'm going after him."

"El will kill you, too, though," I say. "You'd only be giving him what he wants."

"Are you proposing I just let the kid die?"

"No. I'm proposing you let me try to save him." I *have* to try. Killing El isn't the solution—bringing him to justice is. "And I'm proposing that you help me."

"I may have something to assist you," says Yves, who has just taken off into the night sky yet again. He's been driving on a seemingly random track and I have no idea where we are, but for the moment, there doesn't seem to be anyone following us.

"How are you going to do that, Yves?" asks Chen.

"I am in possession of something that's important to Percy. He wanted Marguerite to have it. At the right time, it might remind him of what he has to live for."

"Okay," says Chen slowly. "I guess we should use anything we have. Now we just need to find him. And that's not gonna be easy."

"Yves, can you take me home?" I ask.

"I can get you close. It would be best if I am not detained by the authorities."

"Then get me close. I appreciate it." I look down at my naked forearm. It feels light without a comband attached, and I feel strangely vulnerable. But I'm not helpless. I know what I need to do.

"Wanna let me in on your plan?" Chen asks. "I'll help however I can."

"Good, because it takes more than one person to start a revolution."

Chapter
Twenty-Five

Percy

I put up a good chase before I let them catch me, because I don't want them thinking I'm doing this on purpose.

I discover something fun in the process: I can climb like a spider up a wall, because my fingers and toes and eyes all work together to find acceptable leverage points with perfect balance, efficiency, and coordination. It's somewhat startling, but all my body's systems are online, and the adrenaline fuels them with urgency. My oxygenation is remarkably efficient. The cannies come after me, but they expect me to function within the limitations of a typical human body, so it takes them a little while to adjust their settings.

When I reach the top of an apartment building at the edge of the Potomac, I look out on the river's glittering expanse and wait. I could jump. It's tempting to hurl myself into space just to see if I could fly. I don't know if my body would survive the fall, though, and I don't have my parents here to put me back together. So I decide this is the place for my capture. It's rather picturesque. I wish I could capture it on vid.

I hold up my hands as the federal units descend. Patrol cannies that have climbed up after me ring me in, aiming their weapons. They are guns this time, not neural disruptors. I am officially an enemy of the state, I suppose. I smile at them as they approach. The bright lights from the fed cars sting my eyes until my pupils contract to pinpoints.

A ladder slides down from one of the hovering cars. They're probably afraid to land—there's no guarantee this old roof would hold the weight of the vehicle.

"You are under arrest," says a voice from above. "Cooperate and you will not be harmed."

"I have no intention of fighting you," I say, knowing the nearest patrol canny is broadcasting my answer to the car. "You've caught me fair and square."

"State your name for the record."

"I think I'll let you chaps figure that one out," I tell them, because I want this. I know that the puzzle will lure in my enemy.

"Climb the ladder, or you will be stunned and lifted."

"Watch me go," I say, striding to the ladder. I climb up easily but at a regular speed.

When I peer through the open door of the vehicle, I see a human officer waiting for me, his Cerepin blinking. "Looking for a match?" I ask.

He frowns. "Get in and hold your wrists out so I can cuff them. Your seat's electrified, so it'll shock you if you fight. So are the cuffs."

"How diabolical." I take a moment to straighten my jacket and smooth my hair, and then I offer my wrists. "Now what?"

"You tell us who you are." He fastens the restraints, thick loops around my wrists with a stiff bar connecting them. I can feel the threatening hum of current within.

"How about I tell you what I am? That's much more interesting."

The officer goes still, and I can easily hear the tiny voice emanating from his ear implant. "Take him to Bethesda. No one climbs like that without illegal tech."

"Bethesda," the officer says to the car. "Medical center."

"Oh no," I say blandly. "What will you do to me?"

"Figure out how the hell you climbed up a six-story building in ten seconds flat," mutters another officer sitting in the front seat. "That was creepy as hell. What are you, some type of canny?"

"Hardly." Sort of. "I'm just in very good shape."

The officer sitting on the other side of the prisoner partition from me snorts. "Smart-ass. You can't hide from a Bioscan."

"Obviously not," I say as we soar over DC. My heart is racing at 169 beats per minute, a combination of exertion and nerves. I'm not scared of what's coming—but I am worried about Marguerite. If everything has gone according to plan, Yves will have given her my paper at this point. And if I know her, she's going to find a way to come and see me. I'm both excited and scared by the prospect. I don't want her too close to me. I'm not sure what's going to happen.

But I've set this in motion, and it's bigger than both of us, and the only thing to do now is see it through to the end. My parents did the same—they spoke out, they did their best to expose corruption and evil, and they died in that fight.

Now it's my turn.

I sit quietly with these thoughts as the patrol car descends. When I focus on what's just outside my window, I see the holographic sign for the Bethesda Medical Center. Where Kyla and her mother are imprisoned. Across the parking lot is a large black vehicle that bears the presidential seal. Part of the official White House fleet.

It could not be more perfect. This is exactly where I needed to come. This is where it ends. Tonight.

Assuming Marguerite gets here before it's too late.

Wearing cuffs and held at gunpoint by at least five patrol cannies, I am escorted into the medical center through an entrance marked "Staff Only." I hold my head high and wish I had used a little more hydrostatic gel spray—there's a stray lock that keeps falling across my forehead. No doubt devilishly rakish, but annoying given I can't sweep it out of my eyes.

They lead me past several closed doors and into a spacious white room containing a full-body scanner . . . and a reclining examination chair with a hole at the back of the headrest and dangling straps to secure uncooperative arms and legs and heads. Perfect for installing a neurostim, I would think. My stomach is tight with rage and, all right, *yes*, a bit of fear.

"Wait here," says one of the patrol cannies.

Its human counterpart, a weary middle-aged officer, looks me up and down. Do I detect disgust? "Just answer his questions when he gets here, all right? He's the kind who likes the ones that don't, if you understand."

Our eyes meet, and suddenly I know. He was there when Bianca was murdered. "The price of defiance is higher than the latest tech, I gather."

"Don't find out," he says, a note of pleading in his voice. I suspect he was once a good man but not a strong one. Not strong enough to resist evil when it came to the door. And now he walks from the room, apparently willing to let whatever happens happen—or too scared to try to stop it.

No matter. He doesn't need to be here for the final act.

With three motionless patrol cannies watching over me, I wait. I know he's here already—he just wants to give me enough time to sweat.

I tap my Adam's apple and feel my body shifting to bring my voice back to its normal pitch. It doesn't matter that they know who I am now. Everybody's going to know who I am if I succeed. And if I fail, I'll be disappeared like Bianca was, so it won't matter. I put my face back in its normal configuration, too. It feels good.

One of the cannies steps forward and uncuffs me. "You are to be scanned now," he says, his voice low. "It won't hurt you."

I eye the machine as all my parents' admonitions run through my head, and then I step into the scanning booth. The clear door slides shut behind me. The beams slide over my body as the walls click softly. And then the door opens again and turns me loose.

When I reenter the room, Elwood Seidel is waiting. He has a smile on his face. "Congratulations on turning the Hethermill family into fugitives," he says to me. "You know, when they're caught, it won't be pretty."

"Which means you haven't caught them yet."

He chuckles. "I've got to say, I didn't expect you."

"No? But I suppose that's not surprising. You're not that terribly clever."

His smile drops away. "I did suspect you for a while, actually, but then that little traitor talked me out of it."

"Or maybe you're silly enough to underestimate a fellow simply because he looks ravishing in a dress."

"But now you're the one in custody," he continues, louder, "and I'm . . . well. I can do more or less whatever I want to you."

I yawn. "If what you want is as unimaginative as your wardrobe, then I expect to sleep right through it. Can you blind me first so that I don't have to look at that shoddy hem?" I give his jacket a look of shock.

He rolls his eyes. "Nice try. I want you to know that my office got a com from the French ambassador tonight. We couldn't help her, but it did help us, *Percy*."

"Oh, dear."

"It seems you've got quite a following online. They'll miss you."

Poor Rosalie. "Doesn't seem like good politics to cross the French president and the most powerful country in the European Union. Will that really help Wynn?"

"But you're American, Percy."

"I am also a French citizen, thanks to *ma mère*."

He shrugs. "You're still subject to the laws of your home country. I hope you didn't let all those diplomatic perks go to your head. I'll admit—I didn't think a teenager would be the one smuggling fugitives out of the District, but then it all made sense. Only someone so young would be so stupid."

I can feel a little smile playing at my lips. "Ah, yes. Teenagers. There's no way we can change the world, so why should we try?"

"You've caused me a lot of inconvenience," he says. "You're going to have to pay for that."

"What about the inconvenience you've caused me?" I ask, breathing slow and deep to deny the urge to leap on him and wrap my hands around his throat. "Shall we talk about the trouble you've caused, Elwood? You see, I don't think the ledger is even. You did, after all, arrange for my parents to be murdered."

His eyebrows rise. "You figured that out? I'm impressed. Or did your little friend Chen help you? I'm going to catch him, you know. And when I do, I'm going to make an example of him."

"Ah. So you haven't caught him yet, either."

"I have you, though." He turns as a medical canny strides in. It holds out a screen. "The results of your scan. Now we can decide where to start." His gaze dances over the readout. "My god, Percy. Your parents were geniuses. I almost regret having them killed."

My fists clench. His eyes flick to my hands, and he smiles as he returns to his reading. "Augmentation chips in your eyes, ears, throat, thyroid, bone marrow, heart, pancreas . . ." He starts to laugh. "Aw, buddy. It looks like the only place your parents didn't augment you was your privates."

I smirk. "Well, obviously that's because I didn't need any help there."

His lip curls. He hates that I'm not afraid of him. "Most of the augmentation is in your brain, I see. So you did need help *there*?"

I lean against the scanning booth. "Ah, that. I needed a bit of patching up after a youthful accident. It's just glue holding me together, really."

"I wonder what would happen if we just plucked those chips out? It wouldn't be hard. We have the equipment right here."

I really hope Marguerite gets here soon, before there's not enough of me left to finish this. "Would that make you feel safer, do you think? Would it finally allow you to sleep with the lights out? I do think darkness is better." I give him my best contemptuous look. "Because I'm sure your sleeping attire is even less stylish than your current ensemble. I am no fan of the president, but doesn't even he deserve a chief of staff with a crisp pleat? A freshly genned shirt?"

In spite of himself, Elwood's hand slides defensively down his chest to his belly. "You're trying to goad me into hurting you before we can extract useful information."

"Like who designed my jacket, perhaps? I'd tell you, but I don't think your shoulders are broad enough to do it justice."

"Like how you're smuggling people out of Arlington," he snaps. "Gia Fortin is now speaking out from the safety of Canada, thinking she's out of my reach."

"I'd be more cooperative if you give me what I want."

"And what's that?"

"You have a classmate of mine here. I'd like to see how she fares."

He grunts. "Kyla Barton? If I let you see her, you'll give me information?"

"I'd be more amenable. I miss her. We had a certain bond, you know."

"You know what? Why not. I'm feeling generous. Just know that if you try to escape or get her to help you, I'll have the cannies hurt her while you watch."

"Good lord." I cluck my tongue. "You truly are a broken little man, aren't you?"

His face turns red. "I'm really going to enjoy taking you apart." He stalks from the room.

There's the slightest release of tension in my chest, but it returns the moment Kyla walks in. Her eyes light on me, but they don't spark with recognition.

"Hello," I say softly. "I missed you."

"You did?" She looks nervously at the examination table as I walk toward her. "You're not going to hurt me, are you?"

"What?" I lift her chin with my fingers, but as I do, I see the flash of something red under her hair. A neurostim. I bow my head until our foreheads are almost touching. "I'm so sorry they did this to you."

"Did what?" She seems more interested in the anime movie playing on her comband than she is in talking to me.

I step away from her. "How is your mother?"

"I guess she's fine." But her brow furrows for a moment, as if she's trying to think her way out of a haze, to remember something important.

Rage tingles up and down my spine. "You're going to be all right, Kyla."

"I'm already all right," she says in a dreamy voice. She reaches up and pushes the neurostim, delivering a low-voltage dose of relief to her amygdala or wherever they've implanted the leads.

Elwood Seidel enters the room again, searching my face for my reaction. "What do you think of the neurostim? Your parents wondered what they could really do," he says. "They were suspicious from the start, you know. Flore reviewed the design and was concerned it had the potential for abuse. Your father had the loudest voice, but really it was your mother who started them both down that road. Tragic, isn't it? If she had been a bit more stupid or content to be at home with you instead of in the lab, she might still be alive."

"And perhaps if *your* mother had found you worthy of love, even a little, *many* people would be alive."

He holds up his comband. "Go ahead. I'm used to being mocked, especially by rich technocrites like you and your parents. It gave me great pleasure to look down on their lifeless, bloody bodies. And you know what? This gives me pleasure, too." He looks down at the screen and appears to scroll through a list of options before his nasty smile returns. Then he taps one section of the screen.

Kyla's open palm comes at my face so quickly that I barely have time to catch her wrist. Her other hand claws at my neck, and she manages to scratch me before I restrain that one as well. Her beautiful face contorts with anger, pink lips drawn back from white teeth, eyes full of fury. She kicks and writhes, doing her best to hurt me, even trying to bite me before I wrap her up and hold her so tightly that she can't get at me.

"Stop this! You can do what you want to me, but she's an innocent, and you've already hurt her enough."

"No such thing," he replies, sinking into a rolling chair and watching me struggle with my friend, who is slamming her heels into my shins and throwing her head back in an attempt to smash my face. "She won't stop until her body gives out, by the way. Isn't that fantastic?"

I look down at the spot on her neck where the neurostim device is implanted.

"I wouldn't if I were you. Pulling it out will do irreversible damage. The human brain is such a delicate thing, as you know."

"Please stop," I say, letting my voice drop, letting my fear shine through.

"Your turn, then. I need information."

I'm sweating and shaking, trying to hold Kyla without hurting her. "What do you want?"

"Where's Chen hiding?" he asks. I don't answer. Of course I don't answer. "Hmm, we'll start with an easier one. How are you getting technocrats across the border?"

Kyla is struggling so hard that I'm afraid I'm going to break some of her bones, but I can't trade her pain for other lives. "I'm sorry, Kyla," I tell her, my mouth pressed to her ear.

She screams, and it is eerie and quavering and full of agony.

"I have to say I'm surprised," Elwood says as a patrol canny appears at the door. "You're really willing to let her die?" He lets us struggle as he turns to the manlike machine. "What is it?"

"Someone to see you, sir."

"I'm a little busy here. Take care of it."

"She'll only talk to you."

"She? Who is it?"

"Marguerite Singer."

Elwood stands up abruptly. He looks down at his comband and taps it, and Kyla goes limp in my arms. As we sink to the ground, he strides from the room. I am not pleased to see that he is smiling.

Chapter
Twenty-Six

Marguerite

As I wait in an empty exam room, I say a little prayer that the vice president actually hates me less than she seems to. Before I got out of Yves, I asked Chen to get me through to the president. If he was the hacking god he was supposed to be, I figured it would be easy.

But apparently Uncle Wynn wasn't at the White House tonight, and guess who was?

"My secretary said it was important," said the veep, her voice low and thoroughly annoyed.

"I need to talk to the president," I said. "And it is important."

"Your mother isn't in the office," she replied. "If you've scraped your knee and need a Band-Aid, I can send a medical canny to make a house call."

"You're not being fair, Madam Vice President." I stayed formal. Unlike with the president, there has been no such invitation to call her Audrey. "This is actually a matter of national security. It's urgent. Which makes it critical that I speak to the—"

"And you're talking to me instead," she snapped. "If you want to reach the president, talk to me."

It might turn out to have been the biggest mistake of my life, but for Percy's sake, I had to be all in. "It's El," I said in a choked voice. "Mr. Seidel. He's off the rails."

She was quiet for a moment, and I swear, I could barely breathe. "Off the rails," she finally said after a full minute of silence. "Can you be more specific?"

"He's done some bad things behind the president's back. He's hurting people. Framing them. He's going after one of my friends. I'm worried he may even kill him. Someone has to stop him."

"Elwood Seidel is the chief of staff," the vice president said. "He has the full trust of the president."

I noticed she didn't say he had hers, and it was the tiniest spark of hope I needed. "Please. I believe in the president's values. I'll support him until the end. But El has to be stopped. And I'm going to stop him if no one else does. I know how this sounds, but I'm not making it up. Please tell the president I need to speak with him and I'll explain everything."

After I hung up, Chen whistled low through the speakers. "Do you think she will?"

"I don't know," I said. "She's never liked me."

"And are you sure you want Sallese to intervene?"

"You don't trust him, do you?"

"He's the father of NeuroGo, Marguerite."

"But there's no conflict. He sold his shares years ago."

Chen let it go. "Okay, are you sure you're ready for this?"

"I'm not sure," I said, "but I'm going to do my best to come out of this alive—and to get Percy out, too."

I have a few ideas about what I need to do, but to be honest, I'm not yet sure how to get it all to work. For now, I'm here, weirdly enough in this exam room, hoping for the best. Then my mother walks in, looking relaxed and happy, and it breaks me. She opens her arms when she sees my face crumple. "Oh, baby, I thought you were out with a friend, but El commed to ask me to meet you here! What's wrong?"

"*Everything*, Mom."

"El just told me we caught the bad guys," she says. "Everything's going to be fine!"

"No, Mom! He *is* the bad guy!" I push myself out of her arms even though I still want and need to be there. "And I think you know it."

She gives me a faint smile. "Marguerite, what on earth are you talking about? He's a good man, and he cares about us." She starts to reach up to push her neurostim, but I grab her wrist. "Stop that," she shouts, slapping my hand. A moment later she's given herself the dose, and her smile grows broad again.

I have to look away. The only way I'll get her back is if I take care of El. I'm afraid that if Percy does his self-destruct thing and kills El, she'll never snap out of this. Because he's controlling her. He has to be. She was different before he had that thing implanted in her head. She didn't even seem to *like* him all that much.

I'll just talk her down until I can get to El. "I'm sorry," I say. "It's been a rough day."

She strokes my hair. "I know. But it'll be over soon, and we can go home. El is so relieved that he's captured one of the terrorists."

So that's how they're spinning it. "That *is* so amazing. Can I talk to him? I don't want to talk to anyone but him."

"I'll go ask one of the cannies if El can be interrupted. I am sure he would want to see you."

"Thanks," I whisper, my heart skipping. If he's in with Percy . . .

But a few minutes after my mom leaves, El comes in with a patrol canny by his side. "Nice to see you, Marguerite. You won't mind if we scan you?"

"Scan me? Whatever."

"Her biostats are significantly out of range," says the canny, and I survive the moment by imagining kicking it in the crotch just to find out if cannies are anatomically correct.

"Not surprising," says El. "She's pretty much proven herself a traitor."

"What?" I give him big eyes, my mouth hanging open in shock. "I risked my life tonight to catch FragFlwr!"

"Who turned out to be one of your classmates," he says drily. "The one you tried to protect."

My cheeks grow warm. "Obviously I hadn't figured it out at that point." Except I had. "But he's here now, isn't he?"

"Oh yes, We cornered him on the roof of a building in Arlington. In the end he wasn't so hard to catch."

"And is he cooperating?"

El loses his relaxed, playful look. "He will."

"He won't, El. He doesn't think like we do."

"Let me guess—you think you can convince him to cooperate?"

"I do."

"Search her," El says to the canny.

I hold out my arms as the machineman goes through my pockets. He pulls out the scrap of paper a moment later and hands it to El.

El starts to laugh. "Paper? Are you serious? Where did you get this?"

"Look at the top."

He runs his thumb over the raised flower design on the edge and peers at it intently. "What is this?"

"A memento from his parents, I'm pretty sure. I think that if I give it to him, he'll talk." At least, that's what Yves said. He said it was what Percy needed.

El hands the scrap of paper to me. "I don't get it, but go ahead. You have ten minutes with him. If he cooperates, it'll help you."

I hold the paper in my hand and stroke its fragile length with my fingertips. "Thanks."

"Don't thank me yet," he replies. "If you can't get him to talk—"

"I get it, El. I'm on a doomed transport back to Houston that will never make it."

For a moment, he regards me, his look conflicted. Then he simply says, "I wanted us to be one happy family, and you've ruined that." He pushes his way through the door, and as I follow, he walks over to my mother, who is standing in the center of the hallway.

He cups her face in his hands.

He tilts her head up.

And he kisses her.

I have never felt this kind of hate before, not even when people threw bodily fluids on me, not even when Gia and Bianca and so many others suggested that I got where I am by sleeping with a man old enough to be my grandfather. None of that compares to watching a murderer control my mom like this.

El pulls away from her. "Oh, are you still there?" He waves a patrol canny over. "Please escort Marguerite to 11A, and give her ten minutes with the prisoner."

"Of course, sir." The canny gestures for me to follow him. I do, because it's my only chance to stop any of this madness.

When I first see Percy, his back is to me. He's standing over a body on an examination chair. But when the canny announces me, he turns, and instantly I see the change in him. He looks stricken, circles under his eyes and horror inside them. My gaze strays past him to the person on the chair—it's Kyla, her eyes closed and her limbs loose. Her arm with the comband is dangling off the chair, playing the same anime movie she was watching when I visited before.

"Is she alive?" I ask in a small voice.

"Yes, simply exhausted, I think," he says, just as small. Because that is what we are, caught up in this huge monster's mouth.

"It's the neurostim," I tell him. "El put one on her."

"And her mother. But that was before, probably to get her to cooperate."

Like he did with Mom. "I know I played a part in this."

"None of this is your fault, Marguerite," he says, leaving Kyla's side. He stands in front of me, his lean frame slumped. He looks tired.

"Have they hurt you?"

"Not yet." He puts his hands on my arms and laughs, almost to himself. "It's good to see you."

My hands touch his elbows. I can feel his warmth. I am amazed that he is here, a miracle wrapped in skin. "Your parents must have loved you very much," I say, taking in his face, the metallic glint in his blue eyes.

"Ah, Chen told you about me."

I nod. "I can't say I was that surprised. It all made sense."

The corner of his mouth rises. "That's nice of you to say."

"But he also told me you were here for revenge," I whisper.

He waggles his eyebrows at me. "And are you here to stop me?"

"Yeah." We are chest to chest now, and he is more human than any human I've ever touched. I put my hands on him and feel his beating heart.

"It's racing. A hundred and fifty-one beats per minute," he whispers. "Because of you."

"I brought you something. To remind you of who you are."

He sets his forehead on mine. "I know who I am."

"And what you are."

He nods. "It's going to be okay, Marguerite. I promise."

"You can't," I say, my voice cracking.

His smile is so sad. "I can. But it will never be the same, and I know that."

"Don't do anything stupid." I pull the scrap of paper from my pocket and slip it into his palm. His fingers close over it. "Your parents worked so hard to protect you. Think of them."

"I know," he says, taking a step back from me. He looks down at the paper. "But they would have understood."

And as he brushes his thumb over the flower on the scrap, I know I have played into his hands. I watch helplessly as the writing appears in big block letters, as Percy's eyes skim over what appears to be code.

Code.

"Percy?"

Because he's not seeing me. He's looking past me. "It'll be okay," he says quietly.

"Stop," I say, moving close. "Stop this. For me. Please."

"This has to happen now. Leave the room if you can."

"I'm not going anywhere!"

He gives me a regretful look and then whispers something under his breath.

I can't make it out, because there's a shout behind me and the sound of the door sliding open. I know El and his canny stooges are in the room. But all I see is Percy's eyes go blank. All I feel is his body go stiff against mine, every muscle turning to steel. I catch him as he falls forward and carefully lower him to the ground as El says, "What just happened? What did you do?"

"I don't know. I—he's not breathing!" Panic strikes as I tilt Percy's head back. He hasn't done it, has he? His lips are pressed tight, his jaw clenched. His eyes are wide open. Glassy and empty. This can't be it. It can't be.

I place my hand over his heart again. Then lower my head and put my ear to his chest.

This time, it's silent.

Chapter
Twenty-Seven

Percy

This was not what I expected to happen.

I knew I needed my internal menu to pop up at just the right time, with all the pieces in place, all the options on the table. I thought I knew what came next.

Sometimes I'm a little too arrogant for my own good.

I lie here, stiff as the floor beneath me. My muscles are screaming. My lungs are screaming. My skin, my teeth, my fingernails, my ears and nose, my eyes. There is not a single part of me that isn't in utter agony.

I wish I *had* triggered the self-destruct mechanism. Surely that would have hurt less.

But no, no. Being the optimistic fellow I am, having faith in my parents and their brilliance, having read all my father's instructions to me before I enabled all the options in the menu, I decided to do something else.

System update.

Now I'm looking at the countdown to completion: nine minutes and forty-two seconds. Until then, I have to lie here and watch

Marguerite, her fear for me, her panic, surrounded by enemies. Nine minutes might be several too long.

"He's dying," she shrieks, her hand on my chest. "Let that medical canny through!"

Standing just behind her, Elwood looks down at me. "I'm thinking this is a pretty deserved fate, Marguerite." He picks up the flower paper. The ink will fade, but he must still be able to see it, because he adds, "For both of you. You tried to help him, didn't you?"

"Please," she sobs, lowering her head right over my face. If I could move my eyes, I'd stare at her lips, but instead I'm a corpse, and my gaze is fixed on the monster over her shoulder. "His heart has stopped."

"That's most unfortunate," Elwood says. "But I'm sure I can find the information I need some other way. You might even be able to help me."

Marguerite is on her feet with startling quickness. She slaps Elwood across the face, and he staggers out of my view. He's back in half a second, though.

And he slaps her right back. "Colette," he calls as he grabs Marguerite roughly by her shoulders. "Marguerite needs you."

"Don't you bring her in here," Marguerite warns, right before she kicks Elwood square in his . . . oh, *ouch*. She stands over him as he collapses to his hands and knees, his eyes bulging, right next to me. "I'd hate for her to see me kill you."

"Restrain her," he wheezes.

Marguerite howls and struggles as the patrol cannies rush her, grabbing her around the waist, holding her legs. Just like they did to Kyla.

"Neurostim her," Elwood says to the medical canny. "Get the other girl off the table and then plug Marguerite in. Now." He coughs and slowly sits up. "I should have done this days ago."

"Mom!" Marguerite screams as a woman with curly black hair and eyes just like her daughter's rushes over to help Elwood from the floor. "Com the med canny for Percy! Please!"

She's not asking for help for herself, even though she's in the struggle of her life.

She's asking her mother to help *me*. Well, now I am genuinely charmed.

Nine minutes and three seconds. I have never felt this helpless. This pain feels as if it will never end, like the little nanodemons inside me are going to burst through my skin, flowing out from my ears and nostrils, surfing gleefully on my liquefied brain matter. Now there are sparks in front of my eyes. I think my visual augmentation chip might detonate.

My ears work perfectly well, though. I can hear a car landing outside, its magnetic wheels touching down on asphalt.

In here is chaos. Two patrol cannies carry Kyla, who is still limp and incoherent, past me, headed out of the room. A medical canny strides by, carrying a sealed tray of medical equipment. "She will have to be sedated," it says. "She is too active for implantation. The risk for brain damage is high."

"Do it anyway," Elwood snarls.

"Mom," Marguerite pleads. I listen to the patrol cannies fastening the straps around her body.

The dark-haired woman stands by Elwood. He puts his arm around her shoulders and pulls her close. "She's going to be fine, Colette. You know this is best for her." He kisses her forehead.

"This is really for the best, baby," Colette says. "You'll feel so much better."

I didn't think this could hurt more, and I was wrong. Eight minutes and thirty-nine seconds.

"Do I have your consent to proceed?" asks the medical canny.

Marguerite screams, "No!"

Her mother calmly says, "Yes."

"You're a minor, Mar," Elwood says. "Your mom is looking out for you. She knows best."

"Or maybe I do," says a new voice. One I recognize.

"Mr. President," Elwood and Colette say at once, turning to the man who has entered the room. Secret Service cannies stride past, standing shoulder to shoulder against the walls.

I see no human agents. Perhaps that's because they'll have feelings about what they see happening. These agents could, but I have no doubt their empathy settings have been dialed to zero.

I hope for all our sakes that the president's have not.

"What the hell are you doing?" President Sallese asks his chief of staff. "I thought we were on the same page, or at least the same side."

Elwood's mouth opens and closes, and then he stammers, "But-but we *are*, sir!"

Wynn Sallese shakes his lionlike head. "I would never condone this."

"Uncle Wynn," Marguerite says with a whimper.

"It's going to be okay, Marguerite," he says gently. "Please," he adds, gesturing to his Secret Service cannies, "get her off that table."

They begin to do his bidding as the president faces down his chief of staff. No one is looking at me, but then again, I'm just the corpse on the floor.

Eight minutes and nine seconds. But maybe it won't matter after all.

"Son, I'm disappointed in you. I trusted you to handle our agents doing the investigation. I trusted you to do a good job."

Elwood points at me. "This is the person who was helping suspects escape!"

Sallese finally seems to notice my body lying at his feet. "Did you kill him?"

"He killed himself," Elwood says. "Proof of his guilt, I'd say."

"So if I hand you a gun, would you kill *your*self?"

"What? No!"

The president gives him a sad look. "That's a shame."

Elwood backs up, out of my line of sight. All I can see is the president now, regarding his right-hand man with disdain. "I've figured out what you've done, and it's broken my heart."

"Wait, what?" Elwood's voice is an octave higher than usual.

"I found the evidence, son. You couldn't hide it forever. How long did it take you to plan the bombings?"

"Mr. President, *Wynn*, you have to know, I-I-I didn—"

"Execute this traitor."

When the Secret Service canny standing next to the president raises its arm, Elwood shrieks. "Wynn! I didn't do it! You know I would never do that! Wynn!"

The president heaves a weary sigh. "Fire."

The blast rings in my ears like a bomb, crackling along the inside of my skull. Marguerite and Colette scream. Elwood must have been standing only a few feet behind me, because as he falls to the floor his arm flops onto my chest. The iron-rich smell of his blood floods my nostrils.

I must confess to being surprised by this turn of events. And shamefully relieved. Also, wishing I could change my shirt.

"Someone please remove Colette from the room," the president says, and a canny ushers the distraught, sobbing woman out.

Seven minutes and thirty seconds left. The pain has turned into a hard tingling, and my mind is like a city ablaze. I'm here, but I'm not completely here. I am trying to focus on the now, on Marguerite and her safety, on the president and what he's saying, but there are twenty other tasks that require completion, that require working memory, that require transmission of information along neurons forging new connections each nanosecond, each one a knife prick in my consciousness. This room is growing dim.

Wait, *am* I dying?

Seven minutes, twenty seconds. Maybe this whole thing is just my personal version of following a path of light to heaven.

Marguerite is kneeling on the other side of me, and her voice cuts through the sizzling of my synapses. She pulls Elwood's arm across my body and looks down at it—no, at his comband. "He's been controlling my mom," she says quietly. Her hands are shaking as she hunches low over the screen and taps at it. "I'm going to release her and Kyla and whoever else he's manipulating with this thing."

President Sallese looks down at the two of us. "I know this boy," he says gently. "I guess it makes sense that he got involved." He shakes his head sadly. "It's a terrible betrayal from El. This is just devastating." He gestures down at me. "The lives lost . . ."

Marguerite stares down at the comband. A horizontal blue line scans down the length of her face. She taps at it a few more times and then raises her head. "You know, you don't seem surprised to find out that neurostim devices can be used to control people." She places her palm on my chest.

I will my heart to beat for her, but it doesn't. *Something* is happening beneath my rib cage, though, something electric and bright and sure.

A tear slips from Marguerite's eye. "I was so stupid. Everyone kept telling me, but I wouldn't listen. I wanted to think you didn't know. That it was all El. That he went rogue. But that's just not true, is it?" She sounds so calm.

"Oh, Marguerite. You're so young," Sallese says. "You can't possibly understand what it's taken to get here. You can't understand how necessary all of it was for the greater good."

"Maybe because it wasn't," she says. "Did El really have Percy's parents killed, or was that you?"

"It doesn't matter. The Blakes wouldn't play the game, Marguerite. And look—they didn't follow any rules but their own." He gestures at me. "We both know they did something unnatural to this boy. They turned him into their own Frankenstein's monster."

"They saved his *life*."

"And how many lives have I saved? How many suicides have the neurostims prevented? How many families have I saved from suffering like you and your mother did? Think, Marguerite—now we're in the position to merge these technologies. Cerepins and neurostims. We have the chance to build this thing from the ground up as one amazing device. Think what that will do for the American people."

She blinks down at Elwood's limp arm, at my chest. "If you combine the tech, you'll have access to the inside of everyone's mind. With the ability to affect their moods, you could control what channels they watch. You could control what they buy. What they do."

"I can make people happy," says the president. "That's always been my goal."

"But what if they want to be *free* instead?" she murmurs.

"Can't have both," the president says, sounding like he carries the weight of the world. "I wish we could, but I learned a long time ago that wasn't possible. Let me take care of everybody, Marguerite. I took care of you, didn't I?"

"You used me," she says. "And I let you."

"Because it got you out of a terrible place. Because it gave your mother a chance—it saved her, and you know that. She would have followed your father long ago if I hadn't raised you both up."

"That might be true," Marguerite says, "and I'm glad she's still alive. But what El did to her was a violation. Doing this to anyone is a violation. It's what you did to Dr. Barton, too. She didn't become your puppet willingly. She might have come to you to try to make peace, but you forced a neurostim device on her, didn't you? My guess is that if that vid is analyzed, people can see it."

Why is Marguerite saying this? Lord, why would she antagonize this man? The canny that shot Elwood is standing only a few feet away. She's on her knees in front of the president. At his mercy. I want to clap my hand over her mouth to keep her silent, which I should be able to do in . . . three minutes and eighteen seconds.

"But they *won't* see it," the president is saying. "Or if they do, they won't care. Because most people want to believe. Because they want to be happy. Because they want to be taken care of."

"You're wrong. They want to stand on their own two feet. They want to have purpose, and the way things work now, they can't compete with cannies. That's the piece that needs to change."

"But it won't. Canny labor is cheap and efficient. It keeps this economy afloat."

"For who, Uncle Wynn? For you? I bet Chen is right and you never actually gave up your stake in NeuroGo. Now you're just going to run the country like it's your company and we're your cannies."

The president sighs. "CEO, father . . . people elected me because they need someone who can get things done. Someone who cares."

"And you do," she says, her head bowed. "You care about your own power. You executed El for those bombings, but I saw the look on his face. He didn't do it—you did. You wanted to frame Gia Fortin so you could take Fortin Tech over without a fight. You arranged for all of it, didn't you?"

"Cannies do come in handy for unpalatable tasks, my dear. And if you trigger their secrecy settings . . ." He pretends to zip his lips together, then smiles. "You wanted to bring down Fortin, too, Marguerite."

"I wanted to help the American people!" she shouts, raising her head. "I wanted a fair playing field. I never wanted *this*!"

"I know, I know. But again, you're young, a child, and you don't understand." He points at the Secret Service canny who shot Elwood and then at her. The canny takes aim at her face. "I'm so sorry, Marguerite. I really cared about you."

One minute and one second. Oh, god.

She stares at him defiantly, ignoring the weapon. "You're going to try to silence me?"

"Yes and no. It's such a tragedy that Elwood went on this rampage. I've told a few confidants that I was concerned about his stability.

Discovering he murdered a girl who has come to be like family to me? Marguerite, your death will move the nation. The flags will fly at half-staff for a week. I'll declare today Marguerite Singer Day. You will be forever a part of history. You will never be forgotten." He takes hold of the canny's wrist and lowers the barrel—so now it's aimed at her heart. "I'll have your body lie in state, so let's keep your lovely face undamaged."

"You can do whatever you want now, Mr. President," she says, and my god, her voice is so steady. Her hand is warm on my chest.

Twenty seconds. My newly connected synapses glow white-hot.

"You should know something before you have me executed, though," she continues, looking him right in the eye.

"And what's that?"

"I've been livestreaming from El's comband for the last several minutes."

Five. Four. Three. Two. One.

Time for a resurrection.

Chapter
Twenty-Eight

Marguerite

Wynn curses and bends down to grab El's arm. His face is purple with anger as he pulls the screen off El, drops it to the ground, and then stomps on it. "Send a message to the tech team that Marguerite's account has been hacked and a fabricated vid was just streamed," he says to a Secret Service canny. "Do it now! Get that video off the Mainstream right now." The canny rushes out of the room, leaving the one who still has a gun aimed at my heart.

Then, unbelievably but unmistakably, Percy's heart beats beneath my palm. It jolts my entire body.

Wynn's eyes go wide as Percy Blake rises from the floor, a real-life Lazarus. I am pretty sure I look just as shocked. "Put the gun away, old man," he says in his usual teasing tone. "Enough people have seen her live vid by now that she must walk out of here alive for you to prove it's a fabrication." He glances at me with an approving smile. "You are *so* good, darling."

"Percy," I say, "what—"

"I know, it has to be asked," Percy says. "What just happened to *me*." He smooths his hand down the front of his bloodstained shirt. "And the answer is most definitely not self-destruction."

"It doesn't matter," the president says. "Because you're already dead."

"No," I say, stepping in front of Percy. "If you touch him, I'll make sure everyone knows."

The president grabs me, and I gasp as his fingers bruise my upper arms. "You were family, Marguerite. Family. Like a granddaughter."

"I won't let you hurt him. You've already done enough. Taken enough."

"You haven't seen anything yet. I can wipe most people's memories of the last five minutes. And if you don't help me spin this, you're forfeiting the lives of anyone in this nation who's wearing a neurostim. And let me tell you, little girl, it's millions at this point. Who do you think holds the master controller? Each device is registered to *my* system. And it works, let me tell you." His smile is hideous now that his mask of statesmanship has been ripped off. "The high voter turnout last November was no accident."

Behind me, Percy chuckles. "You just make it worse and worse for yourself."

"I could say the same for you, boy." Wynn sneers. "You should have stayed dead."

"I don't find that descriptor precisely on point. It was more . . . a state of suspended animation. I think I pulled it off rather gracefully."

His flip tone seems to throw the president off. But then Wynn looks down at me. "I can't kill you right now," he says. "You can still help me, especially if you start to behave yourself. But him?" His face is so close to mine, I can smell his minty breath. "I think it's time to bring back the old-fashioned firing squad."

He yanks me away from Percy. "You," he says to one of his guards. "Hold her. But keep her facing the boy."

The Secret Service canny wraps one arm around my chest and another around my waist. I stare at Percy, whose gaze flicks from the canny restraining me to the other cannies in the room.

"Line up in front of the boy," the president says. "Shoot on my command."

I start to struggle as the cannies move to obey. Percy stands calmly in front of the Bioscan machine. "This is not going to solve all your problems," he says to Wynn.

"You're right," Wynn says. "It will only solve one. But it's been a bad day so far, so I'll take what I can get."

Percy's eyes close as the cannies take their position in front of him. And then he opens them and looks at me. "I've decided I'd like to ask you out on a date," he says. "I know exactly what I'll wear."

Tears are streaming down my face. "So you're assuming I'd say yes?" I ask with a watery laugh.

His smile is etched with sorrow. "Really, how could you resist? You're intrigued. Admit it."

I sniffle and roll my eyes. "Fine. But I'm not fashionable enough for you."

"I'll send over a dress. You'd look lovely in violet."

"I'm not much for dresses."

He arches an eyebrow. "You'll make an exception for this one."

"Enough fun and games. I need you to understand that I mean what I say, Marguerite," the president says as the last Secret Service canny steps into place. I can see only Percy's head and shoulders now.

"Uncle Wynn," I beg, as my chest constricts with grief I'm not ready to bear again today. "*Please* don't do this."

"You don't have to watch, Marguerite," Percy says softly. "It's all right."

"Raise your weapons," the president says.

They obey in perfect unison.

"The vice president is going to figure out what you're doing, if she hasn't already," I say, struggling ineffectively against the canny.

"She knows which side her bread is buttered on. Aim."

They do. At Percy's chest. I wait for him to do something. Anything. But he simply stands there, looking defiant. Chen said Percy doesn't think quite like a human, that he's more rational, but this? This isn't rational!

"I'll do anything you ask," I say loudly, desperately. "I'll be your mouthpiece. I'll help you get what you want. I—"

"Fire."

Chapter
Twenty-Nine

Percy

Marguerite screams into the silence that follows. Wynn Sallese blinks and cranes his neck to see beyond the machinemen surrounding me, checking to see if I'm hit. "I said, fire!"

The cannies just stand there, waiting for an authorized order.

From *me*.

This room is in such vivid color. I can see the baby hairs along Marguerite's hairline, which I'd love to smooth with my fingertip. I can smell the sweat on the president's upper lip, and it makes mine curl. I can feel the hum of every single artificial brain in this room. They're connected to me now.

I am online.

"Lower your weapons," I say. "We've had our fun."

They comply and stand aside. "Oh, and please restrain the president if he attempts to do anything rash."

They close in.

"Stop," he shouts. "Execute him, dammit!"

"They won't listen to that kind of nonsense," I tell him. "Not any-more." Lord, I can feel them all. Every thought. The sensation is like streaking through the sky, moving at lightspeed, everything a blur . . . and yet I'm aware of all of it in intricate detail, fully immersed in every moment as it happens.

"How are you doing this?" he roars as cannies take hold of his arms.

"I upgraded my systems, old man. I'm on the network now." I think I *am* the network.

"Why did you go through all that pretending, then?" Marguerite asks, still pale and breathless. Poor dear.

"Oh, come, Marguerite. I had to let him have a moment of victory." I smile at our soon-to-be ex-president. "Sadly, I didn't have time for more than that."

Chapter Thirty

Marguerite

I tuck my hair behind my ear, feeling it curl against my chin, and grin at the screen. "It's been a busy few weeks, but I wanted to let you all know how I'm doing."

I glance across the room at Mom, who smiles.

It's a real smile this time, one generated under her own power. And yes, it looks weary and a little sad, but it's better than nothing.

"I know it must feel like the world's been turned upside down. I believed in Wynn Sallese as much as I've ever believed in anything. I believed he would fix our economy and help us achieve our dreams of tech equality—and then total equality." I sigh. "I was wrong. I'm so sorry for my part in everything that happened and in the lives lost. But we're already on the road to healing, I promise you."

I sit up straighter. I can see my image in the streaming box. He was right. I do look good in violet. "This afternoon I met with President Savedra. She restated her commitment to increasing tech access for all Americans, to working with leading tech companies to incentivize them to help her, and to preserving our safety, health, and security while she does it."

My mom winces and rubs at the nape of her neck. With the neurostim device gone, she experienced withdrawal that lasted a week. People who have had them longer, like Orianna, will need more help. There was a rash of impulsive self-removals just after I streamed my last vid, but our new president addressed the nation that night, imploring people to stay calm and wait to have the devices removed by medical professionals, promising that any external control signals had been disabled.

I believe her. It took me a while, and I still don't like her that much (the feeling is fairly mutual), but I do think she's telling the truth. Still . . .

"You don't have to trust her blindly. I'm not going to. I'm never going to let myself do that again. Instead, I'm going to work toward the same goals myself while keeping an eye on those in power. You can join me. We can figure this out together, as ordinary citizens holding our leaders accountable."

And there's so much to be done. Wynn is in solitary confinement, awaiting trial for ordering El's murder and the bombing of the Department of AIR. Apparently the attorney general is also looking into whether he should be charged for ordering the murder of Valentine and Flore Blake.

Wynn Sallese is going to face justice.

But that doesn't mean justice for the rest of us, not yet.

"President Savedra has asked me to serve as her advisor for youth outreach and relations," I say. "After talking it over with my mom today, I've decided I'm going to accept. That means I'll be traveling all over and posting more vids and asking you for your input—input I'll take straight to the president. Change isn't going to happen overnight, and I know that's what we all wanted, but it was an illusion. A trick. Now we need to face reality—things will only change if we *all* work at it every day. I know we can do it, though. I've got some exciting initiatives to talk to you about tomorrow. But I'll give you a hint.

"The new president sees things differently. I know this might sound scary, but she thinks it's pointless to fight the idea that cannies can do some jobs better than humans can. She wants to empower and regulate cannies to handle that stuff—and to have Americans focus on finding purpose in other ways, through initiatives to help each other, beautify our surroundings, create art, preserve oral histories. 'Nurturing our collective soul,' she's calling it." I bite my lip. "I'm not sure what I think. And I'm still advocating for a better subsidy system, if that's the case. But it sounds hopeful. Like the beginning of a good conversation. I hope you agree."

I sign off and upload the vid to the Mainstream.

The views start to tick up, and the comments start to roll in. People are still scared and skeptical and grieving, but some, at least, seem open to a change.

It's all we can ask for, really.

"That was perfect, Marguerite," Mom says. "The president is going to be grateful."

"I'm not sure." I told her I was going to speak my mind. I made it a condition of her hiring me. And she readily accepted, but I'll wait and see if she means it.

"I think you'll be pleasantly surprised," Mom says. "What are you up to now?"

I glance down at my screen, and my heart skips as I read one of the comments that just appeared.

FragFlwr: We'll see. You look lovely in that dress, by the way. Cheers to your wardrobe consultant.

I snort. "I need to go thank my wardrobe consultant."

She gives me a sly smile. "Be back by ten. It's a school night."

"Ten it is." I grab a jacket and head outside.

The embassy car is waiting, front door open. I get in and find Percy with his hands on the control panel. "What are you doing?"

He flashes a bright smile. "It's called driving, my dear. I could teach you, if you like."

"Please make sure we are in a nonresidential zone when you do," says the voice I recognize as Yves.

"Oh, stop," Percy says. "She'll be marvelous." His hair is blond tonight, and his fingernails are blue. His cravat is relatively toned down, but his stockings are rainbow hued.

"Happy birthday," I say, leaning over and kissing his cheek. His eyes close, and I feel a rush of anticipation in my chest as my lips graze his skin. "I thought I was supposed to give *you* presents." I touch the lace at the edge of the newly genned dress he sent over this morning.

He waggles his eyebrows. "You just have." Still grinning, he taps one of his fingers and twists his right hand over the panel, and we hook a sharp left turn before speeding down the road. "Speaking of appearances, a very compelling presentation tonight, my little political operative. And how is the new president?" he asks as he pokes his thumb at the panel, sending Yves rising into the air.

"Wary. Frazzled. But she has the chops to do the job." I glance at him. "She'd still like to meet you."

His smile fades. "Hmm, I have to think about that. I think I may prefer glorious anonymity to being summoned to the queen's court."

The president recognizes that Percy and I brought down a corrupt regime that was about to swallow her, too. Percy found and countermanded an order to assassinate her that had been given to a set of Secret Service cannies by El the night he died. I guess she'd gotten in his way one too many times. I sent her the evidence of it and the proof of what Percy had done, as a show of good faith.

"She wanted me to thank you," I say. "I think she meant it."

"Tell her she's most welcome."

After Wynn was in custody and the dust started to settle, Percy erased any trace of his activity from the cannies' memories and disconnected himself from all networks. The two of us are the only ones besides Wynn who know what really happened in that room, and with what the president did and all the lies he told, who would believe him?

Percy's off-line again, but I know he can connect anytime he wants. I saw it with my own eyes—he can control cannies. He can probably control AI programs, too, or at least communicate with them in their language. The language of machines. He's extremely dangerous, so much more than Wynn ever was, and he knows it.

I know it, too. But I also know that unlike our former president, Percy is, at his core, selfless, willing to risk everything to save others and do what is right. He proved it. I think he's going to figure out the best way to deal with the enormity of his power, even if it takes him a while. I'm not going to leave him alone in it, though. He's been alone for too long.

"Are you ever going to show the world what you can do?" I ask. "Or is it going to stay between you and me forever?"

He reaches over and strokes my face with the back of his fingers. "I would prefer to have *nothing* between you and me, actually . . . except maybe that."

My cheeks are warm even in Yves's temperature-controlled cabin. "Do you miss it?" I ask. "The subterfuge? Saving people? Being FragFlwr, the way you were?"

"If I do, will you find me another cause to fight for?"

"I might."

"You will," he says as I scoot closer to him. "And I think I might follow you anywhere. You are, after all, *very* good at persuasion."

I put my hand on his thigh.

The car dips and bobbles. "Yves, drive," he says. "My heart rate is just a bit too high right now."

"Yes, sir," Yves replies.

"Where to?" I ask.

Percy slides his arm around me. "Somewhere with a nice view."

"I could gen one and project it onto the windshield if you like," Yves offers.

We both laugh. "No," I say. "I'd prefer something real."

Percy touches my forehead with his. "Me too," he says. "But I think we might have that right here. No Mainstream, no Cerepins, just you and me."

"Yeah, and your super-hearing, super-smell, super-eyesight—"

He bows his head and puts his hand over his heart. "You have slain me."

I tip his chin up with my fingers. "I guess I'll just have to bring you back to life, then."

His eyes glint metallic in the starlight as Yves soars over DC. "You already have."

ACKNOWLEDGMENTS

This book was a true collaborative effort, and so my first thank-you must go to the editor who joined me to hone and grow the idea: Courtney Miller. Courtney, your excitement over this story's potential, and our conversations that forged its backbone, kept me going through the challenges of writing it. Thank you so much for your belief in me and your willingness to take on this project. Thank you also to the amazing team at Skyscape, and to Jason Kirk for stepping in to help usher the book through its final steps toward publication. Thanks to Janice Lee, my copyeditor extraordinaire, for caring about all the details and for reminding me that there are only five weekdays per week. Thank you to Phyllis DeBlanche for final eagle-eyed typo assassination. Thank you to Devon Fredericksen, my production editor, for keeping the project on the rails. And of course, I am grateful once again to Leslie "Lam" Miller for guiding me through the developmental editing process. As always, Lam, you helped me make the book so much better while also helping me stay sane, which I fully realize is not always an easy task. My gratitude also goes to my tireless agent, Kathleen Ortiz, for providing any and all manner of support and organization.

Thank you to my mother for bringing into my life *The Scarlet Pimpernel*, the movie that became one of my all-time favorites (and eventually inspired this book), and to my sisters for watching it with me dozens of times—and then reciting lines that brought us mutual joy for years. Dad, thank you for being so incredibly supportive no matter which way I seem to be headed. Asher and Alma, thank you for being so delightful and tolerating your fuzzy-brained mama. Lydia, thank you for being such an amazing, constant friend. Peter, just . . . thank you (you know why). And readers, you will always have my gratitude and my commitment to creating more stories for you to enjoy. You make it all worthwhile.

ABOUT THE AUTHOR

Sarah Fine is the author of several popular series, including the Impostor Queen and Guards of the Shadowlands. And while she promises she is not psychoanalyzing those around her, she manages to use both her talent as a writer and her experience as a psychologist to great effect. Sarah's stories blur lines, challenge convention, and press boundaries. Her mash-up of seemingly disparate genres yields stories that not only are engaging but will keep readers guessing.

Sarah has lived on the West Coast and in the Midwest, but she currently calls the East Coast home. She confesses to having the music tastes of an adolescent boy and an adventurous spirit when it comes to food (especially if it's fried). But if her many books are any indication, writing clearly trumps both her musical and culinary loves.